What to expect when you're not expecting...

LITTLE BLUE LINES

TARA WYATT

For the one in eight. You're not alone.

Everything will be okay in the end. And if it's not okay, it's not the end.

JOHN LENNON

1

September - Now

"So, what kind of porn are you going to watch?"

From behind his desk chair, I wind my arms around my husband Scott's neck. His computer screen is filled with racy thumbnails, the Pornhub.com home page flickering with skin and sex. An empty, sterile plastic jar sits on the desk beside the mouse, ready and waiting.

I run a hand through Scott's thick, dark hair, the softness reassuring between my fingers. He's dressed for work—almost. Dress shirt, tie, boxers and socks. The flap of his boxers is open just a bit.

"Girl on girl?" I tease. "Threesome? Ooh, maybe an orgy."

I try to force a brightness into my voice that I don't feel. I hate this. Not the porn. I mean, I watch it too, sometimes. Porn is not the problem here. No, what I hate is that we're reduced to sterile plastic cups, masturbation and fertility clinic trips if we have any hope of having a baby. We don't even have to touch. Sex—aside from the porn and the jerking off—has been wholly removed from the equation. The real problem is that my eggs are most likely pure crap. I may be thirty-five, but my eggs are practically geriatric; Jurassic remnants of my fleeting fertility.

"Hmmm, how about this one?" Scott points at a thumbnail on the screen, the bright orange letters beneath promising a "filthy anal gong show."

I laugh, and it's real this time. "Whatever floats your boat, sailor," I say, giving him a kiss on the cheek.

He spins in his desk chair and hauls me into his lap. "You float my boat." He kisses the tip of my nose and an ache blooms in my chest. Sometimes I wonder how he can still love me, defective as I am. Most of the time I don't love me. Or, at least, I don't love all these broken little pieces that live inside me. Shards of hope and disappointment and fear and longing, jagged and uneven and surprisingly heavy for invisible things.

I lean forward and kiss him, wishing we could just get pregnant the old-fashioned way. I don't even know how many times I've fantasized about going away for a romantic weekend, drinking wine and walking along the beach, making love under the stars, eating delicious food as we remember why we fell in love in the first place. In the fantasy, we come home and two weeks later, I'm holding a positive pregnancy test in my hands, joy erupting out of me. I imagine all the fun, creative, painfully cutesy ways I could tell him that he's going to be a father. That our weekend of love making created a life.

But after three years of trying and failing, over and over again, I know that fantasy is dead, and it makes me feel inadequate and jealous and resentful and angry, all at the same time. This is where I live, and have lived, for over thirty cycles now, the last four of which have all involved Clomid and porn and plastic cups and intrauterine insemination.

Reluctantly, I stand. "Do your thing. You'll be late for your board meeting."

His eyes flick to the clock in the bottom right hand corner of the computer screen. "Right. I'll, uh, see you in a few minutes."

Trying to ignore the awkward tension suddenly filling the room, I nod and shut the door behind me, leaving my husband to masturbate into a little cup. I used to stay and help him, but I don't anymore. There's nothing sexy about any of this, especially after so long. Scott's coming doesn't even feel like a sex act. It's clinical and stale. Our marriage vows didn't cover ejaculation on demand, but he does it anyway. For me. For us.

Maybe this fifth time will be the charm. I bounce back and forth between hope—because hope, like an insidious weed, crops up again and again, no matter how many times I try to crush it in the name of self-preservation—and a sort of dull, achy resignation to the fact that this probably won't work.

I make my way to the kitchen and pour myself half a cup of coffee, scanning my emails on my phone as I wait for Scott to finish. I start tagging the new ones, sorting them into color-coded folders, my inbox a fleeting panacea against the chaos of the rest of my life. The phone buzzes in my hand, a text message filling the top of the screen.

Mia: Good luck today! I'm sending good vibes your way.

I set my coffee down so I can text her back. The very faint sounds of female moans and male grunts float down into the kitchen through the vent, and I wonder what kind of porn Scott chose. I text Mia back.

Thanks! Fingers crossed this is it.

I add a smiley face and a crossed fingers emoji, faking an enthusiastic optimism. I don't really have any hope, but I don't want to be the perpetual Eeyore I'm afraid I've become. Over the past three years, I've learned more than I thought there was to know about hope. To some, it's a fuel that pushes them on through life's challenges, giving them strength and energy when they should be running on empty. And I guess maybe that's true for me, but I prefer to think of hope as a rose with thorns. Beautiful and full of promise, but painful to grasp. The more I reach for it, the more I get pricked. The longer I hang on, the deeper the thorns sink. I'm scarred and callused from hanging on to hope for so long. But I can't let go. If I do, I know I'll stop, and I'm terrified of stopping. It's easier to hold on to that painful hope, the kind that maims, than stare into the nothingness that threatens to envelop me when I think about giving up.

For Scott, I think hope is more like a spring. It doesn't seem to matter how many times it gets squished down, pressed almost flat until it's unrecognizable. Scott's hope always bounces back, shiny and resilient, as though it had never been flattened in the first place. After each failure, I don't understand how he can stay so damn positive. But I'm glad he does. One of us has to.

I move over to the Keurig, insert a fresh pod, and slip Scott's travel mug underneath the spout. The orgasmic sounds from upstairs have stopped; he's either finished, or he turned it down. Or maybe that clip wasn't working for him, and he knows I need to leave for the clinic with his sample ASAP. If I don't get it to the clinic within an hour, the sample will be useless, and our cycle will be wasted.

I never would've thought that trying to have a baby would entail spending time thinking about my husband's porn watching habits, but here we are.

I hear footsteps on the stairs and Scott deposits a small, brown paper bag that may or may not contain the future of our family inside on the island. He grins at me, his expression sheepish.

"Mission accomplished," he says, his lopsided smile emphasizing the dimples slashed into his cheeks. I give him a thumbs up and finish the rest of my coffee.

If we have a child, I sincerely hope he or she inherits Scott's unfairly symmetrical features. His dimples, his square chin with the slight cleft, the strong jaw, the straight Greek nose, large brown eyes, all topped with thick dark brown hair. His face is kind, open, easy. Even when he's angry or upset, he looks more like a wounded puppy dog than anything else. My face doesn't have the kindness of Scott's. It's angular—sharp cheekbones, pointy chin, high forehead, thin lips—and even though I try to soften it with makeup, it's easy for me to slip into resting bitch face. When I'm angry (or thinking, or hungry, or tired, or bored), I have a tendency to sport a pinched expression that looks as though I've just stepped in dog shit. Together, Scott and I are a perfect sock and buskin in which I am Melpomene, the sour-faced Muse of Tragedy.

"Love you, Claire," says Scott, screwing the top on his travel mug and then leaning forward to give me a kiss on the forehead. "I gotta go. Good luck."

I smile and nod. "Love you too. Text you later."

I grab the bag from the counter, not even a little put out at what's inside. This is normal for us now. Sperm in a cup is just part of the routine. For us, sperm in a cup is practically a love language.

I gather up my phone, purse and laptop bag and we each head to our separate cars. Once I'm settled in the driver's seat, I tuck the little brown bag between my legs to keep it warm. The car's a little stuffy, but I don't roll down the windows to let in the cool morning air or crank the AC for fear of damaging Scott's sample and ruining our cycle. If I'm sweaty by the time I reach the clinic, so be it. Being sweaty is a far preferable alternative to having wasted weeks of blood draws, vaginal ultrasounds, and pills that give me hot flashes, nausea, headaches and make me cry at the tiniest thing. I will endure mild discomfort to preserve the hard work that's gone into this cycle, this chance at having what so many others have without effort.

One after the other, we pull away from our house, Scott turning left to head downtown to the office where he works as a corporate investment advisor, and me turning right to wend the familiar path to the fertility clinic. It's the Friday before the long weekend, and the traffic is light this morning, making the drive less stressful than it can sometimes be. A few errant drops of rain splatter against my windshield, and according to my car, the temperature has dropped a few degrees, as it often does when rain rolls in across the lake. Summer's almost over, and I'm grateful for the slightly cooler temperatures. Having Clomid-induced hot flashes during the peak of summer isn't something I would wish on anyone.

As I drive, I listen to a podcast, wanting to think about something else besides our three-year struggle to have a child. I worry that I'm becoming obsessed, that my goal to get pregnant is slowly squeezing everything else out of my life. That this need to get pregnant, to have a child, is a boa constrictor, and I'm its prey. It's wrapped around me so tightly that I can't tell anymore where it ends and I begin. If I let it, it will squeeze me until there's nothing left of me.

Behind me, red and blue lights start flashing and even though I'm pretty sure the police officer isn't trying to pull *me* over—I'm in the far-right lane, driving the speed limit—my heart vaults into my throat anyway. I pull to the shoulder, hoping he'll whiz past me on his way to something far more pressing. My eyes are glued to my rear-view mirror and my heart sinks, plummeting like a rock from my throat to my stomach as the cop pulls in behind me. I glance at the clock on my dashboard and squeeze the sample between my legs a little bit tighter. I don't fucking have time for this.

With nervous hands, I fumble for my license, my registration, my proof of insurance. If I'm getting a ticket for whatever traffic sin I committed, fine. I don't care. I just want to get to the clinic so I can drop off Scott's sample. A tiny little drop of desperation blooms within me, like a bead of blood hitting water.

The police officer takes his time getting out of his cruiser, and when he finally does, he ambles toward my car as though he's got all the time in the world. And maybe he does, but I don't. I power down my window and attempt to school my features into something non-bitchy. When he finally reaches my window, I paste a smile on my face and try to relax, even though I can feel my pulse jumping in my throat.

"Good morning, officer," I say, making my voice as bright and chipper as possible. "What seems to be the problem?"

The police officer is young—younger than me—with closely cropped black hair, tanned skin and a kind smile.

He hooks his thumbs in the arm slots of his bullet-proof vest and rocks back on his heels, his assessing gaze sweeping the inside of my car. My legs tighten around the bag a little more. *Oh, God,* I think. *What if he confiscates the semen?* I know the thought is ridiculous—I mean, really, why the hell would he do that? I'm no expert, but I'm pretty sure it's not a crime to have a jar of your husband's jizz in your car—but my stomach clenches just the same.

"You've got a taillight out." He jerks his head toward the back of my car. "You have your driver's license, registration and proof of insurance with you?"

I nod and hand him the documents I've been clutching in my sweaty hand. "I'm sorry, officer," I say as he scrutinizes my driver's license. "I didn't realize the light was out. I promise I'll get it fixed right away." *Please just let me go now*, I silently beg. *Don't make me have wasted the past two weeks over a goddamn taillight.* I glance at the clock again. I've got about fifteen more minutes to get Scott's sample to the clinic before it becomes useless.

He rocks back on his heels again and sends me a perfunctory smile. "Be back with you in a moment, ma'am."

He heads back to his cruiser at a slow, leisurely pace that makes me want to throw something. I watch him in the rear-view mirror as he enters my information into his computer. A heavy weariness overtakes me and I drop my forehead to my steering wheel, letting it rest against the clammy leather. I stare down at the little brown bag, taking deep breaths and trying not to cry.

I hear the officer's door close and jerk my head up off the steering wheel. "I'm not gonna issue you a ticket or anything, but you really do need to get that taillight fixed."

I glance at the clock again. If traffic is on my side, I might only be a minute or two late, and that'll have to be good enough. "I promise I will, officer. Thank you."

He nods and moves to turn away but then pauses and frowns. "What's in the bag between your legs?"

Blood rushes to my face and I force my mouth to form words I don't want to speak to a complete stranger. "It's my husband's sperm sample. I'm on my way to drop it off at a fertility clinic."

He scratches the corner of his square head. "It's a what?"

I speak a bit louder, desperate to leave. "A sperm sample. It's for fertility treatments." As he looks down at the bag again, I see understanding followed almost instantaneously by disgust twist his features. Like a sunrise illuminating a toxic waste dump.

"Uh, all right then," he stammers, taking a step back from my car. "You drive safe now." He scurries back to his cruiser, unable to get away from my car and its contents fast enough. Huh. I guess he can move faster than an arthritic turtle after all.

I put my car in drive and pull back out onto the road. I'm going to be five minutes late, and even though I'm not religious, I send up a silent prayer that the sample is still usable. In my rear-view mirror, I see the officer turn down another street, and watching his cruiser, a wave of shame-fueled anger pummels me, making my jaw ache, my fists wrapped a little too tightly around the steering wheel.

"Asshole," I whisper.

I pull into the clinic's parking lot, drop off Scott's sample, and head to work, knowing I'll be back here in a couple of hours for the actual insemination. Our Hail Mary, last ditch effort before moving on to IVF. But like everything else on this fucked up "journey"—God, I hate when people call it a journey—the outcome won't be up to me. In this situation, I'm powerless. A prisoner of circumstance in a situation that makes me feel as though I'm invisible to the rest of the world.

2

We're all under the illusion that we're in control of our lives. That we choose our behaviors, and therefore choose our consequences. That our circumstances are a product of past decisions—decisions over which we had control. Bad things—hard, heartbreaking, tragic things—don't happen to *us*, because we're in control. They happen to other people, either because they made poor decisions, or simply because of their otherness. And then when those bad things—those hard, heartbreaking, tragic things—*do* happen to us, or to someone we love, we don't know how to cope because we've spent our entire lives with our heads in the sand, ignoring the plights of those around us while claiming to be caring, empathetic people. This ignorance, this lack of compassion, is part of being human. We're selfish creatures, and it's how we survive. I've learned this over and over again over the past three years. Maybe that sounds harsh, but it's a conclusion I've come by honestly.

"Claire Stanhope?" Nearly three hours after dropping off Scott's sample, I'm back at the clinic. The nurse calls my name and I rise from my seat near the back of the waiting room. Rain beats against the wall of tinted windows looking out onto the parking lot, drenching the cars, the trees, the little concrete medians with their sad strips of trodden grass. There are several other women seated apart from me, apart from each other. No one talks, no one makes eye contact, no one smiles. I pass by them, my presence completely inconsequential to them. A couple of them watch the flat screen television mounted to the wall above a never-lit gas fireplace, currently tuned to a news station. Others stare down at their phones. A lone man sits in a chair against the wall, staring at the wall of rain-streaked windows. He looks tired.

I wonder if these people hate this place as much as I do. I wonder if they feel the same sense of dread and panic every time they set foot inside and smell the hand sanitizer and coffee scent of the waiting room. I wonder if they get the same sick little churning in their stomachs while waiting for one of the young, beautiful nurses to call their names. Do these women hurt as badly as I do? All of us carrying our pain around silently, smiling politely at the receptionist while we're all screaming on the inside? I wonder if they're able to pinpoint the exact moment this building, with its padded vinyl chairs, fluorescent lights, overly chipper staff, and banal floral paintings became a symbol not of hope, but of defeat. Of a trudging, despairing, resentment that festers inside this building. Inside of us. It happened so gradually for me that I don't remember the transition at all. It just happened, and all I can do is keep going. Like when you're running and you have to find the stamina and the will to just keep going, otherwise you'll never finish the race. And in a way, infertility is like a marathon, except you don't know where the finish line is, or if you'll ever get there. But you keep running anyway, because the only way you lose is if you stop.

I follow the nurse down the long, winding corridor, still not quite knowing my way through the windowless labyrinth at the center of the building. She walks quickly, and I'm grateful. My bladder is full nearly to bursting—an uncomfortable but necessary step in the procedure— and I just want to get this over with so I can go back to work and bury myself in other thoughts. Ongoing projects. Scott. Weekend plans. My mom. At the thought of my mom, I try to find that kernel of hope that lives somewhere deep inside me. If this works, if I could just give her this, maybe it would be enough to convince her to hang on.

The nurse opens a door to a small examination room and gestures me inside. A thin sheet lies folded neatly on the examination table. "Go ahead and undress from the waist down. The doctor will be in shortly. Any questions?" the nurse asks.

I shake my head and shoot her a rueful smile. "No, I'm good. Not my first rodeo here."

She squints at me for a second and then smiles. As though she doesn't know what to say in the face of my repeated failure, my body's stubborn refusal to get pregnant. I slip out of my nude-colored pumps, black skinny pants, and underwear, folding my clothes and laying them on top of my oversized powder blue tote, which sits on a plastic chair against the wall. I tuck my shoes underneath, neat and out of the way. In nothing but my drapey light blue silk blouse, I hop up on the examination table and begin the work of peeling the sheet open and then wrapping it around my waist.

I hear my phone buzz from inside my tote, and for a second, I debate hopping down off the table to get it, but then decide I don't care right now. I shift on the table, trying to take some of the pressure off my bladder, the paper crinkling beneath me. The sheet is scratchy against my ass. I rub my fingers over it, trying to guess the thread count. Any guess I come up with feels too generous.

The room is cool, and I tuck the sheet around my bare bottom half a little bit tighter. Tinny pop music plays over the sound system: Katy Perry's "Roar." The song ends and segues into Kelly Clarkson's "Stronger." These girl-power pop anthems sound naïve and silly to my jaded ears, and that makes me feel old. I wonder if they pipe them in on purpose.

I stare at the plaque mounted posters on the wall, one outlining the anatomy of a sperm, the other showing the various steps in the IVF process. My eyes wander over it as I wonder if that's what's next for us. Neither of these posters are new to me. I've stared at them dozens of times over the past several months. I should practically have them memorized by now. As Rachel Platten's "Fight Song" comes on, I read them again.

Finally, after a brisk knock on the door, Dr. Kane comes in, a clipboard and a small vial of clear liquid in her hands. Scott's sperm have been washed; I don't really know what this means, and it's one of the details I don't care about. I like to imagine the sperm going through a little tiny washing machine, circling around each other on the spin cycle. She has me verify that it's Scott's name on the vial—it is—and sign a consent form.

"The count and motility were on the low side today," she comments as she sets the vial down on a small metal tray beside the speculum. She doesn't offer anything further. I don't tell her about getting pulled over because she won't care.

"But it's still usable, right?" I ask as I lie back on the table, the paper crunching beneath me as I scooch my ass toward the edge.

She shrugs. "Sure. Can't hurt."

I slip my feet into the stirrups, adjusting the flimsy sheet, and open my legs. I wonder how many people at this clinic—doctors, nurses, ultrasound technicians—have now seen my vagina. It's got to be somewhere around a dozen by now. More than double the number of people I've had sex with, and at least two of those guys never got a good look at my vagina.

She inserts the speculum and I stare up at the ugly drop ceiling, letting the tiny little black dots go out of focus. Dr. Kane threads a catheter through my cervix. It scrapes at my insides like a straw against the raw innards of a pumpkin, and I start to cramp. She moves the catheter in even further and I inhale sharply. One thing I've learned over the past year: apparently, uteruses (uteri? That can't be right) really don't like to have foreign objects shoved inside them. Go figure.

The cramping peaks as she sends Scott's washed sperm through the catheter and into my uterus, where they'll hopefully find the perfectly mature egg I've grown with the help of drugs. A tear slips down over my temple, a tightness settling in my chest that I recognize as grief. Even though I should be hopeful—the hope always peaks right after this, I find—I can't help but mourn everything that's been taken from us. The intimacy of having sex to get pregnant. The so-called fun of trying (although I sincerely believe anyone who thinks trying for a baby is "fun" never really had to try that hard). The loss of dignity that comes with the invasive treatments.

I wipe at my cheek, not wanting Dr. Kane to see.

"All done," she says, removing the catheter and the speculum, leaving me with that deflated feeling I hate. She pulls off her gloves and tosses them into the bin in the corner. "Lie still for a few minutes and then you can empty your bladder." She pats my shoulder. "Good luck and enjoy your weekend!" And then she's gone, the door clicking behind her and leaving me alone in the room.

I press my knees together, hiding my vagina from the empty room. I try to think positively, to imagine the sperm swimming toward the egg and everything going as it should. Immediately, a cynical voice inside my head chimes in. *If it didn't work the first four times, why would it work now?* I dig and dig for that seed of hope, the one I'll cling to over the next two excruciatingly long weeks, until I'm lying there, fully excavated, with nothing to show for it this time. Over the sound system, Sara Bareilles tells me that she wants to see me be brave.

"Shut up," I whisper at the ceiling.

Half an hour later, I'm back at the offices of Carlisle and Winter, ready to throw myself into work, not wanting to think about my body, and if it's doing what it's supposed to do. With a cup of coffee in hand, I pace back and forth in front of the design firm's impressive swatch wall. It's divided both by textile type and color; I'm on the hunt for the perfect shade of millennial pink. My latest client, a newly divorced woman in her early thirties named Jillian, wants a "light, airy, and feminine" bedroom for her new home. I've promised her I'll have a concept board ready for her next week. I reach out and rub a square of poly-blend between my fingers and frown. Poly-blend doesn't exactly scream light and airy. My heels click against the concrete floor as I move down the wall. I smile when my eyes land on a pale pink square of linen. I slip it off the wall, the little metal ring dangling from my finger. I want the tufted, upholstered headboard to be the focus, and covering it with this delicate pink linen will pull the whole room together. In order to keep the room light and airy like she wants, I'm planning to keep the furniture white, the bed linens the palest yellow and the accessories to a minimum. I've also already sourced a gorgeous Turkish rug—off-white, shot through with hints of rose gold—that will ensure the space looks grown up and not childish.

I think about Jillian and the change she's gone through, the upheaval of the divorce. Her life is changing and new, and I get to be a part of it, however small and temporary. This is often the way it goes—people use color, use design, as a sort of demarcation line between the past and the future. They use it as a way to mark a change, to either move past or move toward something. A fresh start after a divorce. Redecorating the home that will see them into retirement. Moving into a new home after the loss of a spouse. Renovating a home in a new city. It's not something we often think about, but color and design are part of our lives; they're part of how we live, how we express ourselves.

A slender arm loops around my shoulders. "Hey, I was looking for you earlier." Mia Corbin peers down at the pink swatch of linen still dangling from my finger. "Ooh, pretty. Headboard for the divorcée?"

I nod and let myself lean into Mia, just a little, grateful to see her. She'd already been working as a designer at C&W for two years when I'd joined the firm three years ago. We'd become fast friends, bonding over our similar aesthetics, love of books, and shared love of our jobs. But beyond the surface stuff, we'd just clicked in a way that's difficult to put into words. We got each other, plain and simple, and these days,

Mia is one of my favorite people on the planet. I think I text her more than I text Scott.

Today, her thick, silky blond hair is straight, falling past her shoulders, her light green shift dress impeccable. I know that my own hair—fine and a light auburn color—is probably fizzing and limp thanks to the rain.

"How did it go earlier?" she asks as I take a sip of my coffee. Mia is one of only two people at work who know about what I've been going through. I haven't told anyone else because it feels weirdly personal—I mean, we're talking about my broken reproductive system here—and also because I don't want the pity, or the prying questions, or the insensitive comments. It's hard not to share sometimes because some situations would be easier if people knew what was going on with me, but it's better this way.

I shrug. "It went. Just have to wait and see."

She gives my arm a squeeze. "I really hope this is it for you. I can't imagine doing everything you've done to try to have a baby. I think I would've given up a long time ago. Or turned into a crazy person. I don't know how you do it."

She means this in the best way possible. I know she does. I know she doesn't have any idea how her comment, meant to bring comfort, makes me feel about three inches tall. I know she's trying to be supportive, but I feel like a shrunken, shriveled version of myself all the same. An infertile *other*, apart from the normal, fertile world. Mia's world, in which she conceived two perfect children with almost no effort. A bitterness rises up in the back of my throat, but I swallow it back and force myself to smile. It's just a comment, not meant to hurt. But I find that things that shouldn't hurt do, like a slide of fabric over sunburned skin. I'm raw, my nerves frayed. I have no protection. My defenses are worn out.

I've waited just a little too long to say something, and I think Mia senses that maybe her comment didn't land quite the way she wanted it to, so she changes the subject with a smile. "Have you seen a pic of the new guy Becca's seeing?"

I have, but I grab on to the subject change like a lifeline. I don't want to feel any of these ugly things about Mia. "No," I muster, shaking my head.

She turns and heads back toward her desk, weaving her way through the open space of the office, and I follow her. Carlisle and Winter is housed in a converted loft in a hip area of town, with high ceilings, arching windows, and concrete floors. The front of the open-concept space is a showroom, with staff desks spread out in the rear half.

I set my coffee and the fabric swatch down on Mia's desk and then peer over her shoulder as she flicks through pictures on her phone. Images of her eight-year-old daughter Ava and her six-year-old son Noah whiz by, but she stops on one: a picture of her husband Tom with Noah on his shoulders.

"Isn't it crazy how alike they look?" she says. My chest tightens. Will I ever be able to give Scott that? I don't know.

I nod. "Totally crazy," I murmur. I'm one hundred percent certain that Mia has no idea how looking at pictures of her kids makes me feel, and really, there's nothing I can say. She's not doing anything wrong, and her wanting to share pictures of her kids with me is completely normal. I'm the one who's not normal. I'm the one with the problem.

I hate that this is who I am now, this hollow person walking around, pretending. Pretending I'm not falling apart. Pretending it doesn't kill me a little bit to hear about Mia's kids. Pretending I'm not different.

"Okay, here we go," she says, stopping on a picture of an incredibly handsome man with thick, wavy black hair and tanned skin. While Mia and I are the boring married ones, Becca is the perpetually single member of our friend group and likes it that way. We, along with Allison Ling, another designer at the firm, all live vicariously through her. In a way, I think we all live vicariously through each other. I'm the one with the good-looking husband and rock-solid marriage; Mia's the one with the adorable kids; Becca's the one living it up; and Allison's the gorgeous one with a trust fund. Sometimes I wonder how much of our friendships are fueled by a kind of aspirational jealousy. I'm jealous of Mia's kids, of Becca's freedom, of Allison's money and looks.

"Wow," I say, even though this is the same picture that Becca texted me yesterday.

"Right? His name's Giancarlo. Apparently he has an Italian accent and everything."

"Lucky Becca. Although I have to say, Scott does a mean Mario impression."

Mia laughs. "You should roleplay with that. You be Princess Peach and he'll come save you from Bowser's castle."

I laugh too, but it's not genuine. If she had any idea about the sad state of our sex life, she'd understand why.

Her phone starts to buzz in her hand and she sighs, rolling her eyes. "It's the school. I have to take this," she says, swiping her finger across the screen and turning away from me to answer. She paces away a few steps, nodding as she talks and then hanging up after a brief conversation.

"They're always begging for volunteers over at that school. What part of 'I work fifty hours a week' do they not understand? I feel bad that I'm not available, but I can't just drop everything to come shepherd the kids to the library." She shakes her head slowly, staring unfocused at the wall. After a moment, she turns back to me and smiles. "Mom guilt. The struggle is real, I'm telling you."

I'm sure it is. I wouldn't know. I try to sympathize. I really do. But I can't quite get there, so I just smile back, not saying anything.

She sets her phone down on her desk, which is strewn with design materials—a couple of tiles, a paint chip sampler, a bound sheaf of wallpaper samples—and turns her gaze on me.

"You're awfully quiet this morning. Are you okay? Oh, shit, how's your mom? I should've asked. I'm sorry." Her brows pull together as she studies me with concern.

I lean a hip against her desk, staring down into my coffee. "No change. I'm going to stop by to see her after work."

"Is the new treatment helping?"

I shake my head slowly. "I don't know. It makes her so sick that it's hard to tell. Helping and feeling better, unfortunately, are on opposite ends of the spectrum."

"Fucking cancer," she whispers, rubbing a hand up and down my back. The gesture is soothing and warm, and it makes my eyes burn. I close them against the tears that want to fall. I cry so often these days that I almost always have tears at the ready, it seems.

"Fucking cancer," I echo, sipping my coffee.

3

I THINK ABOUT DYING A LOT. I THINK ABOUT WHAT IT MEANS TO not exist anymore, how our lives are nothing more than a flash in the cosmic pan and then it's as if we never existed at all. Sometimes I look around me when I'm in a public place—the mall, the grocery store, a park—and watch all the people. A hundred years from now, none of us will be here. The world will be entirely filled with new people—people who, with the exception of a few especially long-lived infants—aren't even here yet.

I think about my own mortality, and how I need to make the most of every day and not wish time away. I think about how this fantastic technicolor trip will one day end in blackness. Will I know when I'm dead? I don't really believe in an afterlife, but a tiny part of me refuses to give up that hope. I think about dying and wonder what the fucking point of it all is. Maybe there isn't one, and that in itself is the point.

Even though I have no say over it, this all makes me feel a driving need to make some kind of mark that will let me say "Aha! And you thought it'd be easy to forget me. Think again!"

I think I dwell on this so much because I've spent a lot of time thinking about what it means to pass on one's own genes, and how it's really our only stab at some kind of immortality.

Or maybe it's because my own mother is dying that I spend so much time thinking about death and what it means and how we live while staring it down. How we bite our thumbs at it and keep going. Somehow. I have to say, she does a better job of facing it than I do.

I pull into the driveway of the sprawling split-level she shares with my stepdad, Eddie. Sometimes it feels unfair to call Eddie my stepdad; he's been far more of a father to me than my biological father, Hugh, ever has. My parents divorced when I was six, and Mom married Eddie when I was ten. Even though we live in the same city, I only see Hugh once or twice a year, and that's plenty for me.

I put the car in park and cut the engine, giving myself a second before heading inside. Mom's been sick off and on for three years now —multiple rounds of chemo coupled with teasing but impermanent bouts of remission—and has been getting progressively sicker for the past several months. Even though she's been sick for years, I still have to brace myself before I see her. I don't want her to see my fear, my worry, my hurt. I don't want to make her feel worse about her pain with mine. I need to be the comfort-bringer, not the comfort-taker, and this is a role reversal for me. Typically, I'm the taker. I'm the taker with my mom, which I guess is mostly the natural order of things, but I'm also typically the taker with Scott, with Mia, with other friends. Especially over the past year or so. I'm aware of this, but I'm not sure what to do about it. I try not to dwell on it because it's just one more thing to feel guilty about. Another way that I'm failing the people around me. Because I don't think I was always this way. I think I used to know how to give.

I walk up the rosebush-lined pathway and let myself in the front door. The scent of pot hangs in the air, mingling with the Carole King music blasting from the living room speakers. I kick off my shoes and take the stairs up to the kitchen. Mom has her back to me; she sways her hips to the music as she stirs something in a bowl with a wooden spoon. She has a blue scarf patterned with golden birds wrapped around her head, and she's wearing a long, flowy blue-and-white striped dress. This is the first time in a while that I've seen her in something other than pajamas or a hospital gown, and even though the dress is too big for her now, I like seeing her in it. For a brief, fleeting moment, I let myself imagine that she's better, but I know she's not. She's just stoned. God bless medical marijuana.

"Hey, Mom," I say from my spot in the kitchen's doorway. She turns, her smile lighting up her gaunt face. When she smiles at me like that, I can picture exactly how she used to look, with her dark blond curls, assessing, shrewd gaze and warm, wide smile. Her face, when full, is so much friendlier than mine; our mouths are where we're most similar. For example, when she's biting back a sarcastic or otherwise snarky comment, her mouth quirks up to the left. So does mine. I wish I looked more like her so that after she's gone, I could see her in the mirror. But I look more like Hugh. Same hair, same eyes, same angular face.

"Hi, sweetie," she says, setting the spoon in the bowl and pulling me into a hug. I hug her back gingerly, afraid to hurt her. Her bones are *right there*, just under the surface of her too-soft, too-thin skin. Her collarbone juts out, bony and sharp, her skin taut over it. She's a shrunken, ravaged version of who she used to be, and I hate it. I hate watching her die slowly, bit by bit, pound by pound, her body disappearing before my eyes, and there isn't a damn thing I can do about it. She pulls back from the hug. "How did it go at the clinic this morning?" She returns to stirring what I can now see is chocolate chip cookie batter.

"I thought you'd sworn off sugar," I say, pulling out one of the stools in front of the island and sitting down.

She waves a hand in the air. "Oh, *fuck* that. I have terminal ovarian cancer. I'm eating whatever the hell I want." My mother never used to swear, but now she could give a trucker a run for his money. As though she's using all the swear words she saved up over the years, letting them pour out of her. I think she likes surprising people, shocking them even. I think it makes her feel a little bit more alive.

I smile. She seems good today. Maybe the new treatment—the Hail Mary treatment—is doing something. "I'm glad you feel like eating."

"So it went okay at the clinic this morning? It's okay if you don't want to talk about it." She samples a tiny bite of her batter and the memory of sitting on the kitchen counter as a little kid on a rainy day, helping her make cookies, licking batter off the spoon, rips through me.

"Yeah, it was fine. Now we wait." I don't really feel like talking about my medical stuff with her; it feels…wrong, somehow.

"Good." She nods and adds more chocolate chips to her batter. She never offers me unsolicited advice or platitudes. She never pressures me for grandkids. She just lets me be, and lets me talk if I want to.

"Where's Eddie?"

"Golfing. Grabbed his clubs as soon as the rain stopped. He'll be home soon. Here, come help me with this." She waves me over and hands me a spoon. We make quick work of placing glistening little balls of dough on the waiting baking sheet. I watch her hands as she works. Her wrists are delicate, and her knuckles look too big for her hands. I try to take everything in because this is all we have left now, but I also know it's not how she wants to be remembered, frail and sick with a scarf around her head. We chat about the weather—this morning's rain, and how Eddie's rosebushes will be happy—and other nothing topics until we finish with the dough and I slide the baking sheet into the waiting oven. We wash our hands and then Mom turns to me, a funny look on her face.

"Come sit with me in the living room. I need to talk to you about something." Her voice is quiet and determined, her expression now serious. Something about her tone sends my heart rocketing down into my stomach.

I follow her in, and she turns the music down before settling herself on the couch. She moves so much slower than she used to—too much life has been crushed out of her. I sit down beside her, focusing on her. Willing this to be anything but what I think it is.

She takes my hand and gives it a squeeze. "I've decided to stop treatment, Claire."

Her words—the ones I'd been both expecting and dreading for some time now—hit me like buckshot, peppering me with pain. Breathing hurts. I swallow and nod, forcing myself to meet her luminous eyes. She's been scared to tell me this—I can see that from the tense, worried look on her face. "Okay, Mom." My throat is so tight I'm not sure how I manage to get the words out, but I do. I can't fight her on this—she's already fought so hard for so long. She doesn't owe me— or anyone—anything more at this point.

Her shoulders relax a bit. "The new chemo isn't doing anything to slow the progression, and it's making me sick as a damn dog. I don't want to spend my last days feeling that way if I can help it. I want to enjoy what I have left, and I can't do that if I'm hunched over a toilet day in and day out."

I brush away a tear that managed to escape, running free down my cheek. "Once you stop, how long will you have?"

"They're not entirely sure. A few months, probably." She says this as though we're still discussing the weather.

A few months. My heart cracks right down the middle. I forget how to breathe. A few months. How can that be all we have left? She's only sixty-two.

Deep down, I've always known this—or a version of this—was coming, but I never wanted to acknowledge it. It was easier to carry on with my head buried in the sand, focused on other things and not the one, big unavoidable thing.

Now that it's here, I am wholly unprepared for it. Unprepared for the intense sense of loss and emptiness that just about swallows me up when I imagine being here without her. I'm not ready.

I will never be ready.

"And you're sure?" I ask because I have to.

She plucks a tissue from the box on the coffee table and dabs at her eyes. "I'm sure. I can't do this anymore, Claire. I'm done. I just want to live out what time I have left as comfortably and peacefully as possible."

My eyes burn and I blink rapidly, but it's not enough. The tears I've been holding back break free, sliding down my cheeks and dripping onto my pants. What she's asking for is completely fair. Completely valid and reasonable. I want to argue with her, but only for my own selfish reasons. So I don't. There's nothing for me to say here. "Okay, Mom. Okay," I manage and then blow my nose, a loud, undignified sound. I cry harder.

Mom's crying now too, and she leans forward and pulls me into her arms. "I don't want to leave you, baby girl. I don't want to go. I don't want to miss out on seeing you do all the wonderful things you're going to do. I want to be here. I want to stay. But that's just not in the cards for me." She kisses the top of my head and I try to breathe around the sobs shaking my entire body. I feel like a child, clinging to her. "I love you Claire. I love you to the moon and back. I will always love you to the moon and back. Even after I'm gone." She pulls away and slips a frail hand under my chin, tilting my face up. "Love doesn't die. I will, but I'll always love you, baby girl."

My throat hurts and I close my eyes, scrunching my face tightly. "I love you too, Mom," I whisper. "I love you too."

For several long moments, we hold each other and cry, grieving and comforting at the same time. I'll soon be both motherless and childless. A lone figure, an outsider to any typical female equation. Anger sparks deep within me at the way our bodies have failed us, have betrayed us. At everything they've stolen from us: futures, and happiness, and normalcy. Our bodies are thieves of life, both actual and potential.

The oven timer goes off and Mom moves to stand, but I wave her off. Wiping at my cheeks with my now crumpled and soggy tissue, I head into the kitchen, shut off the timer and pull the cookies from the oven. I test one with a toothpick and then move them onto the cooling rack. I'm hungry and they smell good, but I don't want them. I have a feeling the smell of these cookies will be one of those smells that will imprint somewhere deep in my brain, forever tied to a memory. For example, lasagna smells like when my parents told me they were getting divorced. The scent of CK One smells like my first high school crush and subsequent heartbreak. Lilies smell like my wedding day. Coconut sunscreen smells like the horrible day on our honeymoon when Scott and I had a stupid fight because we were jetlagged and had too much to drink. The petrichor scent of wet concrete after a summer rain smells like the day I won an award for one of my designs. And now, chocolate chip cookies smell like my mom telling me she's only got a couple of months left to live.

I'm not sure how long I stand there, staring at the tile backsplash, cataloguing these olfactory memories as mascara crusts beneath my swollen eyes. I move some cookies onto a plate and take them into the living room, where mom is listening to Carole King with her eyes closed. I set the plate on the coffee table in front of the couch, and we eat the cookies in silence while Carole croons sympathetically that it's too late now.

It's all too late.

When I finally walk through the front door after a day that's felt like a week, the house smells like garlic and bacon and cheese. I know these smells; Scott's making his homemade macaroni and cheese. Comfort food. I wonder if he suspects what a horrible day I've had, or if him making one of my favorites is a happy coincidence. In either case, I'm happy to try to temporarily find comfort in carbs and fat. Despite my mood, my mouth waters and my stomach rumbles.

I kick off my shoes, drop my bag by the front door and make my way to the kitchen. I rub absently at my face. My eyes still feel swollen, my cheeks sticky with dried tears, even though I washed my face at Mom's before heading home. The macaroni is already in the oven, and

Scott is standing in front of the sink in a T-shirt and jeans, barefoot, as he washes dishes. For just a moment, I stare at his broad back, and a tingling wave of something hot and almost sad washes over me. I rise up onto my toes and kiss his cheek, and then pick up a towel to dry. I don't deserve him. I feel this more keenly now than I usually do. He's good to me in a way that makes me feel self-conscious sometimes, that makes me feel that I'm not worthy of him and all his easy goodness.

"Hey," I say, feeling guilty that I didn't text him at all today. Taking and not giving, yet again. "How was your board meeting?"

"Fine. They were happy with the fourth quarter forecasts. How did it go at the clinic today? I got a little worried when I didn't hear from you." My guilt multiplies.

"Sorry. It's been a…actually a pretty horrible day." As I dry, I tell him about getting pulled over on my way to the clinic, about the insemination, about work. And then I pause, not wanting to say the next words because I don't want them to be real. "I stopped by to see my mom after work."

"How is she?" Scott's brow is furrowed in concern.

I shake my head, the familiar sting pricking behind my eyes. "Not good. She's stopping treatment."

Scott's eyes go wide. "What? Shit."

All I can do is nod. "Yeah. It's not helping anymore and it's making her sick. There's nothing more they can do for her. She has a few months left, maybe."

Scott takes the towel from me, dries his hands and pulls me into his arms. My head settles into his chest, into the groove that feels as though it was made just for my head.

"I'm so sorry, sweetheart," he murmurs into my hair. I slide my arms around his waist and soak up the comfort of his body. He rubs a hand up and down my back, and the tenderness of that gesture, coupled with the emotionally exhausting day I've had, sends fresh tears down my cheeks. I wipe them on his T-shirt.

"Everything's such a mess," I whisper. "I don't know how to…to…"

But I can't finish my thought because I'm crying harder now, and I can't breathe and talk at the same time.

Scott lets me fall apart in his arms, holding me tightly so that when I'm finished, my shattered pieces won't have gone far and I can put myself back together again. He doesn't tell me that everything will be okay because he can't, and I appreciate that. Everything is decidedly not okay.

The oven timer dings and after a final kiss on top of my head, Scott moves away to rescue our dinner before it burns. I head to the fridge and retrieve a bottle of white wine from the top rack. I pour us each a glass, a little less in mine than in Scott's, and bring them to the table. I sometimes feel guilty about drinking while trying to get pregnant, but then I think about all of the drunken one-night stands that end in pregnancies and figure a half a glass of wine probably isn't hurting anything. Cutting out alcohol cold turkey isn't going to suddenly make my eggs less shitty. So whatever. Cheers.

As Scott dishes out the heavenly smelling macaroni and cheese, I duck into the bathroom to once again wash the tears off my face. I'm so sick of crying. I'm so sick of having so much to cry about. I'm sick of hurting. I'm sick of feeling as though every time I think I see a light at the end of this tunnel, I get hit with a goddamn train.

I think Scott senses this and as we eat, we talk about anything but cancer and infertility. This is actually harder to do than it sounds because these two topics have sunk their snaking, slippery tentacles into pretty much every aspect of our lives. But somehow, we manage, dancing around them artfully. We've had lots of practice. We talk about work, about weekend plans, about the news, about if we want to get a dog. Anytime we start to veer close to one of the shadowy giants looming over us, we scurry quickly away, escaping before we can get sucked in.

When we're finished eating and the rest of the dishes are done or tucked away in the dishwasher, I slide my arms around his waist and kiss him. For once, I'm actually interested in sex. I want Scott to use his body to shut off my brain. I don't want to think anymore today. I just want to feel, to give myself over to something good and life affirming. I want to remember what it feels like to want and be wanted. I want to have sex because it feels good, not because it might lead to a baby.

This last bit is easier said than done, I realize, as Scott takes me by the hand and leads me up the stairs to our bedroom. Sex has become this unspoken, looming presence between us. I'm well aware that both the frequency and the variety have dropped off considerably over the past year. It's not that I'm not attracted to Scott; I am. But it's hard to feel both sexy and like a science experiment at the same time. The invasive tests, constant doctor's visits and disappointment after disappointment have bit into the intimacy between me and my husband, leaving teeth marks that haven't quite healed. While we've been trying to get pregnant, sex has become timed and clinical. My orgasm is irrelevant to the process, and all spontaneity and fun has shriveled away. I'm too tired, too frustrated, too lost for spontaneity and fun. For years now, our sex life has been based on a simple equation: if I'm in my fertile window, we make love. If I'm not, what's the point?

Dr. Kane has seen more of my vagina over the past several months than Scott has, and I don't really even like her. Sometimes it feels like my vagina isn't a sex organ anymore; it's merely a defective part of my body not deserving of attention or pleasure. And honestly, sex is the last thing I feel like doing when I've spent every other morning with an ultrasound wand up there, probing me to check on the sad status of my ovaries. There are days when I don't even want to be touched; it feels like the only way to really be at home in my own body.

Slowly, over time, sex has become a reminder of what my body can't do. My body has become a battle ground, covered with invisible scars, each one making it harder and harder to let go. To enjoy. To revel in feeling good in my body that has failed me. Failed us.

Worst of all, I worry that whether or not we're ever successful in conceiving, the damage done will be permanent. I don't want it to be, but I don't know how to recover from this and simply go back to what we once had. Maybe we can't. Maybe a fabulous sex life is just yet another thing infertility has stolen from us. I don't know.

But today, I feel as though maybe there's a glimmer of hope, even if that glimmer is fueled by the weight of grief. I'm not wanting to have sex to get pregnant right now; I'm wanting it because I need Scott. I need to not feel alone and scared for a few minutes. I need to remember that I'm alive, here and now.

Once we're in our bedroom, I pull Scott's shirt off over his head and drop it on the floor. We kiss as he eases me down onto our bed, his weight solid and reassuring above me as I sink into the mattress. He kisses my neck, my ears, my face and I close my eyes, trying to concentrate on just feeling. Just being.

Between kisses, we shed the rest of our clothes. Scott begins to kiss his way down my body and I tense up, grabbing at his shoulders. "No," I say, more of a plea than a command. "I just want you."

He stops his downward trajectory but frowns. "Claire, I want to. It's been a long time since…"

I push up onto my elbows. "I know, but I just…"

I see the truth written on Scott's handsome face. All that damage I'm worried about? One way to make sure it's permanent is if I keep pushing him away. That's not fair to him, or to me. We deserve better.

I lay back down on the bed and open my legs a little for him. "Okay," I say, breathing deeply and trying to relax. Trying to ignore the way having my legs spread makes me feel as though I'm in stirrups, ready for my clinical closeup. Spreading my legs used to be sexy. Now it's decidedly not, even though I'm spreading them for my husband who wants to make me feel good.

I don't come. It's not Scott's fault. It's mine. Even though I'm the one who initiated this, I can't get out of my head enough to enjoy it. And even when I do seem to shut off the leaky faucet of my constantly dripping thoughts, my body doesn't respond the way it used to. I don't know if Scott takes this personally or not. I don't ask because I'm afraid of the answer. Afraid of what it'll reveal, and what it might change.

We move on from my failed orgasm and have sex. I wrap myself in the scent of his body, the taste of his skin, clinging to him, desperate to get what I'd wanted out of this. I'm not sure that I do, but at least we tried.

When we're finished, we go downstairs to find something to watch on Netflix, not discussing the very mediocre sex we just had. I'm relieved.

4

Before

Claire steps into Grinders Café and collapses her umbrella, flinging drops of water through the air. The air outside smelled like spring and worms; the air inside smells like coffee and carbs. Claire shakes out her umbrella, frowning at the length of the line snaking up to the counter. With a resigned sigh, she joins it, tapping her foot impatiently. She's on yet another errand for one of the senior partners at her design firm, running across town sourcing rugs and lamps for a project. She knows she won't get any credit for her work. Frankly, she's getting frustrated with how little designing she does. She's tired of being an errand girl for the "real" designers. She has big plans. Her own clients, her own designs. Maybe even her own custom items, like wallpaper and fabric. She's starting to realize none of that's going to happen at her current gig.

The line moves and she shuffles forward with everyone else. A man turns and looks over his shoulder, scoping out the line behind him. His eyes meet Claire's and they linger for a moment. Claire tucks a strand of hair behind her ear and smiles. He's cute. Really cute. He turns back around and Claire shuffles sideways a little, trying to get a better look at him. He's tall—over six feet, for sure—and nicely dressed in a black suit, light blue shirt and dark blue tie. His shoulders are broad, his waist is narrow. His hair—thick and dark brown—is just a little too long, covering his ears.

It has been nearly four months since Claire's last relationship ended. If you could call a string of increasingly boring dates a relationship. For the longest time, she was happy to date around, experience life, not be tied down. But now, in her late twenties, the allure of that is definitely wearing off. She wants something steady. Something serious. Something real.

The guy turns around again and Claire smiles. He smiles back and her heart picks up speed. Okay, he's more than cute. He's gorgeous. Big brown eyes. Amazing smile. Strong jaw. She glances away, biting her lip, and then looks back, deliberately flirting. He's still looking. She's about to wave when the man behind gorgeous guy taps his arm. It's his turn to order. He turns back around.

Claire watches as he places his order, pays, and then moves to the side to wait for his drink. His phone rings and he answers it. He picks up his drink and moves away.

He's still on the phone when Claire orders her vanilla latte. She waits for her drink, trying not to stare at him. He slips his phone back into his pocket and then walks to the little table with milk and sugar and stir sticks to fix his coffee. Claire doesn't need anything in her latte, but she heads over to the table anyway.

She steps up beside him and sets her latte down, watching his hands —his really nice hands, big and masculine—as he stirs milk into his coffee.

"Hi," she says, toying with the cardboard sleeve on her cup.

He looks over at her, killing her with that smile. *Oh God, he has dimples.* Dead. She is dead. "Hi. Sugar?" He tries to casually, smoothly, slide the sugar bowl across the table toward her. Tries, and fails, and the white bowl bumps, stops and then crashes to the floor, breaking in half and spilling sugar across Claire's beige flats.

His eyes are wide and he's completely frozen in place. Claire throws her head back and laughs. After a second, he joins her, the sound rich and sexy.

"I'm so sorry," he says, crouching down to pick up the broken pieces of the bowl. "You must think I'm the biggest dork." He sets the shards down on the table and dusts his hands off.

"I think you're really cute," she says, holding out her hand to him. He blushes, and it's completely endearing. "I'm Claire. Claire Dailey."

He takes her hand and shakes it, zings of electricity shooting up her arm. "Scott Stanhope."

Now - September

A week later, on Saturday morning, I'm at my friend Becca's shop before it opens for the day, along with Mia and Allison. Becca Montgomery is my age, and she runs the home décor store Nest and Nomad, which is a large, airy space in one of the old, renovated riverside buildings in the revitalized shopping area known as Sawmill Commons. Ten years ago, this area was full of crumbling stone, aging vernacular architecture, abandoned industry, and a few struggling businesses, but thanks to a series of grants and local investment projects, the late 19th century buildings have been restored, the streets cleaned up, and businesses lured with low rents and other incentives. There are dozens of other stores besides Becca's, including an independent bookstore called Paper-house where I often spend both too much time and too much money.

I first met Becca about five years ago at a local design trade show, back when she'd been the buyer for a large home décor chain, and I'd been working at a different design firm, a bigger one in which I'd just been a cog in a wheel, spending most of my time sourcing for more senior designers. About a year after that, she'd quit to pursue her dream of running her own store, and she hasn't looked back. I introduced her to Mia and Allison when I started working at Carlisle and Winter a few years ago, and the four of us have become a solid group of friends. We have breakfast together every other Saturday morning and then hang out in Becca's shop, talking.

Within our group, Becca's the worldly, interesting one. Mia's the mom, Allison's the straight talking, no-nonsense friend who'll give you a swift kick in the ass when you need it. I'm not sure who I am. Mostly, I just feel like the broken one. The taker, who leans on these women. They've been with me through all the shit of the past couple of years— the infertility, Mom's cancer. And yet I still feel like kind of an outsider. I know they don't really understand how hard things are for me sometimes. Mia's kids came easily to her, and neither Allison or Becca want kids. All of their parents are still alive and well. But I know they try. It's not fair of me to want something they don't know how to give. I never used to have these unrealistic expectations of these women who love me. Then again, before the infertility and the cancer, I didn't feel like an outsider, either.

I sip my coffee in its cheery yellow and orange retro-style paper cup from Grinders Café next door and watch Becca as she flits around her store like a fairy, the effect emphasized by her blond pixie cut, enormous eyes that dominate her delicate face and slender, almost waifish figure. She's wearing a simple linen dress, no jewelry, and no makeup except for her usual cherry red lipstick. Sometimes, I want to *be* Becca, with her ease, her confidence, her worldliness. Her delicate femininity. But I know that's a childish fantasy. I can't be anyone else, as much as I might want to.

"So, tell me more about this Giancarlo," says Allison, taking a delicate sip of her macchiato.

Becca smiles coyly, fluffing a pillow and setting it down on an armchair. "What do you want to know?"

"Becca, I haven't had sex in eighteen months, three weeks and six days. I want to know *everything*."

"A lady doesn't tell."

"Oh, come on," says Mia, gesturing with her steaming cup of Earl Gray. "Throw a girl a bone."

"Especially since it'll be the only bone Alli's getting right now," I say, and we laugh again.

"It's true. I'm such a poor unfortunate soul," she says, flashing a puppy dog expression at all of us.

To my surprise, Becca actually blushes. "I know that I'm normally willing to share, but things are…I don't know. They're different."

"Oh my God," says Mia, pointing a red-nailed finger at her. "Are you in love with this guy?"

My mouth falls open. Becca does not fall in love. Love is gauche. Love is a Hallmark cliché. Becca is above the plebeian act of falling in love.

"I don't know," she says, her voice coming out like a little croak.

Allison sighs, shaking her head slowly, her beautiful thick black hair fanning out over her shoulders. "Don't do it, sweetie. Stay strong. I don't care how many inches are in his pants or zeroes are in his bank account, he's not worth it." I can feel Alli ramping up to one of her men are trash rants, and I know that's not what Becca needs to hear right now.

"What's different about Giancarlo?" I ask, trying to redirect the conversation.

Becca flashes me a grateful smile. "Everything." She continues to putter around the store as she extolls his virtues—his sense of romance, their shared interests and worldviews, the out of this world sex, the way she misses him when she's not around him.

I walk beside her as she talks, my eyes landing on every object she touches. I could live in her store. I almost always come away with something either for myself, or for a design project I'm working on. Today, I've already spotted and claimed two pillows I think will look fabulous on the tufted bench I'm planning to put at the foot of my client Jillian's bed. One is a soft pink with a champagne-colored game of tic-tac-toe painted on it, and the other is a creamy gray embroidered with an intricate mandala in white and blue thread.

Becca stops suddenly, her shoulders falling. "But he's here on a work visa, and he's only got three months before he has to go back to Italy."

Allison frowns, but Mia's face lights up with a dawning understanding. "So you think you need to figure out what you want by then."

Becca nods. "Normally I'm fine with an expiry date, but like I said, everything's different with him. I've never really wanted to get married, but what if the only way to keep him in my life is to marry him after only knowing him for a few months?"

"Get a prenup." Alli shoots her a look. "Best thing I ever did, aside from divorcing Calvin."

Finished with her puttering, Becca returns to the front desk and picks up her coffee, taking an aggressive sip of her cold brew and leaving a red lipstick ring on the plastic lid. "Anyway, I'll have to figure it out," she says, ignoring Alli's comment, and then turns to me. I can feel the subject change coming like a drop in air pressure. "Have you decided if you're going to test at home this time?" she asks me. With some cycles, I've taken a home pregnancy test about ten days after the insemination. Other times, I've waited the full two weeks for the blood test at the clinic. Neither method of testing has been lucky for me.

"I haven't decided yet. I think I still have at least one test kicking around in the back of the bathroom vanity somewhere. If I can find it and it's not expired, I'll probably use it. I don't know that I'll go buy more though." I shake my head and let out a little snorting laugh. "I should've bought stock in Clearblue. I don't even want to think about how much money I've spent on pregnancy tests over the past three years."

She smiles sympathetically. "Well, you've been investing in hope. I get it." She takes another hearty sip, as though she can't get the caffeine into her system fast enough. "If you do test at home, when can you?"

"I guess Monday, at the earliest." As I say this, I know I probably won't be able to hold out and wait for the blood test on Friday. The worst part of the blood test is waiting for the phone call, which comes hours and hours after the blood draw, leaving me on pins and needles all day, jumping every time my phone buzzes.

"So…do you think you are?" asks Allison. Direct almost to a fault, as always.

I shrug. "I don't know. Maybe. Maybe not." I fiddle with my coffee cup. "Probably not." Although the wait is agonizing, there's also an odd kind of comfort in it. Until I test, I'm both pregnant and not. I have no evidence to prove or disprove either one, and both paths are still open to me, at least in my mind. A Schrodinger's pregnancy, of sorts.

We talk some more, even though the topics are distinctly Claire-focused. Once again, I'm in the role of taker, not giver. We talk about my mom and her decision to stop treatment. (Becca suggests taking her on an exotic trip). We talk about my mediocre sex life and how I don't know how to fix it. (Allison suggests sex toys and role playing, which brings Mia back to her Mario/Princess Peach fantasy). We talk about my fear that I'm never going to get pregnant. Well, I talk, and they listen. And this is what I need. There's nothing anyone can do or say to make any of this suck any less.

A rustic wooden picture frame catches my eye from another display, and I wander over to it, running the tips of my fingers over the rough-hewn wood. I pick it up, savoring the heft in my hand, allowing myself to fantasize. Empty picture frames are so full of possibility. They're these empty spaces frozen as if caught mid-yawn, waiting for a story to tell others. Waiting for a cherished memory to guard. Before I can talk myself out of it, I take the empty frame to the cash register, placing it on the lacquered counter.

Becca looks at me, a tiny frown on her red lips. "You're still doing this?"

"Guess so," I say, trying not to feel put out by her judgment.

She hesitates, and for a second I wonder if she's going to refuse to sell me the frame. She picks it up and enters the price into the cash register, ringing up my purchase. I hand her some money and she starts wrapping it in tissue paper. She pauses mid-fold.

"Just promise me you're actually going to use it. Okay?"

"Using it is the whole idea," I say. But I know what she means. I have a collection of empty picture frames, probably at least a dozen of them at home. Empty and waiting, just like me.

"Use it right away," she clarifies, slipping the tissue-wrapped frame into a small brown paper shopping bag stamped with the store's logo.

I nod, but I know I won't. It'll join the others in the chest. Waiting expectantly.

Becca's phone chimes, warning her that it's now 9:59 AM and time to unlock the door. The front of the store looks out onto a little courtyard of sorts, and several people stand around, admiring the displays in the shop windows. A busker, a young guy with a guitar and a little stool, has set himself up in the middle. I can't hear what he's playing.

Mia and Allison say their goodbyes, but I stay behind, wanting to visit the bookstore before going home.

As soon as Becca unlocks and opens the door, several customers bustle inside, eager to begin their shopping. Two women approach the counter, one middle-aged, the other in her late twenties and very obviously pregnant. Her hand rests smugly on her protruding belly and she beams first at Becca, then at me. The sight slices through me like a hot knife through butter, burning me from the inside out. It's a mocking tableau, a reminder of what I'll never have, even if I do somehow manage to get pregnant, which feels just shy of impossible most days, despite the shaky hope of my ever-growing picture frame collection. But even if I'm successful, my mom won't be here for it. There will be no shopping trips, no teary phone calls, no deciding what she'd like her grandparent name to be. She'll be gone.

"Hi, we're looking for some nursery décor for my daughter," says the woman. She has a full head of graying hair, an appropriate amount of flesh on her bones. Her eyes are bright, cheery. She gives her daughter's arm a squeeze, pride and delight practically oozing from her. For an irrational split second, I hate these women. I feel slapped in the face by the abundance of fertility around me, by the cruelty I'm supposed to quietly carry so as not to disturb others during their moments of joy.

"That's my cue," I mumble to Becca, who smiles sympathetically. I grab my cup of coffee, the little brown bag with my frame inside, and my purse and then step out into the fall sunshine coating the courtyard. The busker is playing "Blackbird" by the Beatles, filling the air with its wistful tune, but I don't linger. I cross the sun-warmed stones and push open the door of Paperhouse.

I smile and nod at the little bald man behind the counter. He starts to smile back, but his expression sours when his gaze lands on my coffee cup. I duck my head sheepishly. I take one final sip of the coffee and then gently place it in the trash can by the desk.

I make my way to a long, heavy table near the front that always holds a display of new releases, both fiction and non. This is where I always start before making my meandering way up and down the shelves. I trail my fingers over the covers, savoring the texture of the embossed words. The scent of paper and ink envelops me as I pick up a few promising titles, reading the jacket copy, my thumb zipping along the edges of the pages as I flip through the book.

I pick out a new historical fiction novel by an author I've read before and head for the shelves, cautiously avoiding the children's section, which is right next to the parenting section, naturally. I remember when I'd once been excited to venture down those aisles, not in this store, but in another, a different one from years ago. I remember perusing the baby and pregnancy books and finally picking out two about conception and fertility, naively wondering if I'd even finish reading them before I got pregnant.

Not only did I finish reading them, but they both wound up in the recycling bin over a year ago. They were too painful to keep.

I turn down another aisle, picking up the memoir of a former First Lady and turning to page forty. Page forty is always my litmus test. I don't start at the beginning. Beginnings are shiny and highly polished and perfect, but by page forty, the actual narrative, the true voice, are in full swing. It's far enough in to get a feel for the writing style, but not so far in that I'm going to spoil anything for myself. Seriously, try it next time you're book shopping. Page forty.

"*Noooooo! I need! I need!*" An urgent toddler scream interrupts my reading, coming from the children's section in the next aisle over. I move into the space between the aisles, still pretending to read my book, but wanting to observe. The mother is younger than me, but her face is drawn in lines of exhaustion and frustration. She plants her hands on her hips, staring at the wailing child, who flings himself onto the floor, kicking and screaming.

"We're here to get a birthday present for your cousin. I told you we're not getting anything to take home today," she says, her voice thin and tight. Her knuckles are white. This only makes the boy scream harder. A book about fire trucks lies on the floor beside him, discarded in his anguish. The mother sighs and moves to pick him up. He flails and bucks like a fish in a net, crashing his forehead against her chin. I wince, imagining how much that must've hurt. Tears roll down his face. He screams, the high-pitched, ear-piercing screams only a small child can make. Others have now started to watch. She begins to maneuver his rigid body back into the stroller when he bucks again, knocking her Grinders coffee cup out of the stroller's cup holder and sending it crashing to the floor. The scent of vanilla hazelnut permeates the air. The mother clenches her jaw, still wrestling her screaming child into the stroller. There is a sizable coffee splatter on her jeans.

"That's enough!" she says to him through gritted teeth. Pink spots rise on her cheeks, and she blinks rapidly, as though holding back tears of frustration.

"Mean Mommy! Mean Mommy! Mean Mommy! No like you! Mean Mommy!" The boy chants as she finally manages to buckle him in, rolling him hastily out of the store, leaving both the book and the spilled coffee behind.

I'm ashamed to admit that there's a gleeful schadenfreude in watching this unfold. Not that I would've had any idea how to deal with that if I were in her shoes—I'm not judging her. And yet, as silence descends back over the store, once again restoring it to the peaceful sanctuary I love, I realize I feel relieved. A part of me—a very, very small part—is happy that I don't have to spend my precious Saturday morning dealing with a screaming child in a public place. I glance down at the two books in my hands, the products of my leisurely browsing. My time and my money are my own, and maybe that isn't the *worst* thing in the world, right here, right now.

Immediately, my stomach tightens and begins to churn uncomfortably. My skin heats as the guilt burns through me. After everything I've gone through to try to get pregnant, it feels supremely shitty of me to even have these thoughts. I should want to trade places with that woman, should want to embrace the struggles and turmoil and hard days that come with being a parent. After all, isn't that what I'm fighting so hard for?

The relief sits uncomfortably beside my guilt, and they whisper to each other, tugging my emotions back and forth. A dull ache takes root just behind my temples. I'm still staring at the empty spot where the mother and screaming child were, the book, the spilled coffee. I walk over and right the coffee cup, and then pick up the book and place it gently back on the shelf. As if this tiny bit of housekeeping can somehow atone for my reaction to the whole thing.

I pay for my books and go home.

When I step into the house, it's completely silent. Sunshine filters in through the windows, slanting across the floor and illuminating the dust motes floating idly in the air. I can still smell the coffee and maple syrup scents leftover from Scott's breakfast. I listen, looking for signs of

Scott, but the house feels empty, absent of the subtle vibrations made by the presence of another person.

"Scott?" I call out, but there's no response. I pull my phone out of my purse to check for text messages, but there's nothing. I shrug, leave my purse and shoes by the front door and head upstairs to put my frame away with the others and to add my books to the shelves in the office. Yes, the same office where Scott jerked off last week. It's a multi-purpose room, okay?

As I slip the books onto the shelf, adding them to my ever-growing collection, I hear the sound of Scott's laughter coming through the open office window, a deep baritone that I would recognize anywhere. I set the bag with the frame down on the desk. The curtains flutter in the breeze as I step towards the window, pushing one of the gauzy panels aside to look out.

"Do it again, Mr. Scott!" A little girl's voice, high with excitement.

I can see Scott's bare back, his broad shoulders, water from his hair dripping down onto his skin. The neighbors directly behind us, the Wus, have a pool and two little kids. Scott gets along great with Rob, but then again, Scott gets along with *everyone*. I get along less well with Sarah, and yes, I generally get along less well with people than Scott, but I struggle with Sarah mainly because all she ever wants to talk about is kids and how we ought to have some "before I get too old and my eggs shrivel up." I think she's trying to be funny when she says this. I usually make some mumbled excuse and try to change the subject. I'm not comfortable enough with them to tell them about our struggle to conceive. And I've learned that whether we tell people or not, we leave ourselves vulnerable to dagger-shaped words disguised as advice. If we don't tell people, we get the inevitable questions about when we're going to have kids, how come we don't have kids, etc. They tell us not to wait too long, often making an infuriating *tick-tock* sound complete with finger wagging. They wax nauseatingly poetic about how one can never truly know what love is until one is a parent (I once got into an argument at a party with someone who'd said that to me. Yes, I'd had some wine. It didn't make their remark any less insulting or condescending).

So, in the past, in a misguided attempt to side-step all of these comments and prying questions, we've tried honesty. But, of course, that almost always blows up in our faces. Here, I now present a list of the top ten worst things people have actually said to us when they've learned we're having trouble getting pregnant. And let me be clear: these conversations all began because someone had asked us about having children, not because we brought the subject up.

1. Why don't you just adopt?/Have you ever considered adoption?/You should adopt because the world is overpopulated anyway. (I have a variety of snarky responses to this one, including "no, what's adoption?" "did you consider adoption before getting pregnant with your biological children, since the world is already overpopulated?" "there's no *just* about adoption, which is often a path just as emotionally fraught and financially draining as infertility treatments," and my favorite, "Oh, we tried that, but the Cabbage Patch was fresh out of healthy unwanted babies.")

2. You're lucky you don't have kids. At least you still get to sleep in! (Yes, a few extra hours of sleep on the weekend are worth more than a *child*. Please, tell me more about how "lucky" I am to be infertile. This is like telling someone with a digestive disease how lucky they are because at least they're skinny.)

3. Just relax! You're probably not pregnant because you're too stressed about it. (You know, I wasn't stressed about getting pregnant until almost two years had gone by and we were starting down the path of expensive, invasive fertility treatments. And honestly, would you say this to someone with a different medical issue? Just relax! Your stress is

probably making your allergies worse! I sincerely hope you hear how ridiculous that sounds).

4. Maybe you're not meant to be a mother. (Yes, someone actually said this to me, and no, I did not punch her in the throat. Gold star for Claire.)

5. You shouldn't have waited so long. (I was barely thirty-two when we started trying, so not exactly a withered up old crone. But thank you for chastising me as I open up about this difficult issue.)

6. So is it your fault, or Scott's? (Asked by a boorish co-worker of Scott's at a company event. I did not throw my drink in his face or tell him to mind his own fucking business. Another gold star for Claire.)

7. Maybe you just don't want it badly enough. You have to manifest the things you want. (Excuse me while I manifest my foot up your ass.)

8. It could be worse. You could have cancer or something. (Is this supposed to be comforting? What are you, the empathy police? Everyone's problems are their problems, and saying it could be worse is completely dismissive and minimizing. Things could *almost always* be worse. That doesn't mean people aren't allowed to be upset about bad things happening in their lives.)

9. OMG, I would *never* do fertility treatments. It's just not natural. (How nice for you that you never had to make that decision.)

10. Whatever you do, never ever give up! (I know this is meant to be reassuring, comforting, inspiring. But it's not. Sometimes giving up is the most humane thing to do. Not that we're there yet, but we might be someday. And no, I don't want to hear your story about your neighbor's cousin's boss's sister who gave up and got pregnant with a "miracle" baby at age forty-nine.)

So, yeah. We don't tell people anymore.

Recently, Sarah revealed to me that she and Rob are trying for a third. Every time I see her, even if it's just a wave across our backyards, I brace myself for the inevitable pregnancy announcement, like a soldier in the trenches ducking and covering in anticipation of a grenade. Lately, I've been avoiding the Wus altogether. It's just too much for me, waiting for her to tell me she's pregnant, watching her adorable kids run around, wondering why it's so easy for them and so hard for us. So it's not unusual that Scott's over there without me.

I watch six-year-old Charlotte Wu climb onto Scott's shoulders. "Daddy, Daddy, watch this!" Rob waves from the deck, smiling at his daughter.

Scott crouches down, Charlotte's little hands enveloped in his. Then he springs up and she jumps, soaring several feet in the air and into the deep end of the pool. She lands with an impressive splash. She pops back up after half a second thanks to her Barbie water wings. Her laughter rings out, filling the warm air. Scott beams at her. My heart breaks a little. I want to give him this so badly. It amazes me that he's able to do this, to play with these kids with a smile on his face. I don't think I could.

Even though we're in this together, sometimes I feel very, very alone. I'm alone in the treatments, alone with the medications, alone, apparently, with my pain and how isolated I feel from the world. Alone in my reactions, alone in how I process things. I never would've thought that trying to make a baby could be so goddamn lonely.

"Marco Polo!" yells four-year-old Silas as he makes his way into the shallow end, step by careful step. With a roar, he launches himself into the water, splashing towards Scott. They start to play, and Scott good naturedly lets them cheat. Lets them win and have their fun. God, he would be such a good dad. And here I am, not even good at *trying* to be a mom.

I still feel a bit shaken from my reaction to the book store tantrum, and I wonder if the relief I shouldn't have felt could be chalked up to mental and emotional exhaustion. Sometimes I don't know if I have it in me to keep going, to keep putting myself through the hope and the heartbreak of cycle after cycle. I'm drained, often running on empty. Coasting on fumes of optimism. Maybe the relief I felt was just a way of giving myself some space from the crushing weight of everything I normally feel—the failure, the emptiness, the isolation. An infinitesimal break from throwing myself repeatedly against the rocks, hoping to someday, somehow, land on the shore with everyone else.

I turn away from the window and take the frame from its paper bag. Opening a chest in the corner, I add it to the collection of empty windows waiting to be filled.

5

Before

CLAIRE WALKS DOWN THE SIDEWALK TOWARD THE THAI restaurant where she's meeting Scott for their first date. The air is warm, fresh green leaves budding on trees. She avoids the puddles left by the spring rain and wipes her slightly damp palms on her skirt, humming to herself as she walks. Anticipation sings through her. There's something about Scott that makes her feel excited. As though she's on the cusp of something big, something important. It might just be the dimples, though. Either way, she's been looking forward to seeing him again.

She sees him before she sees her. He's standing just outside the restaurant, his hands in his jean pockets. He rocks back and forth on his heels, and she takes a moment to appreciate him before he sees her. His dark blue Henley shows off his body, and her own body tightens in response. His hair is a bit shorter than when she saw him at the coffee shop. She wonders if he cut it for their date.

He sees her and waves, and she smiles and waves back.

"Hi," she says, and stretches up on her toes to give him a kiss on the cheek. She is bold, and sure, and isn't playing games.

"Hey," he says. "You look great."

She swings her skirt a little. "Thanks. So do you." For a second, they stand there, just looking, and then he pulls open the door to the restaurant.

"After you," he says, ushering her inside.

She glances back at him over her shoulder. "You either have very good manners, or you want to check out my ass."

He leans forward. "Maybe it's both," he says, his voice low. A warm shiver works its way down her spine.

They sit down at one of the empty tables, and they talk. They drink tea, eat spring rolls and pad thai and beef curry and talk. And talk, and talk, and talk. About their jobs. About their families. About places they've traveled, music they like, favorite movies. About where they went to school, about their friends. They talk and talk as Claire's foot finds Scott's calf under the table. They talk and talk as the restaurant slowly clears out and the staff begin shooting them dirty looks.

Claire feels as though she's known him for a long time. It's so easy with him.

Scott pays for their dinner and they step out into the still warm night. It's obvious neither of them want the date to be over.

"Do you want to go for a walk?" Claire asks, already knowing he'll say yes.

He takes her hand, lacing his fingers with hers, as they make their way toward Washington Park.

"Thank you for dinner," she says, swinging their joined arms.

"You're welcome."

For the first time that night, a silence falls between them, but it's not awkward. It's a content silence. Like everything else tonight, it's easy. She feels so good with him.

"What are you thinking right now?" she asks him. She is alive, her heart beating hard and happy in her chest.

"That this is the best first date I've ever been on."

Her insides glow at his words. "Ever?"

"Ever."

"That's high praise. I hope our second date isn't a total let down," she says in a light, teasing tone.

"Pretty sure that'd be impossible, Claire." He squeezes her hand and they stroll down a softly lit path in the park. Lightning flashes through the sky and thunder cracks above them just before the skies open, and a hard, heavy rain starts to fall. Claire shrieks and Scott pulls on her hand. They run toward a nearby gazebo, the rain soaking their clothes. When they reach it, they're both breathless with exertion and laughter.

Claire leans against the inside of the gazebo, catching her breath. Scott has stopped laughing, and he's studying her intently. Slowly, he moves toward her and places his hands on either side of her head, leaning close.

"What are you thinking right now?" he asks.

"I think you know," she says, her breasts pressing into him with every rapid breath.

With agonizing slowness, he leans down and kisses her. The kiss is everything Claire's ever wanted. It's sweetness and heat and promise, all rolled into one. He slips his arms around her and pulls her close, her body melting into his.

Claire knows she's going to fall in love with him.

Now – September

Years ago, before we were married, Scott and I went to a wedding, as you do several times every summer between the ages of twenty-six and thirty-two. You do it so many times that it becomes a ritual: put on a pretty dress, do your hair and makeup, paint your nails. Arrive at the wedding and pretend to pay attention to the ceremony. Ooh and ahh over the bride's dress. Drink the wine set out on the tables. Eat chicken and potatoes and wedding cake. Dance to "Love Shack" and "Don't Stop 'Til You Get Enough." Go home with some new tchotchke in your purse. Lather, rinse, repeat.

It's really kind of an odd way to celebrate two people committing their lives to each other, when you think about it. At least, it always felt that way to me. The weddings are all so similar that they become impersonal. I guess that's why when Scott and I got married five years ago, we slipped away to the south of France with only our parents, Scott's brother and sister, and a handful of close friends. I'd been to so many weddings at that point that I was scared my own would blend in with the others and that ten years down the road, I'd barely remember it. I didn't want the day that marked the start of married life with Scott to be like that.

Anyway, at this particular wedding, the groom was Scott's roommate from college, a recent law school grad. Neither of us knew the bride very well, whom the groom had met during law school. But a lot of Scott's friends from college were there, so while he was spending time shooting the shit and catching up, I was mostly left to my own devices.

We'd been seated with three other couples, all of whom were perfectly nice in a sort of pleasant but highly forgettable way. I'm not saying this to be mean; I'm sure we were just as forgettable to them as they were to us. As the evening progressed, we had the kind of conversations you can only have with strangers who've become situational acquaintances: the falsely cheery, overly interested, laugh a minute kind fueled by wine and the desire to make a good impression, if not a lasting one.

I can't remember the name of the woman sitting next to me. I think it might've been Jennifer, but I'm not sure. Jessica? Julie? Jill? I'm almost positive it started with a J. Even though I don't remember her name, I do remember what she looked like. Curly light brown hair piled on top of her head in an elegant updo, sparkly black dress, pretty makeup. Maybe five years older than me. She'd been telling me about her three-year-old daughter and showing me pictures on her phone. I took a sip of my wine and asked what I'd thought at the time to not only be a perfectly innocent question, but a wholly appropriate one.

"So, do you think you'll have another?" I asked. I cringe now, remembering how'd I'd thought that was any of my business. But I'd been conditioned to think it was a totally reasonable question. Maybe I'd become numb to the way people pry into women's personal lives, asking almost thirty-year-old me with increasing frequency when Scott and I were going to get engaged. (For the record, people were not asking Scott this question, and I resented the assumption that because I'm a woman, my primary goal was obviously to get married, but naturally, the same wasn't true for Scott.)

With my question hanging between us, the woman's face fell and she put her phone away, slipping it almost guiltily back into her evening bag. She glanced off, her eyes bright, the shining lights from the dance floor catching the beads on her dress. "I don't..." She stared unseeing into the distance for several more seconds before meeting my gaze. "Things don't always work out the way you want, you know. Excuse me." She'd picked up her clutch from the table and headed for the bathroom, her feet moving quickly despite her towering heels, leaving me gaping in my seat. What the hell had I said?

Now, I know and I feel like a jerk. I don't think I'd ever even heard of secondary infertility then, but in hindsight it's obvious that's what she was dealing with. I think about her sometimes, this woman whose name I don't remember, and the pain I caused her. How blithely clueless I'd been. I get it now.

I wish I knew who she was so I could apologize. However things ended up working out for her, I hope she's okay. If she is, maybe that means that someday I will be too.

When my alarm goes off on Monday morning, I'm already awake. I've been lying here for the past ninety minutes, trying to fall back asleep, all while imagining what it'll feel like if the test turns out to be positive. A jolt of excitement runs through me every time I picture the lines I so desperately want to see appearing on the test. I already know how I'll feel if it's negative. Been there, done that, bought the damn T-shirt.

I lie in bed, staring at the ceiling, weak, early sunshine creeping in around the edges of the blinds. The windows are open to let the cooling fall air in, and our street is quiet. I hear the distant rush of traffic, leaves rustling in the trees, birdsong, and not much else. It's a morning like any other, but I need it to be different. Just once, I need things to not go the way they always go.

Scott rolls over in bed next to me and runs a hand up and down my arm, his skin warm with sleep. "Are you still going to test?" he asks, his voice low and croaky.

"Yeah," I say. I have to will myself to throw the covers back, lower my feet to the floor and head into the master bath. I shut the door quietly behind me, sealing myself in. I feel like I'm on autopilot now, letting familiar actions take over. I have to be on autopilot, otherwise I might chicken out, wanting to continue existing in the gray area of not knowing. In the not knowing, I still have something to hang onto, even if it's a thread of hope thinner than a spider's web. It's still something, both anchoring me and pulling me through each long day.

With jagged movements, I open up the vanity and pull out the Clearblue box I'd bought at Walmart, with one test remaining. I have a feeling I don't want to know. I glance at the expiration date on the box, a tiny part of me hoping the test is past its prime and I'll have an excuse to throw it out, but it doesn't expire for another year and a half. Damn. With the test in my hand, my heart rate spikes. The moment feels heavy, as though I could scoop up armfuls of the air around me and mold it into something.

I pull my panties down, sit on the toilet and start to pee, holding the test strip under the stream for several seconds. I'm good at this now, I've done it so many times. I don't splash, I know just how long to keep the test there, and I know how to wait. I slip the cap back over the test strip and set it on the back of the toilet. My heart is beating so hard that it almost hurts. I hate this, the anxiety that comes with testing. It's as though a fork in the road lies before me, and I'll be going down one path—pregnant!—or another—not pregnant, again, for the thirty-seventh time—and I know which path I want, but it's not up to me. I don't get to choose. I'm subject to the lines on a test, as is everything that will unfold in the aftermath.

I flush, wash my hands, brush my hair, brush my teeth. Floss. Rinse with mouthwash. Procrastinating with little tasks that keep me from looking at the test. The longer I wait, the more hope creeps over me, filling up the dark little crevices until I feel light as air. I let myself imagine walking over to the toilet, picking up the test and finally seeing the little blue lines I've been hoping for for years. I let myself imagine it until it feels real. A certainty.

A gentle knock sounds against the bathroom door. "Claire? You okay?" Scott asks, and I know I can't put off looking at the test any longer. With a shaky breath, I force my legs across the tile floor and pick up the test.

One blue line, surrounded by a deathly white, signifying the absence of life. Not pregnant.

I stare at the result window, willing a second blue line, intersecting the first, to appear. Hoping against hope that maybe I've looked too early, but I know I haven't. I feel numb, heavy with it, my limbs each a hundred pounds as all that airy hope leaves my body. I let myself stare at the test for another moment before I bury it in the graveyard of tissues in the garbage.

Emotions flash through me one after the other; anger—at myself for letting myself hope, at the unfairness of the situation, at Dr. Kane —frustration, sadness, desperation, hopelessness. It all crests over me like an ocean wave, pulling me under and suffocating me as I'm battered by the undertow. I wait for the tears to start, but they don't come. I'm too angry. *Of course* I'm not pregnant. Pregnancy is something that happens to other people. Not to me. Stupid, stupid, stupid Claire.

I open the bathroom door to find Scott on the other side in his boxers, his hair rumpled, his bare skin still lined from the sheets. Our eyes meet and I shake my head. He deflates a little, his shoulders lowering, his head bowing. I hate that he has to feel this way because of my defective body. That I'm the one constantly throwing a bucket of ice water on the simmering coals of his hope. I don't know how he doesn't hate me for it. It's honestly a tiny miracle.

"I'm sorry," he says, his voice rough around the edges, and he pulls me into his arms. I go willingly, needing his comfort. Needing to not feel alone. As he strokes my back, my throat tightens and my eyes sting, and the tears I've been waiting for come.

"Me too," I say, my voice a shivery whisper. I cry harder, grieving for something that never was.

How many times can a heart break before it stops healing? Before the cracks become scars? Before they become permanent changes?

I don't know. I don't know. I don't know.

Going to work is the last thing I feel like doing today, but I have a full day, and maybe being able to bury myself in work will be the distraction I need, although I doubt this is true. With each failed cycle, my ambition and drive have died a little more. I used to take on more challenging projects. I used to pursue clients. I used to go to conferences and work to build up the brand of both the firm and my own designs. I don't do any of that anymore. I just don't have the energy, but maybe today I will. I don't want to think about pregnancy or babies or fertility or motherhood. I want to avoid those topics the way a liar avoids the truth, dancing and dodging and twisting away. Easier said than done, I know, but today I need to lodge my head in the sand, to blot out everything I can't handle. This failure is too raw, too painful for me to fake anything today.

I go through the motions of my morning routine, feeling empty and depleted. I shower, dress, do my hair and makeup. I glance at the little garbage bin, where I buried the hope of our latest cycle. I try to focus on what I'm doing to prevent my mind from wandering down painful paths.

I drink my coffee and eat my toast slathered in peanut butter. I check my work emails on my phone, sorting them as I do every morning. Scott gives me a kiss before he leaves for work, his hand lingering on my lower back, his eyes filled with concern. But he doesn't say anything and neither do I. We're old pros at this, and we both know there's nothing either of us can say or do to make this hurt less. This grief will be a part of our lives for the next couple of days, until we rally, put it behind us and move on to the next step.

I get in the car and leave for work, flicking through radio stations with the little button on the steering wheel, trying to find something to distract me. But nothing works, and despite my best efforts, I can feel the tears starting to well behind my eyes. I try to swallow them down, but then a Dixie Chicks song that always wrecks me comes on the radio. I don't change the station.

Now, before you start to worry for my safety, please know that I have crying while driving down to an art. Between being an infertile woman and having a parent with a terminal illness, I've had *a lot* of practice. The key, I've learned, is to find a balance between letting myself cry just enough that I get relief from the pain inside me, but not so much that I can't see. It means letting the first few tears fall, like popping a too-tight blister. The release is almost instant, cathartic, and with it comes clarity. Carrying around pain makes you foggy.

I clench and unclench my fingers around the steering wheel, the stitching digging into my skin. "Why is this so hard for us?" I ask the empty car, my voice thin and reedy. "Why is this so fucking easy for everyone else?

Why?" The lone anguished syllable seems to hang in the air, shimmering and ghostly. My throat is getting tighter and tighter, and a weight presses down on my chest, making it harder to breathe. Tears cling to my eyelashes, slide down my cheeks and into the hollow at the base of my throat, making the skin there itch. My nose runs. I switch the radio off, knowing I'm too close to the edge, too close to the point of no return. To sobs that I can't control.

I pull into the parking lot behind the Carlisle and Winter building and park in the back corner. I pull Kleenex, eye drops, mascara, and concealer out of my purse. Like I said, I know what I'm doing. Using the mirror on the back of the sun visor, I fix myself up, doing my best to conceal my red-rimmed, puffy eyes. I am not a pretty crier. When I cry, I get red and blotchy, the skin around my eyes swells, the whites become bloodshot. My nose runs like a broken fire hydrant, my mouth dries up. Classic ugly cry.

Popping a breath mint in my mouth, I go inside, ready to lose myself in the busy day ahead. I head for my desk, keeping to myself to avoid making conversation. I'm shit at small-talk on good days; who knows what gleaming gems of conversation I'd come up with today. Once my laptop is up and running, I go through my schedule for the day. My client Jillian is coming in at ten so that we can finalize the concept board and start ordering items for her bedroom makeover. If everything's in stock and we don't have any hiccups, we should be putting the final touches on her room within a week or so. Then, at two, I have another meeting on my calendar, scheduled by Janet Carlisle herself. The details are skimpy, but it looks like she, along with me and Mia, will be meeting with a new potential client. Then, at four-thirty, I'm having drinks with a few people from Aurora Construction. They're building new luxury townhomes by the river, and I'm pitching them on hiring Carlisle and Winter to put together the interiors of the show homes. Gavin was supposed to do it, but he's been scaling back his workload and passed the meeting off onto me. Most days, I'd be excited and energized by this kind of opportunity, but today I'm dreading it. I'm not in a rubbing elbows, schmoozing kind of mood. I hope the drinks don't go too late. All I want to do tonight is put on sweats, order takeout, open a bottle of wine and watch trash TV.

Schedule for the day squared away, I make my way to the Keurig, select a pod, and wait for it to brew. I hear Mia before I see her. There's something distinctive about the way her heels click against the concrete floor. I take a deep breath and try to school my face into something neutral. It's not that I'm not going to tell her that our final attempt at IUI failed. I just don't want to get into everything right this minute. It's still too fresh and raw for me. I need to sit with this failure for a day or two.

"Oh my gosh, did you see the new flooring samples Gavin brought in? This new supplier has some absolutely gorgeous patterned tiles I'm dying to use somewhere," she says, opening one of the cupboards and pulling out a bag of English muffins.

I turn to her and shake my head. "No, I haven't had a chance to look yet. I'll check them out later."

"They're stunning. It's making me want to rethink the design plan of the grand foyer in the Curtis house. Maybe I can find a way to incorporate them…" Her voice trails off as she starts making notes in her phone.

"Hey, do you know what that meeting in our calendars is about?" I ask, blowing steam away from the top of my mug. "There were almost no details beyond a time and location."

Mia shakes her head, her silky blond hair sliding over her shoulders. "I overheard Janet and Gavin discussing something late last week about a local celebrity, so it might be related to that. But I don't really know." She looks up from her phone, pausing as she looks at me. "Were you crying?" she asks, lowering her voice. Her brows knit together in concern. "You're all red. What's wrong?"

Well, shit. I press my lips together, debating whether to tell her or not. I don't know why I'm being weird about this. I wrap my fingers around my mug, letting the warmth seep into my skin.

"I took a test this morning. It was negative." Each word cuts into me as I speak it, reopening the still-fresh wounds. I can still see the single blue line, the space where the other should've appeared blank and empty.

"Oh, shit. Honey, I'm sorry." Before I can stop her, she wraps her arms around me, hugging me, and it takes me a second to relax into the comfort she's offering. After a moment, she pulls back, shaking her head. "You'd think those doctors would've figured out how to knock you up by now."

I wince at her words, and then try to hide my reaction with a sip of coffee. *Guess I'm just so damn infertile that I'm practically a medical mystery.* I'm suddenly angry. Beyond angry. My face heats, my heart speeds up, my thoughts scatter.

An awkward silence hangs between us and she shifts her weight from one foot to the other. I stare into my coffee. I get the sense that she's waiting for me to say something to bail her out of the verbal mess she's made, but it's not my job to rescue her right now.

"Well, that really sucks," she finally says. "I'm sorry."

"Thanks." My voice comes out flat, but she doesn't seem to notice, or at least she pretends not to. I wish I hadn't said anything. I've clearly made her uncomfortable with my silent, unfair anger, which is only making me feel worse. Another silence falls between us.

She turns her phone toward me, a professional photo of her daughter looking like a beautiful ballerina filling the screen. "Didn't these turn out nice? They're from the ballet clinic the other week."

I stare, unseeing, at the picture. I feel like I'm being strangled from the inside out. My skin is too hot. My chest hurts. "Gorgeous," I say, fighting back whatever's cresting inside me right now.

Her face lights up. "Isn't she? I was wary about spending the money on the photos, but decided to splurge."

"It's a beautiful picture," I say. In this moment, I don't care. I know that's shitty of me, but it's the truth. My insides feel like sandpaper, rough and raw and gritty.

Mia smiles and puts her English muffin into the toaster. "I'm sorry it didn't work out for you this time," she says, her tone light, easy, casual. "But you have other options, right? You'll be okay?"

"Oh, sure," I say. I nod. I purse my lips together in a thin smile. Mia seems content with my answer, so I turn and walk back to my desk, wishing I'd kept my damn mouth shut.

6

It's five minutes after two and I'm sitting in Janet Carlisle's office in one of the stunning but horribly uncomfortable chairs facing her desk. They look like egg chairs, but with the top half cut off, leaving just the bottom half to act as a suction cup for your ass. Maybe it's Janet's subtle way of letting people know that if you're in her office, a little ass kissing would go a long way.

Mia sits in the other ass-sucker chair, her attention focused on her phone. I twist and glance behind me, looking for any sign of Janet through the glass walls, but I have no idea where she is. The chair makes a soft squeak as I pivot in Mia's direction. She doesn't look up, and I open and close my mouth. I say nothing and pivot back in the other direction. She's sitting only a few feet away from me and I miss her.

The glass door to Janet's office swings open and she strides in, trailed by someone who I immediately recognize. Her dark brown pixie cut, perfectly styled, gleams with the kind of preternatural shine that can only be achieved with expensive smoothing and gloss treatments. Her medium-brown skin is flawless, her eyebrows arching delicately over her huge brown eyes, which sport the perfect amount of smoky eyeshadow. Her smile is a little too white—her teeth have an almost ghostly glow to them. Like that episode of *Friends* where Ross overdoes it with the teeth whitening. It was a joke back then, but people actually look like that now. She's wearing a red shift dress with a black leather moto jacket over top, and honestly, she looks a lot like Halle Berry in person. Mandy Sinclair, host of the incredibly popular morning TV show *Morning Chat* turns, and as her jacket gapes open, I see it. My stomach clenches and then drops, making me feel a bit sick, and sweat prickles along my hairline. Anxiety floods me like a tidal wave, with a strong jealous undertow. I don't watch *Morning Chat*, and I don't really follow celebrity gossip, so it's news to me that Mandy Sinclair is pregnant. But with that perfectly round stomach straining against the red fabric of her dress, there's no denying it. Janet ushers Mandy inside and then swings her office door shut. Mia and I both stand.

"Mandy, I'd like to introduce Mia Corbin and Claire Stanhope, two of our most talented designers. I think they'll be the perfect fit for this project. They both have several years of experience, and I believe their aesthetic will match up nicely with yours. Here, why don't you sit down, get off your feet," Janet says, gesturing to the chair I'd just vacated.

Mandy smiles and extends a hand, offering it first to me, and then to Mia. "It's so great to meet you," she says, everything about her friendly and relaxed. Mia sits back down in her chair, her face bright with excitement. I can practically feel her vibrating with it.

"I just need to tell you that I *love Morning Chat*," she says, her hands fluttering in her lap as she speaks, the words tumbling out of her mouth in a rush. "I record it every morning, and I watched it all the time when I was home with my kids."

Mandy smiles again. "Thank you so much! It's always nice to connect with a fan of the show." She eases back in her chair and crosses her legs. "How many kids do you have?"

"Two. Is this your first?" asks Mia, gesturing at Mandy's unmistakable bump. I feel that gesture like a kick in the stomach.

"It is! We're so excited." Mandy rests her hand on her stomach protectively.

"Oh, I can imagine. Your whole world is about to change, but it's absolutely amazing," Mia gushes. "It's the best thing in the world." I'm burning from the inside out, little coals of jealousy and bitterness igniting somewhere deep within me until I feel scorched.

"I just can't wait to meet her," Mandy says, rubbing her hand in a circle over her belly.

Mia lets out a little squeal. "So you know it's a girl? Omigosh, girls are so much fun."

"Claire." Janet's voice cuts through the haze of jealousy I've fallen into. I'm surprised to hear my name; I'd started to feel invisible. "Please go get an extra chair for yourself."

I nod and scurry out of Janet's office, heading for the supply closet where I know we keep a set of stylish white folding chairs. My mind races in time with my heart as I carry one back to Janet's office. I hate that just seeing a pregnant woman spikes my anxiety, making me feel shaky and small. But I can't help it. It's not like I *want* to feel this way. But the longer we try without success, the harder it gets to face what I might never have. Time doesn't make it easier. It makes it worse, as though my defenses are worn down after all this failure.

Mia and Mandy are still gushing over the wonders of pregnancy and motherhood while Janet watches impassively. I open the chair and it makes an ear-splitting *screeeee* sound. The conversation in the room stops as everyone turns to look at me and my creaky chair. I want to pat the chair, thanking it for the distraction. Feeling oddly satisfied with my little interruption, as unintentional as it was, I sit down.

"As I'm sure you've guessed," Janet begins, picking an imaginary piece of lint off of her designer blouse, "Mandy has hired Carlisle and Winter to design her nursery."

My stomach sinks. I plaster what I hope is a professional smile on my face. "With all due respect, I'm not sure you need two of us on this job. I have a full plate right now, so I'm more than happy to hand the project over to Mia…" My voice trails off at the stony look on Janet's face.

"You two work well together, and Mandy is an important client, worthy of our best efforts and utmost attention and care. Claire, if you can't handle your workload, then—"

"No, no! It's not that. Sorry. Continue." I feel the blood rush to my cheeks, heat creeping over my neck. Mia shoots me a *what the hell, Stanhope?* look. I don't react and slide down in my chair, just a little.

We spend the next half hour going over the details of the project. Mandy shows us pictures of the room, and we discuss ideas around the color palate, theme, furniture style, and budget, all in very broad strokes. When Mandy says she's hoping to keep the total cost under $30,000, I nearly choke on my tongue. I can't really fathom spending that on a nursery, but then again, I can't really fathom having a nursery at all.

I try to muster some enthusiasm for the project, but I can't. I don't want to do this. By the time the meeting wraps up and Janet is walking Mandy to the door, I've sunk into a sullen silence.

Mia glances over her shoulder, through Janet's open door and then spins to face me. "What's up with you today?" she hisses.

I don't even know what to say to that, so I say nothing at all.

Mia stares at me blankly and after a few seconds, I see the lightbulb come on, her features twisting themselves into a wary expression. "Are you…upset because it's a nursery?" She says this with a tinge of disbelief.

"Yes. It's really difficult for me to be around stuff like that." I'm both surprised and not that I have to explain this to her.

Mia arches an eyebrow, her lips pursed in an impatient pucker. "Not everything is about you and your infertility, Claire. God." Her words come out in a sharp, staccato burst. The cruelty of them is unexpected, and I don't know how to react. So I don't, I just sit there, staring at her, trying to think around the anger, the frustration, the hurt, clouding my senses. She pushes out of her chair and starts towards the door, but Janet comes back in. She sniffs, as though she can smell the tension in the room.

"Mandy was happy with your ideas. Claire, I know you're busy, but she's a huge client. You don't have many family-oriented projects in your portfolio, so this is a great opportunity for you to flesh that area out." She levels her steely blue gaze at me. "Next time someone does you a favor like this, you could try a little gratitude, hmm?"

I feel like a brat, even though I'm not entirely sure that I *am* one. But she's right. Mandy Sinclair *is* a huge client; she didn't have to give me this opportunity. "Right. Yes," I say, taking a deep breath. "Thank you for the opportunity." The words are like sour milk in my mouth, sickly and hard to swallow. It's hard to feel grateful for an opportunity you don't want.

Janet simply nods and then waves her hand, kicking us out of her office. Mia walks past me, striding toward her desk, her back straight, her shoulders rigid. She doesn't say another word to me, which, honestly, I'm pretty fine with right now. We both need to cool off. And yet I can't stop replaying her words, turning them over in my palms like river rocks, weighing them, absorbing their texture, looking for flaws.

Maybe she's right. Maybe I *do* make everything about infertility. But Mia's words had hit me like an unexpected slap, and the fact that they were so startling makes the slap sting all the more. She's seen me go through month after month of failure. She's seen me go through the invasive testing. She's seen me take the fertility drugs. She's seen me come in late after countless trips to the clinic for bloodwork and ultrasounds. She's seen me fall apart after yet another negative test. I would've thought that she, of all people, would at least *try* to understand. I mean, I don't think it's rocket science for her to wrap her brain around why I wouldn't want to spend the next several weeks putting together another woman's nursery when every day I live with the fear that I'll never put together one of my own.

I don't look in her direction as I head back to my desk, and a prickling sense of shame creeps over me. I'm horribly embarrassed at everything I've shared with her, thinking she was an ally. Thinking I could lean on her for support, when clearly, she's sick of hearing about it. Fuck, I'm sick of talking about it, but unlike her, I don't have the luxury of just switching it off, saying that I've had enough. For me, infertility thoughts are like the CNN ticker that runs along the bottom of the screen, a constant unspooling of distracting words. They might not be the big picture, but those thoughts are always there, running underneath everything, chattering mindlessly somewhere in the recesses of my brain.

I decide that I need to get out of the office and head to my next meeting. I don't care that I'll be almost an hour early. I'd rather sit alone and drink coffee while answering emails than stay here, trying to avoid Mia, trying to pretend that everything's fine. My face will give me away, if I stay. I know it was just one comment, but I feel betrayed, and I need some space. So, I gather up my things and leave.

When I get home from work, I'm tired, grumpy, and sad. The last meeting of the day went well, and honestly, it was a welcome distraction after the shit show my afternoon turned into. The reps from Aurora Construction seemed pleased and impressed with what I had to show them; at least that part of my day didn't end with me wanting to cry, scream, or hit something.

I let the front door fall closed behind me, dropping my things on the bench by the front hall closet. All I want to do is put on my rattiest, comfiest yoga pants, Scott's old UCLA sweatshirt, open a bottle of wine and watch junk TV. But when I see Scott, I know that he has other plans. He emerges from the back of the house wearing a maroon-colored button up that makes his brown eyes look like melted chocolate, and a pair of black pants. He's carrying a bouquet of white flowers —lilies of the valley and peonies. Our wedding flowers.

He steps towards me and gently sets the bouquet in my hands. His large, warm hands rub the backs of my arms. "I love you, Claire. No matter what. Okay?" He tucks a strand of hair behind my ear, ducking his head to try to catch my gaze. I'm staring at the flowers, tears welling in my eyes. "For better or for worse."

"I'm sorry we've had so much of the worse lately," I say, my voice cracking. It's my fault. I don't deserve this kindness.

Scott smiles. "Better's coming. I know it is." He leans forward and kisses me on the forehead, the gesture sweet and reassuring. I bury my face in the flowers, inhaling deeply. They smell like hope. They smell like promise. They smell like love, and happiness. They smell like me and Scott, before we dared to want a child of our own. I carefully set the bouquet down on the bench and wrap my arms around Scott's neck, holding him close.

My eyes land on the little table by the stairs. It holds a clear blue glass vase with silk cherry blossoms sticking out of it, a little stack of purposefully chosen books, a silver ampersand paperweight with our names engraved along the bottom (a wedding gift that we use as our "note-leaving/mail gathering" spot), and a framed wedding picture. Scott in his perfectly cut black suit and I in my dusty blue wedding dress, are standing on a stone cliff, beaming at each other as a terra-cotta-colored village rises up behind us, a glimmering blue ribbon of Mediterranean Sea rippling across the top of the photo, beyond the village. I stare at the wedding picture and all the happiness it contains. At a younger, much less burdened Claire and Scott, who never spent time discussing things like infertility and cancer. I look at the picture and while the happiness is there, all I see is two naive people totally unprepared for the years of heartbreak ahead of them.

Beautiful, happy fools, ignorant of pain. I wish I was still that happy fool.

"I thought maybe we could go to The Oak," he says, naming our favorite restaurant. I pull back from his arms and nod. It wasn't what I'd planned for the evening, but Scott's trying so hard. I'm unworthy of the effort; the least I can do is say yes.

"Let me go change and put the flowers in some water, and then we can go," I say. I give him a kiss on his smooth, warm cheek and head upstairs. I quickly change out of my cream-colored pantsuit and yellow silk blouse and pull on an emerald green cocktail dress. It's one of my favorites, with its short skirt, long sleeves, high neck and open back. The material is simple, the cut one of playful contrasts. The color brings out the red in my hair and makes my bluish-gray eyes look green. I slip on a pair of strappy black heels and a set of big hoop earrings, and then duck into the bathroom to brush my hair and touch up my makeup. When I see myself in the mirror, my skin isn't as blotchy as I think it will be, and I take that as a good omen.

As I make my way down the stairs, Scott grins up at me, the dimple in his right cheek making an appearance. I see that he's put the flowers in water for me—the vase is on the dining room table, just visible from the stairs. When I get to the bottom of the stairs, he pulls me against him and kisses me. This isn't the chaste, comforting kiss of earlier. This is the kiss of a man who likes what he sees. There's a hunger to it that warms me from the inside out. When he pulls away, my skin is tingling. I don't remember the last time he kissed me like that. I also don't remember the last time I put on a sexy dress for him, or the last time I didn't automatically shy away from overtly sexual physical affection.

"I like this dress," he says, running his thumb under my bottom lip, fixing where he's no doubt smeared my lipstick. "This is the no bra dress." His eyebrows bounce up and down and I laugh, a real, genuine laugh that feels like a tiny miracle. I didn't expect to have a laugh like that in me today.

I need to try harder for him. He deserves more than what I've been giving him. He deserves a wife who smiles more often than I do, who's more engaged than I am, who puts his needs first sometimes. Someone who he can have good, fulfilling sex with. Someone who's pulling her weight in the relationship. I know I'm not any of these things, and haven't been for a while. But he deserves these things, and I want to give them to him. I want to feel worthy of him and his kindness, and his optimism, and his unwavering way of loving me, even when I don't love me. I've been failing him as a wife, not because I can't get pregnant (well, not *only* because), but because I've pulled away and retreated into myself, leaving him to carry our marriage by himself.

The Oak isn't far from Sawmill Commons, in the older part of town. The restaurant is in a gorgeously restored century home, and I've always thought that its peaked dormers with their ornate gable decorations, coupled with the bright red door, make it look like a luxurious gingerbread house, tempting passersby with the mouthwatering scents wafting from it. A massive oak adorns the front lawn, surrounded by an impressive circular garden. Orange chrysanthemums, red pansies, and black-eyed susans, all blooming in neat circles, patches of color, sway gently in the quickly cooling evening breeze.

The inside is just as inviting, with cream colored walls topped with ornate crown molding, lush burgundy carpet and elegant brass chandeliers, all dimmed to give the room a warm, intimate glow. The tables are covered in white cloth and surrounded by crimson-colored leather dining chairs. Paintings from local artists hang on the walls, and a black and gold bar lines the far back wall. Jazz floats on the air. As we're shown to our table, I can smell garlic and roasting meat, making my stomach rumble in anticipation.

"I can't remember the last time we went on a real date," I say, smiling at Scott, being the Claire who tries. "Thank you for this. It was a great idea. Far better than what I'd had planned."

He grins. "Let me guess. Sweats, chips and dip, wine, and a *Ghost Hunters* marathon?"

My lips twitch. "I will neither confirm nor deny that." Guilt tugs at me as I realize that my plans didn't include him, even though he had his heart broken this morning, too. Meanwhile, he's gone out of his way to give me this—the flowers, the nice restaurant, the night out. I'm thirty-five years old and I continue to be struck by the depth of my assholery at times.

The waiter comes and we order wine and a charcuterie board to start. Scott excuses himself to use the men's room before our food comes, and I fish my phone out of my purse, wanting to make sure there aren't any crucial follow ups from any of today's meetings I've missed. My inbox is clear—for once—but I do have a couple of text messages from Mia, sent over the past hour or so.

Mia: I'm really sorry I said what I did. I shouldn't have snapped like that and I didn't mean it.

Mia: Claire? I'm sorry, okay? Please text me back. It was a dumb thing to say. I love you.

I set the phone down on the table and take a sip of my wine. For some reason, her apology isn't making me feel any less shitty about the way things went down today.

The thing is, I'm so emotionally worn out from spending the past few years both watching my mother fight for her life and trying and failing to get pregnant that I'm running out of steam when it comes to making other people feel okay with hurting me. I'm sick of pretending that my feelings don't matter; that their comfort is somehow more important than the pain I'm in. If someone makes a dumb cancer joke, I'm expected to laugh it off so that they don't feel like a class-A jerk. If someone says something insensitive about infertility, I'm supposed to take the comment with grace so as not to make them feel uncomfortable.

I dismiss Mia's texts and don't reply. I'm on a date with my husband, and I don't feel like getting into some protracted text conversation meant to assuage her guilty conscience. Maybe that's unfair of me, but it's what I need to do right now. But a tiny part of me does feel better knowing she apologized, even if I'm still hurt.

Scott returns from the men's room and sits down across from me.

"So, how was the rest of your day? After..." He trails off and then takes a sip of his water, not needing to finish his thought.

I shake my head. "It was kind of one of those 'good news/bad news' type days. The good news was that Mia and I have been assigned to design for Mandy Sinclair."

Scott's eyebrows inch up his forehead. "The talk show host?"

"Yeah."

"And what's the bad news part?"

"We're designing a nursery for her."

"Oh." Scott's features soften with understanding. "I'm sorry. That must be shitty."

"It is, and to make it even shittier, Mia doesn't get why I'm not into it. We had kind of a fight about it after the meeting."

"Really, Mia? But you guys are so close."

"I know." I play with the edge of my thick cloth napkin.

"I'm sure you guys'll work it out. And you can get through this nursery project." He reaches across the table and lays his hand over mine. "Just treat it like any other project, any other client."

I rub my thumb over his knuckles. "You're my best friend, you know that?" I say, and just like that, there's a lump in my throat and a stinging in my eyes, as though I'm reciting wedding vows. Maybe in a way, I am. "I love just being with you, talking to you. I'm so lucky to have you."

He smiles, his brown eyes warm and soft. "Well, I *am* pretty awesome." I laugh, and he squeezes my hand. "You're my best friend, too, Claire."

"I'm sorry things have been so hard lately. That I haven't been—" I swallow thickly, unable to get the rest of the words out. I feel oddly compelled to recite a litany of my failures, to lay them all at his feet in an act of atonement. But I can't seem to make the words come.

"Hey, don't do that. You've had a lot of shit to deal with. I know you're doing the best you can." He gives my hand a reassuring squeeze. "I know you're trying."

I shake my head slowly. "That's just it; I don't think I have been." A tiny part of me wants him to be mad at me, to be frustrated and annoyed. As though I deserve to be punished for my behavior, my selfishness, my failings. I want the way I feel about myself to be justified. Validated. *Yes, Claire, you are a selfish, self-absorbed person, and a pretty terrible wife when it comes down to it. I'll prove you right with my anger.* But, of course, because Scott is a better person than me, that's not the response I get.

"Don't be so hard on yourself, sweetheart. You should be proud of how strong you are. Most people would've crumbled a long time ago facing what you've had to face."

"You haven't crumbled," I say, my voice quiet. "I know you want a baby as much as I do."

He pauses, his expression thoughtful as he takes a sip of his wine. "No, but I'm also not the one with a dying parent, or who's getting poked and prodded every damn morning. You're so incredibly strong that you amaze me, every single day."

I blink and a tear slips down my cheek, landing on the white table cloth. I press on the wet splotch with my finger, feeling its coolness against my skin. "You would be such an incredible dad," I say, my voice barely above a whisper, as though saying it too loudly will entice the universe to snatch it away completely.

"And you'd be an unbelievable mom," he says. "Look at everything you've done, everything you've endured and sacrificed just to *try* to get pregnant."

I study him across the table, tenderness along with an empty ache blooming inside me. I take a shaky breath. "Let's do IVF," I say, Scott's words giving me the strength to throw myself in front of yet another proverbial train. IVF is the only thing we haven't tried yet. The big guns, so to speak. I'm scared to venture down that path, not only because of how invasive and expensive it is, but what if IVF doesn't work? What then?

"We don't have to decide anything tonight," he says. "I know you have mixed feelings about it."

"It's our only shot at this point. Am I thrilled about giving myself injections and having a surgery to suck the eggs out of my ovaries?" My skin tightens uncomfortably as I say the words. "No. And it's expensive and not covered by insurance. But it's our only chance now."

Scott chews his bottom lip, his gaze faraway. "We could go back to the adoption agency…" It's a half-hearted suggestion on his part, the lack of enthusiasm evident in his voice, in his posture.

More than anything, I want my own biological child. I want to experience pregnancy with a child that is half me and half Scott. This is one of the few beliefs I hold that I don't think is selfish. It's perfectly natural for me to want my own biological child. Most people get to have one, or two, or three, without even thinking about it.

And so, I look at Scott and tell the truth. "I don't just want any baby, Scott. I want our baby. I'm not ready to let go of that yet. I'm not saying never to adoption; but right now, my focus is on getting pregnant with our child."

He looks relieved. "I'm not ready either. I just didn't want to take it off the table if you wanted to pursue it."

I shake my head. "Not right now, no."

"Okay, so IVF it is."

I raise my wine glass and clink it gently against his. "IVF it is."

When we get home, I'm buzzed, both from the wine and the conversation. Nervous excitement dances through my blood at the prospect of starting IVF and the idea that maybe it'll be the treatment that finally works for us. I feel hopeful, and I let that feeling fill me up until I'm almost giddy with it.

Scott misunderstands my dizzy mood and backs me up against the wall in the foyer, his hands on my shoulders, his hips pressing against mine. "I miss you," he whispers right before his mouth connects with mine. It's a continuation of the kiss we'd shared earlier, hungry and simmering with warmth. I suddenly want to convince him—convince myself, too—that I'm still the same Claire he married. That I still want him and deserve him and need him.

"I know," I whisper against his mouth, my fingers going to the buttons of his shirt. "I'm sorry. I miss you too."

"I don't want to miss you anymore. I don't want this to…to wreck us. I love you. I love us."

My throat tightens and guilt churns through me as I continue to work on the buttons of his shirt until it hangs open. "I'm right here," I say, and he nuzzles into my neck, making me shiver. Maybe, just maybe, if I can let myself enjoy this, if I can get out of my own head, if I can revel in feeling good in my body, I can move past it all. I just need to know that it's possible.

Scott pulls away from me and takes my hand, leading me upstairs to our bedroom. We don't turn the lights on, stumbling through the dark towards our bed, kissing and touching. I close my eyes, trying to focus on the warmth of his mouth on mine, the slide of his palms over my skin. My body heats and I feel a tingling, tightening pull between my legs that I haven't felt in a long time. And yet…it's not the same as it used to be. I'm working so hard to get turned on. So, so hard. As though I've forgotten how to use my body for this.

I shed my dress and push Scott back on the bed, kissing my way down his body and then taking him into my mouth. He moans and holds my hair out of the way. I haven't done this in a long time. I've forgotten about foreplay, about arousal, about anything not directly related to getting pregnant. It feels both foreign and familiar.

Scott's breathing becomes labored and he pulls me up. "I need you," he says, his voice a husky whisper, and I can hear the longing in his voice. I can almost taste how much he's missed me, how much he's missed this.

I straddle his hips and take him inside me. It feels good, but not the way it used to. It's as though everything is slightly dulled, less vibrant and intense than I remember it. Like I'm filled with some kind of numbing agent. Scott reaches between us, touching me. It doesn't feel like anything. There are no sparks, no twinges, no flares of pleasure. It feels…nice. But I can't stop thinking about where I am in my cycle;

how many people at the clinic have seen my vagina; how many times I've had a phallic ultrasound wand inside me. How we can do this a million times and I won't get pregnant, even though this is how almost everyone else does it.

I ride him, feeling broken and empty, knowing that this joining of our bodies can't make life. I know I need to stop thinking about this. I know, I know, I know. I try to focus on the pleasure, but the creeping, antsy thoughts push back in, spiraling, sucking me under in a wave of debilitating sadness.

"Are you close?" he asks, and I feel the anger flare through me, like a piece of paper catching flame. How can he think I'm close? How can he be? How does he not feel the same aching melancholy that I do? For me, this is a reminder of every failure. For him, this is something else entirely.

I don't say anything, just moan and ride him harder, wanting this to be over. It's not Scott's fault—he's a good lover. It's mine. It's always mine.

He comes and I lean my forehead against his, trying to breathe around the ache in my chest. I kiss him and then climb off of him, ducking into the bathroom.

I sit on the toilet and cry.

7

Before

CLAIRE AND SCOTT EMERGE FROM THE MOVIE THEATER HOLDING
hands. It's their fourth date, and Claire is a bundle of nerves and anticipation. *Ask me,* she thinks. Hopes. She shaved her legs. She put
condoms in her purse. *Ask me.*

They make their way back to Scott's car, a tension zinging through
the air between them. She wonders if he can hear her heart pounding.
She wonders if he wants this as badly as she does. He holds open the
passenger side door for her, and she pauses, lingering. She runs her
fingers through his hair and kisses him, slow and deep.

Ask me.

Scott brushes her hair away from her temple. "Do you want to
come back to my place? No press—"

"Yes. Yes, I do."

They both laugh, and Scott practically jogs around to the driver's
side. They drive in silence to Scott's apartment. They hold hands in the
elevator, sneaking glances at each other like excited teenagers on prom
night.

Scott unlocks his door and turns on the light. It's a cool, loft-style place, completely open and airy. It's masculine and grown up. Her eyes land on the king-size bed and she reaches for him. He kisses her, and as the kiss grows in intensity, he presses her into the wall. She can feel him through his jeans. Her body feels like one giant throb. He drops his head and kisses her neck, and she threads her hands through his thick hair. His hand skims over her hip, down her thigh.

He pulls back, breathless. "We don't have to…" He licks his lips, his eyes dropping to her breasts. He backs away, just a little. She slips her arms around his waist and pulls him close.

"Stop being such a gentleman, Scott, and fuck me."

His eyes widen and then go molten at her words. "Oh, thank God," he murmurs, his mouth crashing back down on hers. With his hands cupping her ass, he lifts her and she winds her legs around him. He manages to walk them to the bed, and they tumble down, a tangle of hungry mouths and limbs. Clothing hits the floor. Skin slides against skin. Claire is flush with arousal. Scott kisses his way down her naked body, parting her legs. Tasting her.

"Yes," she moans, her back arching off the mattress. She's so primed, so desperate for him that it doesn't take much to send her over the edge, and she comes, moaning and trembling. She's still pulsing when he sheaths himself in a condom and slides into her. It has never been this good with anyone.

"Oh, fuck, Claire," he groans, and she twines her legs around his waist, urging him deeper. It feels so good. So right. It's perfect, and addictive.

"I want you inside me all night," she says, her hips meeting his as they move together. She doesn't want this to end. Just wants the plea-sure, the connection of Scott inside her. He moans and kisses her.

She comes again before it's over. Her body is limp, wrung out with pleasure. After, Scott traces his fingers over her arm and tells her she's beautiful.

"I think I'm falling in love with you," he whispers just before sleep pulls her under.

October - Now

It's a Saturday morning, the weekend following that hellish Monday. I had my blood test at the clinic yesterday; even though I'd known I wasn't pregnant, they still need to officially confirm for their own records. While I was there, I signed Scott and I up for the upcoming IVF education night. I'm still nervous (although nervous seems too small a word for it) about moving ahead with IVF, but it's our only option now. I'd once thought I couldn't imagine doing something as drastic as IVF. Funny how our perceptions change along with our circumstances.

The air is cool this morning, and the leaves on the trees are a riot of flaming color. Mom's backyard is home to a birch, an ancient maple, and a slender aspen. We're tucked into two matching white wicker chairs on the back deck, letting the sun warm our faces. I glance over at her and catch her rubbing her arms.

"I'm going to go get you a wrap, okay Mom?" I ask in a way that isn't really asking as I push up from my chair. She clearly knows there's no use arguing, because she just smiles up at me and nods. Her face is fuller than it's been in a while, and her skin has lost that sickly waxy sheen. Her energy is better, too, and she seems to be getting around with a bit more ease. I know none of this means she's better. She will never be better. It just means she isn't constantly fighting with the nasty side effects of the chemo anymore. She looks healthier, but she's still dying.

I open one of the French doors and slip into the kitchen. It smells like coffee and toast, and Eddie turns around from where he's fiddling with the Keurig. "You want some coffee? I know it's a bit cool out there this morning, but she loves to be outside." A little silence falls between us, his unspoken words heavier than the spoken ones. *It doesn't matter if she's cold, if it makes her happy, let her do it. She doesn't have much time left to enjoy things like fresh air and hot coffee and sunshine.*

"Sure, some coffee would be nice." I move into the living room and grab Mom's red and yellow patterned wrap from the couch. "Want some help?" I ask as I re-enter the kitchen. Eddie waves his hand, shooing away my offer.

"No, it's all right. I'll bring it out in a few minutes." He smiles at me again, but in a way that pulls his features down. The air around him practically radiates sadness, and that's not something I'm used to with him. I set Mom's wrap on the table and loop my arms around Eddie. He doesn't say anything, but he hugs me back. After a moment, we separate, and Eddie's eyes are bright.

"I don't know what I'm going to do," he says. "The thought of being here without her…" He shrugs, a helpless gesture. "It's over-whelming."

I reach out and rub his arm. "I know. I know." There's nothing else I can say. I don't know how I'm going to manage, either.

Eddie sighs heavily and shakes his head, as though trying to pull himself out of staring down the barrel of future grief. "Coffee'll be out in a minute."

I nod, pick up Mom's wrap, and go back outside. Eddie has always reminded me a bit of Mr. Rogers, and I don't mean that in a snarky, mocking way. Maybe it's his carefully combed dark hair, shot through with threads of pure white. Maybe it's the fact that he can't resist a good cardigan. Or maybe it's that he's one of the kindest, most thoughtful, caring men I've ever known. Maybe it's because it's so unexpected and refreshing for a man born in the 1950s to be so in touch with his emotions. He was more than a breath of fresh air when he came into the picture when I was nine; he was a revelation. For me to see and understand that my dad—my biological dad—wasn't the only kind of man there was probably saved me from a lot of heartbreak and daddy issues down the road. Eddie's influence allowed me to choose well for myself, because I knew that men like him existed. Sometimes Scott reminds me a bit of Eddie, and I mean that in the best possible way.

I lay the wrap around Mom's shoulders, which are still bony and too-thin, even if she feels less breakable than she did a few weeks ago. She pulls it tight around herself and then pats my hand. "Thanks, sweetie."

I sit back down. "Eddie's going to bring us some coffee."

She smiles brightly. "Oh, how I've missed coffee. For so long I couldn't drink it because of that damn metallic taste in my mouth. It made the coffee taste horrible, and it usually just made me sick anyhow." She sighs, staring distantly at some sparrows flitting through the trees, free and light as air. "It's nice to be able to taste things again, to enjoy things." She settles back in her chair, and says in a quieter voice, "Even if it's only for a little while."

I want to wrap my hands around time and squeeze it, putting so much pressure on it that it stops, strangling it so that it can't move until I release it. I don't want to watch her get sicker and weaker. I don't want to figure out how I'm supposed to make my way through the world without her.

Eddie steps outside and presses a warm mug into each of our hands, our coffees doctored exactly the way we like them—Mom's with French vanilla coffee creamer, mine with milk and a little sugar. He kisses the top of Mom's head and smooths her brightly colored scarf before disappearing back inside, giving us time alone together.

"Scott and I have decided to move forward with IVF," I say, blowing away steam over the rim of my mug.

Mom doesn't say anything, and for a moment, I wonder if she didn't hear me. Finally, after a tiny sip of her coffee, she nods. "If you're sure."

It's not quite the response I'm looking for—although, if I'm honest, I'm not 100% sure what kind of response I *am* looking for—and I frown slightly.

"We are. It's the only option left now. There's an IVF information night at the clinic this week, so we signed up."

Mom doesn't say anything for a few moments, just sips her coffee again. "So, I guess that means more hormones, right?"

"Yeah. And needles and an egg retrieval procedure."

Mom sighs, and I don't understand why there's suddenly a tension in the air. "I guess I was just hoping for a little more time with the normal Claire. The hormone-free Claire."

Something cold and heavy sinks in my chest. "What do you mean?"

"I'm just so happy to see you when you're yourself. The hormones change you. Make you different."

"Different how?"

She waves a hand. "It doesn't matter."

"Uh, no, you don't get to tell me that and then say it doesn't matter. How do they make me different?"

She turns to look at me, and I can tell she regrets saying what she did. Regrets her honesty. "You're just so emotional and bitter and unpleasant. I know it's not your fault, it's the damn hormones. I hate to see you go down that road again so soon." She says the words all in a rush, as though she's pulling off a verbal Band-Aid.

But it doesn't matter how fast she says them, they hurt all the same. Am I really that different when I'm on hormones? I know they make me more emotional. I mean, the other week I cried at a toilet paper commercial because the animated cartoon bear family made me ache for a family of my own. But I didn't realize they turned me into some kind of ogre that people don't want to be around.

Under normal circumstances, this would be grounds for an argument. But I don't want to argue with her. Not when our minutes are slipping away, one after the other.

"I'm sorry. I'll..." I wrap my fingers tightly around the mug as I flounder for words. "I'll try not to be that way. I really will. But we need to move forward with this. The longer we're in it, the heavier it gets."

Mom reaches forward and puts her hand on mine. She feels bad, I can tell. "But couldn't you take a break? Just a short one?"

"I'm scared that if we take a break, we won't start again. It's like pushing a boulder up a hill; we've got momentum right now. If we stop, it'll be that much harder to get it moving again."

She shakes her head, her expression thoughtful. "But a break might be good. You know, for you and Scott."

"Scott and I are fine." Where is all of this coming from?

She purses her lips together in a thin line. I know that look. It's her patented *should I tell Claire this questionable thing I'm about to tell her* look.

"I've never told you this, but your father and I tried and tried to have another child after you. We started when you were around two and never really gave up. Back then, fertility treatments weren't as widely available. We tried different things, but nothing worked, and I never got pregnant again. I think...I mean, the marriage wasn't good, but not being able to give you a sibling didn't help. It just piled stress and tension and blame on top of an already bad situation, and that's the last thing I want for you and Scott."

I lean back in my chair, staring absently at the sun dappled leaves of the birch tree as I take all this in. I need a minute to process all of this, to untangle her experience from mine. I can't help but wonder if I inherited my shitty eggs from her. Maybe I *was* a shitty egg who defied the odds.

"I appreciate what you're telling me," I finally say, "but Scott and I are not you and Hugh. Not by a longshot. Scott and I aren't already having problems—in fact, we're pretty solid. He's been a huge support through all of this. We need to at least try IVF. We need to know."

"But sometimes you have to let things go, Claire. I did, and I was fine. I just don't want you to spend time and money and inject yourself with hormones and go through all the grief and the stress for something that—" She cuts herself off abruptly.

For something that isn't going to happen.

She doesn't say the words, but I hear them anyway, clear as the blue sky above us. Because it didn't happen for her, she assumes it's never going to happen for me. I know it's just her opinion, but it makes me feel like a failure all over again.

I take several deep breaths before I trust myself to speak. "I'm sorry that it didn't work out for you. But my situation is different. My marriage is different. The treatments available are different. I know all of this is coming from a good place, but you're kinda pissing me off."

Mom smiles a lopsided smile, staring down into her coffee. "It's not my intention to piss you off. I just…I know it's maybe selfish, but I don't want this to color the time we have left."

"But it's because of the time left that I have to try. If it works, wouldn't you at least want to know?"

She stares off into the distance and doesn't say anything, an oddly peaceful look on her face.

I swallow past the lump in my throat. For several minutes, we sip our coffees without speaking. Life ticks by around us, beat by relentless beat. In the past, I might've made an excuse and left, but I can't do that now. I won't.

"I want to have a party," she says, her face tilted up to the sun, her eyes closed.

"What?" I think that I must not have heard her right. Her words have caught me off guard.

"I want to have a party." She finishes her coffee and sets the mug down on the little glass table between our chairs. "A celebration. Come see me one last time before I die."

The casualness of her words makes them feel even sharper. I have no idea how she can be so cavalier about her own death, but then again, I'm not the one facing it.

"You want to have a party so people can come see you before you die?"

"Yeah. Maybe we could rent one of those giant bulldogs with the signs attached to them. You know, the ones that people put on their lawns with signs like 'Lordy, lordy, look who's forty.'"

My mind is scrambling to keep up with her. "Don't you think this is a tad morbid, Mom?"

She shakes her head, her silk scarf spilling over her shoulder. It shimmers softly in the sunlight. "No, I think it's honest. And fun. I want to see people before I go. I want to laugh and dance and eat and drink and savor being alive. I'd rather be here to enjoy my celebration of life as opposed to who knows where." Her eyes mist over and she swallows, her throat working. She's so thin that I can almost see its internal mechanisms through her skin.

My chest hurts. There's a bittersweet finality to throwing a party like this. Like a pre-funeral. But if this is what she wants, I can't deny her. My own mixed emotions don't matter. What matters is that for now, she's still here, and she wants to live it up while she's living at all.

"What would you want the sign on your bulldog to say?" I ask. She turns to look at me, her expression brightening.

"I don't know, maybe something like 'let's go crazy before she's pushing up daisies?'"

I sputter on my coffee. "Jesus, Mom!" I cough, trying to clear coffee from my windpipe.

"What? Too shocking?"

"Pushing up daisies? Really?"

"What, I can't make a joke? I don't want this to be some kind of sad drag with crying and misery. Miss me when I'm gone. Save it for the funeral."

I blink, trying to get my bearings. This is all a little too much for me.

"We could play songs like 'Highway to Hell,' 'Another One Bites the Dust,' and 'Stayin' Alive.'"

I stare at her incredulously. "You're kidding, right?"

Her lips twitch. "About the music, yes. About having a party, no."

I hold up my hands in front of me in resignation. In surrender. "Okay, weirdo, we'll have a party."

Mom sits up straighter and does a content little head bob, her body rocking from side to side, as though this is the best news she's gotten all year. Hell, maybe it is. I don't want to plan it for her, not because of the work involved, but because of what it signifies. I thought stopping treatment was the beginning of the end, but somehow this feels more like it. Once we pass these goalposts, there'll be nothing left to do but wait. I don't know how I'll bear it.

<hr>

Before

Claire steps into the offices of Carlisle and Winter, wiping her slightly damp palms on the skirt of her red shift dress. Her purse is slung over her shoulder, the strap digging in a little. She glances around, not entirely sure where she's supposed to go, or what she's supposed to do. The space buzzes with activity, but no one seems to notice her. She stops the first woman who rushes by her.

"Excuse me, I'm here for an interview. Do you know—"

The woman smiles; it's warm and reassuring, "Sure. Conference room at the back there," she says, pointing. She winks. "Good luck. And fantastic dress, by the way."

Claire feels some of the tension leave her shoulders. Her neck feels looser. "Thanks. I got it at this little boutique in Sawmill Commons."

"Oh, Blush?"

Claire nods.

"I love that store! I just got the prettiest black and white polka dot blouse there. Anyway, I shouldn't keep you." She gives her a thumbs up, and Claire squares her shoulders and heads for the conference room.

"Oh hey, wait!" the woman calls out. Claire turns, but the woman rushes behind her, a flurry of blond hair, red lipstick and high heels.

Claire feels the upward tug on her dress's zipper, the metal cool against her slightly overheated skin. "Your zipper was down a bit."

"Thanks," Claire says, shooting the woman a grateful smile.

"No problem. Oh, and if Gavin asks, your favorite contemporary designer is Kelly Hoppen. I'm Mia, by the way. Hopefully I'll see you around!"

Now — October

On Monday morning, I sit at my cluttered desk, staring at my computer screen as I idly rearrange pieces of digital furniture in a room. I've spent the past week focusing on finishing up Jillian's bedroom, supervising the painting and the installation of the new hardwood flooring. I'm not normally quite so hands on, but after the Mandy Sinclair visit, and the thing with Mia, I've been avoiding the office.

But Jillian's room is just about done now, and I have to admit, I'm quite pleased with how it turned out. Soft white walls with ash gray hardwoods. The beautiful Turkish rug. Cream colored linen over the windows. The pink tufted headboard, the bed piled with blankets and pillows, making it cozy and inviting. The antique beaded chandelier hanging above the bed. It's dreamy, ethereal, and peaceful, and will hopefully give her the fresh start she needs. We're still waiting on a few small details—the matching lamps for the white nightstands are supposed to come in this week, and two beautiful antique prints of horses are currently being framed—but it's mostly done. I can't use Jillian as my excuse for avoiding everything else anymore.

I did end up responding to Mia's text messages, the morning after my date with Scott. I didn't really know what to say, so I told her not to worry about it. So, not really a blank slate "I forgive you" statement, but one that let her off the hook all the same. Because I love her and don't want to fight. I can't afford to ostracize my allies right now.

I close out the design program and click back to my email. I answer a couple, delete a few others. I'm still waiting to hear back from Aurora Construction about the model house project. The meeting went well, but I also know we're far from the cheapest design firm in town, which could hurt us. This isn't a client who wants the best for their beloved home; this is a corporation who wants to sell things. Completely different interests.

I open my calendar, and my heart sinks. Mia and I have a meeting with Mandy Sinclair on Friday to show her the concept board. We're supposed to meet with her today to further discuss ideas, even though I'd rather swim with disease-ridden crocodiles than work on planning another woman's nursery. And yet, I know there's no way out of this project. Not after the way everything went down in Janet's office last week.

I'm so sick of feeling stuck inside my own life.

A manicured hand slides a Starbucks cup in front of me, and I look up to see Mia standing beside my desk.

"Hi," she says, looking uncertain. We've barely spoken over the past week, which is weird for us. Even weirder is that I've both missed her and welcomed the space. There's been this unsettling push-pull inside of me, wanting both to reach out and to keep my distance. I don't think there's been a time in our friendship when I've ever *not* wanted to tell her everything going on in my life.

"Hey," I say, swiveling around in my chair to face her. "This is for me?"

"Yeah, a vanilla latte. Your favorite." She smiles tentatively. She has a little streak of red lipstick across one of her front teeth. I curl my lips back and ostentatiously rub my front tooth with my tongue, one of our unspoken "check yourself" gestures. She rubs a finger across her front teeth. Even though I'm hurt, it's so easy to slide back into these small signals of friendship.

"Thanks," I say, picking up the coffee cup. I don't know what else to say, so I stay quiet. I want to give her the chance to talk.

"It's, um, a peace offering," she says, and I can see how hard this is for her. Mia's not the type to eat crow of any kind, and apologies are hard for her. She's stubborn and proud, sometimes a little too much. It's one of the things we have in common.

I'm still not entirely sure what to say, partly because I don't want to make a big thing out of this, especially at work, and also because I know I'm not blameless in this. I know that she's trying, even though she doesn't know what to do or say. But is that her fault? Trying to talk to me must be like trying to pick up a cactus; it doesn't matter how carefully you come at it, you're likely to get pricked. I hate that I'm like this, but my needle-sharp defensiveness is the only way I can cope. It's the only way I can make it through some days with my sanity intact. I feel bad that she's gotten more than her fair share of jabs.

"Thanks," I say, which I know is lame, and take a sip of my latte. "Really, let's just forget about it and move on."

For a second, she looks relieved, but then the relief written across her face is replaced with something that looks a lot like determination. The back of my neck prickles.

"Claire, I really do feel bad about what I said, both about your cycle not working out, and for snapping at you in Janet's office. I've been on edge lately because of some…some personal stuff, and I think I've maybe been taking it out on other people. You know I don't do well with surprises."

"Is everything okay, with you and Tom? The kids?"

She nods, a faraway, thoughtful expression on her face. "Yeeeeeahh-hh," she says stretching the word out so it sounds completely uncertain. "Just a lot going on right now, and I'm not really ready to talk about it."

I don't know why, but a cold, hard lump of something that feels like dread drops into my stomach. I take another sip of my latte, trying to chase it away.

She opens her mouth to say more, but then shakes her head and closes it. Instead, she tucks a sleek strand of hair behind her ear and nods. "So what's next for you guys now?"

I toy with the sleeve wrapped around the Starbucks cup. I notice that they've spelled my name wrong: *Clare*, without the *i*. I want to open up to her, but my trust is a little shaken. It would be so easy to say that we haven't decided yet, or that we just don't know. But it's Mia, and in the past I've always told her everything. It feels weird, unnatural to hold back.

"We're going to move on to IVF," I say before I can talk myself out of it.

Mia lets out a happy little squeal that has my eyebrows furrowing together. "Oh my God, Claire, I'm so happy for you! That's so exciting. Really. It's totally awesome." She beams at me with her hands clasped in front of her chest; she bounces a little on the balls of her feet, like a Tigger in Michael Kors heels. Her reaction is as though I've told her I'm pregnant.

"What's awesome?" asks Allison, a mug of tea clutched in her hands. Her long hair is pulled back in a high ponytail, and she's wearing a forest green shift dress with bright, sky blue pumps. Immaculate, as always. Two interns, their arms laden with binders and textile samples scurry past, their eyes darting further away from Alli.

"Scaring the interns again?" I ask, grateful for the excuse to shift the conversation away from my ovaries.

Alli glances over her shoulder and then rolls her eyes. "They're here to learn, and I'm here to teach them. I don't have time to hold anyone's hand or listen to asinine chit chat about what they did on the weekend, or what they ate for dinner. I don't care. I guess that makes me an ogre." She laughs into her tea, clearly not feeling bad about the situation.

Allison is that rare breed of workaholic who works a lot not because she needs to, but because she wants to. Work *is* her play. If she's not working on something, she doesn't know what to do with herself.

"So, fill me in," she says. "What's exciting, or awesome or whatever?" She glances at her watch, as though she's making sure she has enough idle minutes built into her jam-packed schedule to talk to her friends for more than thirty seconds.

"Claire's going to do IVF," Mia says, still beaming with happiness for me.

"Oh, hey, that's great," says Allison, squeezing my arm. "Congrats."

I take a breath, and then another. Every single word that hangs on the tip of my tongue is sharp, or sarcastic, or unkind. I force a thin smile to my lips. The muscles around my mouth twitch uncomfortably. I take another sip of my latte before I speak.

"I appreciate the enthusiasm, but I really don't think it's awesome. In fact, I think it fucking sucks that it's come to this."

Mia waves a hand in the air, batting away my comment like a mosquito that won't quit. "I know it sucks that this is the route you have to go, but at least now you'll finally be able to get pregnant." If I'm not mistaken, there's an undertone of relief in her voice.

My teeth grind together, and I really, really wish I'd kept my mouth shut. "There are no guarantees, here. We could spend all this money, I could go through all the shots and everything and we could still end up with no baby. Maybe we don't end up with any viable eggs. Or maybe the eggs won't fertilize. Or maybe they fertilize but don't develop into actual embryos. Or maybe they do but the transfer fails. Or maybe the transfer works, but I miscarry. So many things can go wrong. This is a total crapshoot."

"Well, maybe on the first try, but it'll work eventually." Allison nods confidently.

"Exactly," Mia nods along with Allison, digging her designer heels into what she thinks she knows.

"Listen, I get that you're trying to be positive and supportive. I do. But I feel like you're not hearing me. This is expensive and scary and odds are it won't work."

She frowns and crosses her arms in front of her chest. "If it's so awful, why are you even bothering to do it?"

At least at that, Alli flinches, shooting a look at Mia.

"Because we need to know. If we end up not being able to have kids, I won't be able to put it behind me if we didn't try everything."

Mia shrugs, her eyes flicking to the ceiling. "Okay. I guess I just don't know what you want from me." Allison purses her lips together, staying quiet.

I don't know how to explain to her that I just want her to stop making me feel so alone.

"Let's just…let's just focus on work stuff for now, okay?" I offer. I'm not trying to make her feel bad, but I also know I can't keep doing this with her. "We've got the meeting with Mandy this afternoon, and we have to come up with a concept board for her by Friday. Let's just focus on that."

Her tone hardens and cools. "If that's what you want."

"I think it's best for now, yeah."

"Sure." She shrugs again. Her mouth purses into a pout and after a second, she heads back to her desk.

Alli takes a sip of her tea. "Well, that took a turn."

"I hate the way she makes it about her." I grimace at my honesty, wishing I could call the words back. I don't want to put Alli in the middle of this.

"Well, that's kinda who she is. It doesn't mean she's a bad person. She means well, you know." Alli sends me a wry smile and strides back to her desk, interns scattering like the parting of the Red Sea as she walks across the office.

8

Before

"You're acting weird," Claire says, tracing her thumb over the back of Scott's hand. She's holding a picnic basket in the other as they walk through Washington Park.

"What? No I'm not," he says, giving her hand a squeeze, but the tension is still there, in his features, the set of his shoulders. Claire decides not to press it. They've had arguments in the fourteen months they've been together, but this doesn't feel like that. It feels…different.

Scott starts to lead them toward the gazebo—their gazebo, as they've come to think of it—where they had their first kiss. Claire's mind starts to race as she wonders if…But she pushes it away. She doesn't want to let herself get excited about something that isn't going to happen. They're here to celebrate her new job at Carlisle and Winter. That's all.

They spread out the blanket and the food and start to eat. Claire forgets about the path her mind had gone down as they talk about her new job. When the food is gone, Scott clears his throat and starts acting weird again.

"Do you want some dessert?" he asks. She frowns—she didn't pack any dessert, but sure enough, there's a little pink pastry box inside the basket.

"Um, yes," she says, feeling a little funny. Maybe it's because Scott's hands are shaking. He pulls out the pastry box and hands it to her. His expression is so, so serious. Claire's heart takes off like a rabbit. She opens the box and there isn't a cake inside. There's a diamond ring inside a white jewel box, nestled among pink peonies. Everything inside her goes very, very still. She looks up, and Scott's on one knee.

"Oh my God," she whispers.

Scott licks his lips and takes her hand in his. "I want to spend the rest of my life with you. I want to see the world and make babies and grow old with you. I want the ups and the downs, the good and the bad. I want anything and everything, as long as it's with you, because Claire Elizabeth Dailey, I love you so much I don't even know what to do with myself. Will you marry me?"

"Yes," she says, and she feels the word with her entire body.

Now – October

Scott and I are in the car, headed home from the IVF education night at our clinic. A folder is sitting in my lap, one of the edges a little warped from where I'd been clutching it in my sweaty palm. My mind races, leaping erratically from one thought to the other until I feel as though I can't quite catch my breath. I think about injecting myself with up to six shots a day—drugs to make my ovaries grow multiple eggs, drugs to make sure I don't ovulate those eggs pre-retrieval, drugs to finish maturing the eggs before surgery. I think about the horrific sounding surgery where they retrieve my eggs with a needle inserted directly into my ovary, piercing the inner wall of my vagina. I think about the potential side effects and complications of all these drugs and procedures—everything from mood swings, headaches and nausea to infection and ovarian torsion (yes, it's exactly what it sounds like). I think about how there are no guarantees and this might not work. I think about how monstrously expensive it is. Thousands and thousands of dollars just for a chance. Christ.

I glance over at Scott, whose eyes are on the darkened road, the divider lines racing towards us in the glare from the headlights and then slipping away, receding back into the darkness. A surge of resentment presses up through my chest and suddenly tears are pricking at my eyes. I look away, staring blankly down at the folder, emblazoned with the clinic's cheery green and yellow logo. It pulses and glows with each streetlamp we pass.

I have to do *everything*. The shots, the appointments, the side effects, the surgery. All he has to do is jerk off into a cup.

"You're awfully quiet," he says, not taking his eyes from the road.

"It's a lot to process." I stare out the passenger side window. Dead leaves fly up around us as we drive past, swirling in the wind created by the car's passing.

"But you do want to do it, right?"

"Wanting to do it and needing to do it aren't the same thing. I mean, no one *wants* to do this."

There's a pause before he speaks, and then when he does, his tone is serious. "You don't have to do it if you don't want to."

"That's not what I said." I fold my arms over my chest. I don't have the energy to argue with Scott right now. I sigh and let my head fall back against the headrest. I'm so tired.

"Jeez, okay. I'm just trying to be supportive." There's an edge to his voice that has me swiveling my head in his direction.

"What's wrong?"

His grip tightens on the steering wheel. "Nothing's wrong."

"Okay, then."

A silence falls between us, only broken by the commercials playing at low volume on the radio. A car dealership. A local winery. Laser eye surgery. A furniture store. Mundane pieces of life that make me wish our lives were mundane. No infertility, no cancer, no drama.

"It'll be okay. We can do this," he finally says, the edge gone from his voice.

I let out a sarcastic snort. "Easy for you to say." My resentment bubbles up and over me, like lava out of a volcano. I don't want Scott to tell me everything will be okay. I want him to understand how freaked out I am about all of this. How absolutely shitty this is. "You're not the one who has to inject yourself and have surgery and have an ultrasound wand shoved up your fucking vagina every other morning."

"Claire, if I could take it on for you, I would. But I can't. Don't blame me. That's not fair."

"I'm not blaming you. I just think it's awfully easy to be a cheerleader when your contribution only involves porn and jerking off."

"You think I want it that way?" Scott's voice rises, and he becomes uncharacteristically loud. "You think I like feeling useless? I'm basically a goddamn sperm bank. Don't assume this is easy for me. Because it's not."

"It's easier for you than it is for me." Physically and emotionally, he seems to glide through all of this while I stumble almost daily. It makes me wonder if he wants this as much as I do, and if he does, why is it so much easier for him? The ease with which he seems to navigate all of this makes me feel lonely.

"Physically, yes. You're right. But you think I'm not scared? Worried? Sad? You think all those failed attempts don't eat at me? They do. And I can't do anything about it. All I can do is watch."

I don't know why I'm picking this argument. Maybe I just need an outlet for everything boiling up inside me. "At least you're not the one whose body is defective. At least all you have to do is watch."

"What is this, the pain Olympics? Fine, Claire. You win. Only what you're feeling matters."

God, I am *such* an asshole.

I start to cry. I've been so wrapped up in my own pain that I never even stop to think of Scott's. Of course this is hard for him too. I guess we're both alone in this. Alone, together, each with our own grief, our own fears, our own ways of getting through each day.

I expect Scott to pull the car over so we can talk, but he doesn't. He just keeps driving, his focus on the road. Looking ahead. Moving forward. We don't talk for the rest of the drive home.

Scott pulls the car into the driveway and cuts the ignition, shuttering the car in silence. His face is drawn, resigned. In the light from our front porch, he looks tired, with deep shadows under his eyes. "I don't want to fight with you about this," he says, his tone weary.

"I don't want to fight, either." I've left several splotchy marks on the front of the folder. I somehow doubt I'm the first woman to cry while holding this IVF packet. "But please don't tell me everything will be okay. If you don't want to be a bystander, then you need to be in the shit, with me, where everything is decidedly not okay." Scott is a relentlessly positive person; I don't know if he can do what I'm asking.

"Okay, as long as we're not going to act like you're the only one suffering here. Sometimes...sometimes I guess I need you to be in the shit with me. And you never are. You withdraw and shut everyone out, including me."

He's not wrong. I know I do this. I wear a mask and hoist a shield, like some kind of warrior. Deflecting and fighting and disguising my wounds. It's how I get by, how I cope. How I function when the pain and grief would swallow me up if I let it. And I can't let it, because I'm so scared I'll lose myself completely to it.

"Okay. I'm sorry. I'll...try to...to not shut you out."

"And I'll try not to be a cheerleader when what you really want is a shoulder to lean on."

I nod. "Okay." I wipe at my face with the heel of my hand. The tears have dried, leaving my skin feeling tight, my eyes swollen. I can feel a clump of mascara binding some of my eyelashes together. "Let's go open a bottle of wine."

"Good idea. I could use a drink." Scott opens his door and heads toward the porch, not waiting for me. As I watch him, a part of me wishes I'd never wanted to get pregnant in the first place. I feel as though the past three years have been stolen from me, from us. We'll never be the same Claire and Scott we were when we got married. That couple, that happiness, it doesn't exist anymore.

Grief has changed us, and I don't think we can ever go back.

9

I don't know where I am.

I'm standing alone in the middle of a forest, wearing nothing but a filmy white nightgown. The air is cold, and a harsh breeze makes the thin fabric swirl around me and cling to my clammy skin. My feet are bare, sinking a little into the loamy forest floor. I look around, but in every direction, all I can see are the black silhouettes of skeletal trees, devoid of their leaves. A full moon lights up the sky, casting everything in tones of black, grey, and white. There is no color anywhere. The forest smells like death. Dead leaves, rotting wood, and underneath it all, a coppery smell that sets my teeth on edge.

I clutch the flimsy nightgown around myself, trying to find even an ounce of warmth in the thin fabric. I listen for signs of life, but the forest is deathly silent. No hooting owls, cracking twigs, rustling brush. Nothing. I'm alone here in this desolate place. Panic surges through me as I try to remember where I am, why I'm here.

The wind picks up, and the branches of the bare trees creek and moan above me. A wave of nausea rolls through me and sweat beads along my hairline despite the cold air. I turn in a slow circle, trying to get my bearings. The moon is huge, impossibly close, luminous. I shiver and swallow against the churning in my stomach. This place feels haunted. It feels like death itself. I don't want to be here.

I take a tentative step forward, no idea how I'm supposed to get out of here. Every direction looks the same. A cold rush washes over me, through me, and I see her. To my right, standing maybe twenty feet away, is my mother. I can only see her in profile, with her curls blowing around her face, but I know it's her. Even though I haven't seen them in years, I'd know those golden-brown curls anywhere. She looks healthier, stronger, than she's been in years. She's also wearing a white nightgown, but hers flutters elegantly while mine sticks to my skin like plaster. The light of the moon seems to infuse her, giving her an ethereal, almost otherworldly glow. I run toward her, relief powering me, making me forget the cold gripping my skin. She'll know where we are, what we're doing here.

"Mom!" I call out, my voice high and frantic. "Mom!"

She turns and I stop in my tracks. There's nothing but smooth, silvery skin where her mouth should be.

"Mom," I say, my voice now a shivery whisper as I force my feet to move, pine needles cushioning my bare feet. "What happened to you?"

She shakes her head and a tear slips over her cheek, leaving a glistening path down her face. I reach out for her, but my hand glides right through her shoulder. She's not really here.

I can't help you anymore, Claire.

Her voice echoes through my head and I pull my chilled hand away, taking a step backward. I stare at the ghostly figure in front of me, and I don't know if I should run or try to help her. As if there's anything I could do. This was always inevitable.

Her expression solemn, she raises a hand and points straight ahead.

Go.

The word stretches into a moan, mingling with the clacking, cracking branches above. I stare at her for a moment, but even though I don't blink, she disintegrates before my eyes. Gone. As though she was never even here. Grief wraps itself around me, but I know I need to do as she said. I need to go.

I spin and start moving in the direction she indicated. The forest floor is damp and cold beneath my feet, the air chilled. A rhythmic clicking noise echoes through my head, and I look around, trying to find the source. It takes me several steps to figure out that it's my own teeth chattering. Goosebumps dot my skin, making it feel tight and overly sensitive, and I move faster, trying to generate some warmth, but I don't think there is any in this gray world.

I don't know how long I walk. It could be minutes. It could be hours. I trudge interminably through the dead forest, not knowing where I'm going, where I'll end up, or how long it'll take me to get there, if I ever even get there at all. I'm about to give up, to cry out for help, when I hear it. A plaintive cry in the distance.

"Mommy!"

My head snaps in the direction of the cry and my chest fills with a desperate, clawing need. That voice belongs to my child. I know it does. He's here, looking for me. I just need to find him. I'm lost without him, just like he's lost without me. Once we're together, everything will make sense.

"Mommy!" The cry comes again, louder, more frightened, filled with need. I start to run in its direction, urging my legs as fast as they'll go. Pain shoots up my legs as rocks and sticks dig into the bottoms of my feet, but I push on. Protruding branches tear at my nightgown, my arms, my face, leaving stinging, raw cuts on my skin. My hair snags and I'm yanked back, held in place by a claw-like branch.

"Mommy!" The child's voice is thin and high, and it gives me the strength to rip my hair free of the branch. A clump of it still dangles there; I can feel wet warmth on my scalp. Pain makes my vision hazy, but I keep moving. All that matters is that I'm free and now I can get to him, this child who needs me.

I run until my lungs are on the brink of exploding when finally the trees thin and I emerge from the forest into a clearing that holds a small lake. I fall to my hands and knees, my body shaking with exhaustion as I scan the scene in front of me, looking for my son.

The moon hovers above the lake, gigantic and still. The surface of the water is flat and calm, untouched by the cool air still creaking the branches of the trees behind me. Like a mirror, smooth, silver, pristine. My breath comes in pants and gasps but I try to listen for another cry, straining to hear anything over my ragged breathing and pounding heart. Blood rushes through my ears. My body is too loud with exertion to hear anything else.

Then I hear it. A soft rippling noise, coming from the lake. I lift my throbbing head and look out. I don't know how I didn't see it before.

A little body, arms and legs outstretched, floating face down in the water. Gone. Grief wraps itself around me, suffocating me, strangling me. I feel crushed beneath the mountain of it, unable to move. I can't take my eyes off of the horror in front of me. I cry out, but the wind picks up and snatches away any sound I make. I let myself fall to the frozen forest floor—

My limbs jolt against the mattress and I wake with a start. My heart throbs in my chest and I feel as though I can't catch my breath. I sit up, my eyes darting around the darkened bedroom, taking it in. My hands start to shake as I push my tangled hair out of my face. A puddle of sweat has collected between my breasts and drips down my torso.

It was a dream. No, a nightmare. I keep looking around the bedroom, centering myself. Consoling myself with the knowledge that it wasn't real.

Holy shit, it felt so real.

I get out of bed and pad quietly into the bathroom, shutting the door with an almost silent snick behind me. I retrieve a washcloth from the open shelves above the bathtub, wet it with warm water and press it against my face, feeling the need to chase away the cold of the dream. As though I can chase away the desperate longing, the agonizing grief, the overwhelming loneliness with a little heat.

My hands are still shaking a little.

After a few moments, the washcloth starts to cool, so I wring it out and hang it over the faucet to dry. Leaning my hands on the cool surface of the marble-topped vanity, I squint at myself in the mirror. My hair is disheveled, my skin pale, dark circles below my eyes. I, too, am wrung out. I let out a long breath, smooth down my hair a little, and then shut off the light.

As I climb back into bed, Scott stirs and pulls me into his arms, settling my back against his warm chest. I stare at the wall and wait for dawn.

Before

Scott's fingers skim down Claire's back, slowly undoing the buttons on her blue wedding dress. She stands at the French doors of their honeymoon suite, the night and the Mediterranean stretching before them in a vast sea of shimmering navy. Claire sips a glass of champagne and sighs. The buttons open and Scott parts the lace, gently pushing the sleeves down her shoulders. She sets the champagne down and carefully steps out of the dress. Scott picks it up and sets it on an ornate arm chair in the corner. He shrugs out of his suit jacket and pulls off his tie, undoing the first couple of buttons on his shirt. He picks up his own champagne and slips an arm around Claire's waist.

"How do you feel, Mrs. Stanhope?" he asks as they stare out at the sea together.

"Like I have everything I've always wanted."

Scott kisses her temple. "Everything, huh?"

"In this moment, yes. And there's so much more to come." Her voice is sleepy, sated with happiness.

"I can't wait to do it all with you."

"Mmm. A house."

Scott finishes his champagne and sets his glass down, wrapping his arms around his wife. "Travel."

"Babies." Her eyes sparkle.

"You're going to make such a good mom, someday, Claire."

"Someday, you'll be the world's best dad." She threads her arms around his neck, nestling her body against his.

"In the meantime, I think we should practice the baby-making part of having a baby."

Claire smiles at him, the coy, achingly sexy smile he adores and sinks to her knees.

Now – October

It's Friday, and I feel like I've run a marathon this week. After our follow-up meeting with Mandy, in which she'd described wanting a "glam, super girly, with a beachy vibe" nursery, I set to work pretending I was designing any old bedroom as opposed to a baby's room, since the design Mandy wants doesn't exactly scream "baby." Clinging to this idea is getting me through, barely. Mia and I have been tiptoeing around each other at work, mostly working on the concept board through email even though her desk is in the same building as mine. I don't know where we stand right now, and every interaction is like walking on eggshells. We'd put the board together yesterday afternoon, making idle chit chat about nothing. I don't offer anything up, and she doesn't ask.

I've been busy planning my mom's morbid "come see me before I die" party, including booking a giant fucking bulldog—just like she'd asked—for the front lawn. Eddie and I have been emailing and phoning people, inviting them to come, and I managed to book a caterer. I'm trying to focus on the minutiae of planning the party, and not on what the party signifies.

I've also been spending time trying not to think about IVF—we can start at the beginning of my next cycle in just a couple of weeks—or the lingering tension between me and Scott. Things have been a little off with us ever since our argument in the car, and I've been feeling distant and emotional after my nightmare the other night. I'm also trying not to think about that nightmare.

I'm completely exhausted from the things I'm avoiding. Like I'm treading water in my own brain, trying to ignore all of the sharks lurking below.

Mia appears at my desk, concept board in hand. "Mandy's waiting for us in the conference room," she says. She flashes me a small smile, but I can't tell if it's genuine or not. I want to tell her that I miss her, but I can't. Things are so different between us lately, as though the tectonic plates anchoring our friendship have shifted. On the surface, everything looks the same, but underneath, cracks, maybe irreparable ones, have formed.

"Great," I say, rising to my feet, grabbing my notebook and returning Mia's smile. She nods, turns and clicks her way toward the conference room where Mandy's seated in one of the white leather swivel chairs surrounding the glass conference table. Large hoop earrings dangle from her ears, and a silk leopard print scarf winds its way around her delicate neck. She's wearing an expensive looking shift dress in a stunning stony blue color, her growing bump clearly visible beneath. Soft pink ballet slippers complete the look. She looks like a real-life Snapchat or Instagram filter, all long eyelashes and flawless skin. I'm kind of in awe of her. I feel suddenly underdressed in my white cable-knit sweater, black skinny pants, and ankle boots.

I shove my sleeves up my arms self-consciously and tuck a strand of hair behind my ear. Oh yeah, now I surely look like a Snapchat filter too.

"Hello ladies," says Mandy. "It's great to see you again." She smiles at both of us, practically glowing. "I've been looking forward to this all week. I can't wait to see what you've got!" She taps the tips of her fingers together in a silent, delicate little clap.

Mia sets the board down on the presentation easel at the front of the room. "How are you feeling? You look *amazing,* by the way. Pregnancy clearly agrees with you."

"Aw, thank you. I definitely don't feel amazing. I have heartburn like you wouldn't believe, I wake up with a sore back every morning, and oh my God, I can't stop farting."

I don't want to like Mandy Sinclair. I don't want her to win me over. I want to keep a professional, polite distance so that this project takes up as little space, both mental and emotional, as possible. But any woman who looks as glam and polished as her while making fart jokes…Dammit, I like her. How can I not?

We all laugh and then I join Mia by the concept board. "All of this is subject to your approval," I say, gesturing at the board. "Anything can be changed if you're not happy with it, or want to see other options." Mandy nods enthusiastically and settles back in her chair. Over the next ten minutes, I walk her through the design Mia and I have cobbled together. Mia is quiet, her weight shifting continuously from one foot to the other.

We plan to install white beadboard wainscoting along the bottom half of the walls, while the top half will be wallpapered. I'd searched and searched for what I'd wanted, but eventually I'd given up and designed my own wallpaper—a soft crepe pink with white palm frond silhouettes arranged in a scattered, organic pattern. I think it suits the girly, beachy vibe Mandy wants without being too grown up or posh to suit a nursery.

The blond hardwood floor is staying the same, and so to complement it, we've sourced furniture all in white with rose gold accents: a dresser with an almost art deco vibe to it, with rose gold lacquer set into the front of the drawers in an expanding diamond pattern, and a little side table topped in white with rose gold legs. I sourced a large circular rug in a soft pink hue made out of natural rope—it looks hand-crocheted, and has a boho, beachy vibe while working with the more glam elements of the rest of the room. The crib is rose gold, with off-white padded and tufted sides, curved at the top into a graceful, royal-looking peak; it looks like something a princess would sleep in. The glider is a posh, straight-backed armchair and matches the crib, done in a classic cream shade with antique brass nailhead detailing along the sides. I've suggested adding pops of green with items like blankets, lamps, and other small décor items in shades like sage and pistachio to balance out the pink and rose gold that could easily overwhelm the room.

Mandy doesn't say anything as she surveys the board, the tips of her fingers pressed to her lips. Her eyes are bright and she blinks rapidly, her throat working against the emotion written plainly across her face. She nods, and when she speaks, her voice is quiet, subdued compared to her usual bubbly tone. "I love it. I really love it." I'm both proud of the work I've done and resentful of the creative energy I've poured into a nursery for someone else.

Mia makes a small sound, halfway between a moan and a whimper, her fingers pressed to her lips. "Excuse me, I'm not feeling well," she manages to squeak out before running for the door. It swings silently shut behind her.

"Is she okay?" Mandy asks, her eyes flicking from the concept board to me, where I'm awkwardly hovering a few feet away from it. I've been avoiding getting stuck alone with her, not wanting to fake enthusiasm for her pregnancy and this nursery project. Not wanting her to see my fake enthusiasm for what it is.

I shrug. "I'm not sure. Maybe something she ate?"

Mandy nods, her gaze returning to the concept board. "You did most of this, didn't you?" she asks, catching me off guard. I'm not sure what to say—is it unprofessional if I tell the truth that yes, I did most of the work on this. Mia contributed, but the overall design plan and most of the sourcing were up to me. She's been distracted this week, often disappearing for long periods of time.

After a few seconds, I nod hesitantly. I don't want to throw Mia under the proverbial bus, but I also appreciate being recognized for my efforts. "Yes, but only because Mia's been so busy, and she still contributed quite a bit, and really this is a team effort..." I'm rambling, and thankfully, Mandy cuts me off.

"It's okay, Claire. I love what you've come up with. I really do. I think it's perfect. You obviously listened to what I wanted and went out of your way to deliver. Where did you find that wallpaper? It's perfect, and I never would've thought of something like that myself."

A slight flush creeps up my cheeks. "Oh. Well, I couldn't find exactly what I was looking for in any of the sample books from our suppliers, so I designed it myself."

"So this is custom wallpaper?"

"It is. A Claire Stanhope original."

Mandy stands, walking closer to the concept board, scrutinizing it. "You're incredibly talented, Claire. Have you ever thought about starting your own line, or company? Or both?"

My head spins. "Not...no, not really." I mean, I've daydreamed about it, especially on days when Janet or Gavin is pissing me off, but I've never seriously considered it. To be honest, it's always seemed completely out of reach. Something beyond what I'd be capable of. I mean, who would want to buy something with my name on it? I'm no one.

Mandy sits back down, swiveling in her chair to face me. She gestures for me to sit down next to her, and I do.

"How long have you been working as a designer?"

I tilt my head, doing the math. "About ten years. I have a bachelor's degree in art and design from Pace University. I've been at Carlisle and Winter for a few of years now."

"So you have quite a bit of experience." She leans back in her chair, tenting her fingers. I feel like I'm on a job interview. "Do you have a design philosophy?"

I know the answer to this question, but I still hesitate momentarily.

"I think design, especially when you're working on someone's home, is so much more than creating something aesthetically pleasing. Our homes and how we feel in them play such a huge role in our lives, and my goal when designing a room for a client is to not only give them something beautiful, but to give them something that makes them feel however it is they need to feel. Calm, happy, excited, energized. There's an aesthetic response, but there's also an emotional response I'm trying to evoke.

"Take your nursery, for example. You said that you wanted something girly, glam, with a beachy vibe. All of that says to me that you want a happy, bright, relaxed space where you can revel in being a mother to your daughter. Where you can treasure bonding with her." My throat aches as I speak.

Longing, deep and raw, fills my chest. I want a room specially made where I can bond with my child. Where I can spend hours feeding and changing diapers and staring down at the tiny person that is somehow half me, half Scott. The life that we made, the two of us together.

The life that might never exist.

Suddenly Mandy's eyes are bright again. She swallows and nods. I give her a moment to work through whatever's going through her mind. I want to ask her if she's okay, but I know how that question wrecks me, especially when I'm trying to get it together, so I don't say anything.

After a moment, Mandy clears her throat, back in control. "You should come on the show. I'd love to do a segment with you. We could have audience members ask design questions, like design therapy, and you could showcase your work. I think it'd be great."

My eyes are probably the size of charger plates. "Seriously?"

"Yeah. Let me talk to my producer about it."

"Mia too?"

Mandy purses her lips together and then tilts her head. "I think the segment would work better with one designer, and I just love your whole philosophy. Are you game?"

"I mean, I think I'd have to run it by Janet and Gavin, but yeah?" It comes out high-pitched, like a question.

Mandy stands. "Great. I'll talk to my producer and be in touch. Let me know when you're ready. Oh, and can't wait to get started on this!" she says, gesturing at the concept board. She smiles and then is out the door.

10

Before

Claire shrieks with laughter as Scott picks her up, lifting her into his arms.

"You're not seriously going to—"

"It's tradition! I have to carry you over the threshold."

"Scott, we've been married for almost two years. I don't think the tradition applies to us." But Claire nestles her head into his neck and he can feel her smile against his skin.

He steps over the threshold and into the empty house that is now officially theirs. Their first home. Maybe their forever home. He sets her down, the heels of Claire's boots clacking loudly against the hardwood floor and echoing through the house. She takes his hand and starts leading him from room to room.

"A big dining table in here for family dinners. A farm style one, with a rustic chandelier overhead," she says, talking animatedly. She pulls him into the den. "A sectional sofa, against this wall here, for family movie nights." Hands entwined, they head up the stairs.

"King size, right here," Scott says, moving them into the master bedroom. "And this shower needs christening."

"Mmm," she says, her eyes lingering on the massive walk-in shower.

They make their way from room to room, ending with the smallest bedroom at the end of the hall.

"This would make a good nursery," Claire says, her voice a little dreamy.

"It would," Scott agrees, his hands on her shoulders.

She turns to him, her bottom lip caught between her teeth. "What would you think if I maybe…stopped taking my birth control?" Her eyebrows raise hopefully.

Scott smiles, big and wide. "Yeah."

"Yeah?"

"Yeah. Let's have a baby."

Claire kisses him. Everything is perfect.

<hr>

Now – October

It's a sunshiny Saturday morning, and like so many other Saturday mornings before, I'm sitting in a corner booth in the South End diner with Mia, Becca, and Alli. It's been a couple of weeks since we've all sat down together, and it feels different than the last time we did. A shift between us, a drop in air pressure, even though we're sitting at our usual table. I don't know how much Becca and Alli know about the lingering tension between me and Mia. On the one hand, I don't want to drag them into it, but on the other, I wish I had someone other than Scott to vent to. Not that Scott isn't a good listener, but like a typical guy, he's not good at just letting me blow off steam without trying to offer solutions to everything. As though I'm full of steam and he's trying to catch it, contain it, mold it with his bare hands. Sometimes I don't need solutions. Sometimes I just need to let it all out.

The waitress comes by, stainless steel coffeepot in hand and pours us all a cup. When she reaches for Mia's mug, Mia shakes her head. "Could I have some mint tea instead?"

"Is your stomach still bothering you?" I ask. After she'd bolted from the meeting with Mandy, she'd emerged from the bathroom about ten minutes later looking shaky and pale. She'd mumbled something about food poisoning and gone home for the day.

She shrugs. "Yeah." Something about the way she looks at me, the tone of her voice, makes the hair on the back of my neck stand.

Becca smiles sympathetically. "Food poisoning is the absolute worst."

"Agreed," says Alli.

The waitress brings Mia's tea, and we all order our usuals: French toast for me, eggs Benedict with extra bacon for Alli, a Greek omelet for Becca, and a traditional two-egg breakfast for Mia.

"So, give us the latest on Giancarlo," I say in a teasing voice, batting my eyelashes at Becca. She's been quiet in our group text all week.

She sighs, tracing her fingertip around the edge of her mug. "His time's running out. He applied to have his visa extended, but it was denied. Even the architectural firm who hired him and brought him over in the first place tried to see if they could sponsor him for some kind of extension, but no dice."

"What are you going to do?" asks Mia, sipping her tea.

Becca chews her lip, shaking her head slowly. "I don't know. I've… I've never met anyone like him before. I've never had this kind of chemistry, this kind of connection with someone so instantly, so easily. There's no guessing, no games. It's all just so simple and clear and wonderful. I don't want to let him go." She sighs and picks up a pink Sweet n Low packet from the little white container on the table. "But what are we supposed to do? Is it fair to ask him to pack up his entire life to move here after only a few months? Assuming he'd even be allowed to come back after getting his visa sorted out."

"Have you thought about moving to Italy?" I ask. The words taste a bit sour as they come out of my mouth. I love Becca. I don't want her to move to Europe. But I do want her to be happy, and I refuse to tether her here.

Becca tilts her head. "I have. I don't know that I'm ready to pack up my entire life, either. Say goodbye to my parents, my friends. Sell the store I've worked so hard to make successful. Move to a country where I don't speak the language." She crumples the packet and smooths it back out. "I don't know. I keep waiting for some answer to fall from the sky and save me from having to make a decision."

"Just get pregnant and then I bet he'll move here for you," says Mia, as though it's the simplest solution in the world. Her words, so cavalier, so casual, are like shards of ice biting into my skin. I look down into my coffee. Becca squeezes my knee under the table.

"I don't really think that's a solution, and besides, I don't want children, and neither does Giancarlo."

"Wow, so you guys have talked about kids and everything?" Allison arches an eyebrow.

Becca nods. "I just wish we had more time to figure everything out."

"I don't envy you," I say. "It's a hard situation. Complicated, even though you obviously love him."

She smiles, her cheeks rosy, but her eyes sad. "Yeah. I do."

I try to put myself in her shoes, wondering how I'd have felt if, just three months into our relationship, Scott had to move halfway across the world. Would I have gone with him? Could I have convinced him to stay? The thought sends a little ache ricocheting around my chest. Three months; just enough time to know what you're losing, not nearly enough time to jump into such huge sacrifices.

Our food arrives and we all dig in, except for Mia, who picks at her breakfast like a bird, nibbling at her toast, poking almost suspiciously at her eggs. When the waitress comes back to check on us, she orders a ginger ale.

"Do you want to go outside and get some fresh air? I'll come with you if you want," Becca offers.

Mia shakes her head, and her eyes dart around the table, spending a second on each of us. When they reach me, there's a flicker of hesitation, and of something else. Something like regret. I feel it right in the pit of my stomach, a startling little punch.

"I have something to tell you," she says, dabbing at her lips with her napkin and then tossing it onto the table. "I'm pregnant."

Becca and Alli gasp and immediately begin heaping congratulations on her, but I can't move. I go numb. I feel as though someone has poured concrete over me, encasing me exactly where I am.

"Was it planned?" I blurt out. I'm in shock. I don't know what else to say. It's a rude question, and yet I ask it all the same.

She shakes her head, smiling and now resting a hand on her still-flat abdomen. "No, it was a total surprise."

The numbness recedes and I feel everything all at once. Shock and sadness and resentment and buried somewhere deep underneath it all, a tiny seed of happiness. I don't know how to grow and nurture that seed, though. I'm too overwhelmed with everything else to dig down deep and find it.

"Well, congrats," I say. My throat hurts, as though there's something stuck in it, and my skin feels too tight for my body.

"When did you find out? When are you due?" Becca and Alli ask at the same time, one question tangling itself with the other.

Mia smiles, patting her belly again. "We only found out a couple of weeks ago. I'm ten weeks along now. We weren't trying at all—I mean, I was on the pill for crying out loud—and then when my period didn't show up and I started to feel sick, I just knew I had to take a test. Sure enough, it was positive." I can tell she has mixed emotions about this. She'd always been happy with her family of four. Distantly, objectively, I know that this must've been a shock for her. I try and try to find some empathy, but I just can't, and that makes me feel like the world's most horrible friend.

The waitress brings her ginger ale and Mia sips at it. "I didn't have a lot of morning sickness with my first two, but with this one I feel sick and gross all the time. And I'm so tired. It doesn't matter how much sleep I get the night before, I feel like a zombie most days. I miss coffee. And wine. And sushi." She laughs, merry with complaint. I clench and unclench my hands in my lap and paste a smile on my face. Trying to put on a happy face for her sake while my insides shrivel up and die.

Becca and Alli continue to pepper her with questions. Are her kids excited? Is she going to find out the sex? What was Tom's reaction? It's this last one that crushes me. I'm an insect under a trash compactor as she speaks.

"It was the sweetest," she says, gulping her ginger ale with more enthusiasm, a weight off of her shoulders now that she's told us all her secret. "I told him I thought I might be, and he went out and bought a test that second. I mean, in the past when I've suspected I might be, I was, so he was already excited. I took the test and showed it to him and he started to cry. Then he dropped to his knees and kissed my belly and said 'welcome to the family.' He keeps touching my belly and talking to 'our little surprise.'"

I can't even fathom what it's like to experience all of this, to have a pregnancy just fall into my lap. To be able to simply have sex, miss a period, take a test and boom. New family member on the way.

The restaurant feels airless and too hot, and I push myself to my feet. My legs are shaky, uncertain beneath me, and my lungs burn with each breath. "Excuse me," I say and head to the bathroom, my eyes fixed on the black and white tiles under my feet. Once inside, I splash some cold water on my face, trying to cool down, and then I lock myself in a stall, letting the tears come.

It's not fair. The words swirl around and around in my head until I'm dizzy with them.

I let myself cry for several minutes, emotions ripping through me, overwhelming me. Everything is so raw and I can't untangle it. I'm jealous and sad, but also angry at Mia and the way she told us. I'm resentful and bitter. A failure. Broken. Abnormal. I don't fit anywhere. Every negative thought I've had about myself over the past three years piles up like a chain reaction accident on the freeway, each one crashing into the last.

"Claire?" Becca calls and I hear the bathroom door whoosh shut behind her. "Are you okay?"

"Yep, I'm fine, just needed a minute," I say, even though I can hear the frogginess in my voice, giving me away.

"Mia left. I think she was upset."

Hurt pushes me up and out of the stall. I lean against the outside of it, staring at Becca. "*She's* upset? Right. Okay."

"I think she was bummed that you clearly weren't happy for her."

I wipe at my cheeks as shame grips me. "Oh. Um…it's not that I'm not happy, I just…"

Becca shakes her head. "No, I get it. She should've told you privately, so you could at least brace yourself."

"That would've been nice, yeah. She's my friend, and I am happy for her, somewhere deep down inside, but I'm so fucking sad for me, Becca. It just kinda cancels everything else out. I hate that I feel this way. That I am this way. But it's just the way it is." I walk to the sink and splash more water on my face.

After I pat my face dry with a scratchy paper towel, Becca wraps me in a hug. "I love you. I'm sorry this was so hard for you." She pulls back and meets my eyes. "I'm sorry for what you're going through. It's so unfair."

Fresh tears spring to my eyes, but they're made of relief and gratitude.

"You're a good egg, Becca Montgomery," I say, running a finger under one of my eyes.

She smiles. "C'mon. Let's go order a piece of cheesecake."

I step into the house and listen for Scott. I can hear the sounds of TV in the den, so I head in that direction. I'm not sure what I'm looking for, what I need right now. All I know is I need to tell him. I need to share this with someone. Maybe then it'll be less heavy. Not lighter. Just…less.

Scott is sprawled on the couch in a T-shirt and a pair of sweatpants, a cup of coffee in his hands and an episode of *The Walking Dead* on TV. It's his latest binge, and normally we binge things together, but I'm not in the mood for zombies lately. It feels less escapist and more depressing. He takes one look at me and shuts the TV off. I wonder what my face looks like right now.

"Mia's pregnant," I say, my voice a little wobbly. My cheeks are hot. I feel like I'm about to start sweating.

"What?" Scott sits up, sets his coffee on the table in front of him. "She is?"

"Yeah. A total surprise. They weren't even trying." Each word is like a knife, and I'm flaying myself with them.

Scott's features tighten into an expression I don't recognize. There's bitterness there. Hurt. He runs a hand through his hair and then rolls his eyes. "Must be nice."

"Right? I can't even imagine."

"Me neither." His voice is far away, his gaze unfocused as he stares at the darkened TV. I've done this to him. I've taken away hope and happiness. I've done this to us with my shitty eggs. Guilt overtakes my hurt and my shock at Mia's announcement, and I sniff, tears slipping down over my cheeks.

This seems to remind Scott that I'm in the room and he holds his arms out to me. "Come here." I sit down on the couch beside him and let him wrap his arms around me. I bury my face in his neck and let it all out.

"I don't know how I'm supposed to cope with this," I gasp out between shuddering sobs. I know, deep down, that this isn't really—or at least, not entirely—about Mia. It's about me. It's about the loss I keep having to face over and over again. It's less about what she has and more about what I lack.

Scott strokes my hair. "You'll get through it. I know you will. You just need to be strong."

I push back slightly. "I'm so fucking sick of being strong."

His face goes blank for a second, and I suddenly see how selfish I'm being right now. Slapping Scott with this news that must be hard for him to hear too, and then expecting him to comfort me. I shake my head. "Sorry. You're right. Hey, do you want to go to a movie?" I shove the subject away, locking it down, pretending it's not there.

Scott shrugs. "Sure. Pick whatever and we'll go." He shifts away from me and turns the TV on.

11

Before

CLAIRE AND MIA STEP INTO THE REVOLVING GLASS DOORS OF THE Marriot Marquis in New York, the lights of Times Square flashing around them. They're both in town to attend the *Architectural Digest* Design Show, a conference they look forward to every year. The streets radiate the summer heat they've absorbed all day, and the air is full of noise and life. Even though the sun is setting behind the towering skyscrapers and bright billboards, the pavement is still warm. The warmth matches Claire's mood as she and Mia wait for the elevator to take them back to their room. She's pleasantly loose with wine and pasta and Mia.

Over the past couple of years, they've become inseparable. It began as a workplace friendship, but then their connection began spilling over from work into their everyday lives. They text almost every day, sharing every aspect of their lives. Fights with their husbands, insecurities about parenting, talks about sex and relationships, the excitement of Claire and Scott buying a house, jokes, and gossip. Sometimes Claire's more excited to tell Mia some piece of news than Scott. The truth was, she adored Mia, basking in a platonic love she'd never experienced before.

She's like the sister Claire always wishes she'd had. A little older and wiser, already a mom, always there with a shoulder or an ear, or advice.

Claire bounces a little as she plops down onto her bed. Mia opens the little bar fridge and pulls out a bottle of wine, uncorks it and brings it over to the bed with two flimsy plastic cups. She fills each and sets the bottle on the nightstand between the beds. As they sit and drink, they talk about work, about new, exciting things they saw at the conference, about Mia's kids, about Claire's new house. Claire is glowing, both with wine and with knowing she has news to share with Mia. She savors the excitement of telling her, of anticipating Mia's reaction.

Claire finishes her wine, licking a stray drop off of her bottom lip. "So…Scott and I are trying. I stopped taking my pill last month."

Mia's spine snaps straight and her hands shoot out, lightly gripping Claire's shoulders. "Ohmigod. Claire! That's amazing! I'm so excited for you! Wait," she says, leveling her gaze at Claire's empty cup. "Should you be drinking?"

Claire smiles. "I'm on my period right now. First month trying was a bust."

Mia smiles sympathetically. "Oh, honey, almost no one gets pregnant on the first try. I'm sure it'll happen soon. We had to try for like three months for Ava, and it felt like a lifetime. Oh my God, I can't wait to see you pregnant. You're going to be the most beautiful preggo!"

Mia wraps her in a hug. Claire is happy.

Now - November

I'm sitting on the edge of the bathtub in the master bathroom with a pair of yoga pants shoved down around my ankles. Scott sits beside me, his hand warm and reassuring on my lower back. My legs twitch up and down in a nervous rhythm I can't seem to stop. Goosebumps dot the bare skin on my legs.

"You can totally do this," Scott says in a soft voice. "The first one's the worst, psychologically. That's what Dr. Kane said."

I nod and force my hands to move. I've laid out everything I need: the preloaded Gonal-F pen, along with a single needle cap, the syringe filled with HGH, alcohol swabs, and my little radioactive-yellow sharps disposal container. With shaking hands, I rip open the alcohol swab and rub it in a slow circle over a fleshy part on my upper right thigh. I include a dark brown freckle in my sterilizing path so that I don't forget where to stab myself. The smell of the alcohol cuts sharply through the air and my stomach lurches, as though the anxious butterflies taking up residence there have rocks tied to their wings.

Scott takes the alcohol wipe from me and throws it in the garbage beside the toilet. I've frozen again, so he continues rubbing my lower back. I think about everything my mom's gone through to try to fight off the cancer—the surgeries, the chemo, the picc line, the infections—and feel like a giant wuss. It's just two little needles in a fleshy part of my leg. No big deal, right?

Working up the nerve to stab myself feels like a big deal.

I pull the little green shield off of the needle. It's small—thin and short—and really not intimidating at all. I try to tell myself that I'm freaking out over nothing, but it doesn't feel like nothing. I close my eyes and take a deep breath as Scott rubs circles on my back. Holding the pen in my right hand, I rest my thumb over the depressor button on the end, like a game show buzzer, and start to lower the needle toward my bare thigh. A tiny drop of clear liquid drops from the needle's steel tip and lands on my skin.

I'm moving slow, too slow, but I can't seem to go any faster. When I get within a few inches of my thigh, my arm seems to lose strength, and I drop it down to my side, pen still in hand.

"What if I can't do this?" I ask Scott, my voice cracking a little. "What if we fail because I can't?"

He slips a hand under my chin and forces me to meet his gaze. "You can. You just need to be strong and power through this. Once it's over with, you'll see that you can do it."

I nod and raise my arm again, taking a cleansing breath. I lower the needle toward my thigh, but trying to close the distance between those last few inches, between metal and skin, is like trying to force two magnets with the same pole together. I can almost feel the repellent force.

"Argh!" I let out a frustrated grunt. Why is this so hard? Why am I so freaked out? I'm being ridiculous.

"Do you want me to do it?" Scott asks. He glances at the needle warily. Given that he's one of the most squeamish people I know when it comes to anything medical, I don't think putting my injections in his hands is a good option.

"No, no, I can do it. I just need to psych myself up."

"Okay, hang on." He pulls his phone out of the back pocket of his jeans. "We're not doing this right." He swipes and taps on the phone screen, and a few seconds later, the opening strains of "Eye of the Tiger" come through his phone's speaker. I can't help but laugh. I definitely do *not* feel like Rocky right now. "Come on, Claire. You've got this."

"Okay. Okay. I've got this." I nod, raising the needle for what I hope is the final time. "I can do this. I can do this. Can you count to three? And I'll go on three?"

"Sure. One, two, three." He says it almost nonchalantly.

I don't move when then countdown ends. "Oh, c'mon! That was too fast!" I give my head a shake. I want this, more than anything. I need to do this. "Count again, but slower. I can do it this time." I adjust my grip on the pen. "Do it."

Scott nods and starts his countdown over again. "One... two...three."

I clench my teeth together and fight against every protective instinct I have, ignoring the tension in my arm and sliding the needle into my leg when Scott says three. There's a slight sting as it pierces my skin, but then it's in. I've done it. There's a needle in me, and I put it there. I didn't think I'd be able to do it, but I did. Adrenaline surges through me. I feel like I've just accomplished something important, or inspirational. I'm about to pull it out when Scott says, "Wait! You didn't press it!"

My face flushes. I'd been so caught up in the victorious thrill pumping through me that I'd been about to pull it out without pressing the button on top of the pen to deliver the hormones. I click the button down with my thumb and count slowly to five. When I'm sure all the medication's been delivered, I slowly pull the needle straight out. A tiny bead of blood wells from the injection site, but I don't think I've done any serious damage. I check the little display window on the pen—it's back down to zero, meaning the full dose was administered.

I pick up another alcohol swab and clean a small part of my opposite thigh, then rip open the packaging containing the preloaded HGH syringe. My hands have stopped shaking now that I know I can handle this. Unlike the friendly pen, this is a real needle, longer and thicker, and with a plunger. But I can do this. I pierced myself once; I can do it again. I actually feel like kind of a badass.

"Eye of the Tiger" is still playing as I position the syringe and just go for it. I gasp in surprise; this one hurts more, and I don't think my technique was very good. I have a hard time getting a grip on the plunger, and then when I do, I shove it down, hard and fast. Liquid fire shoots into my thigh, spreading beneath my skin.

"Oh, shit, it burns!" I gasp, yanking the needle out. More than just a dainty drop of blood comes out and I fumble for the box of tissues on the back of the toilet, knocking them over.

"Oh, gross," says Scott, going white at the sight of the blood. He turns away and picks up the tissue box, shoving it at me. I grab one and press it to my thigh. Blood wells, a small bit of red blooming against the white. My thigh burns and feels heavy and tight. I let out a pitiful whine as I bounce my leg up and down, trying to get the burning sensation to subside.

"I did it too fast," I pant. Sweat beads along my hairline. "She said to inject the HGH slowly. Now I know why they tell you that." I take several deep breaths, in through my nose and out through my mouth, the tissue still pressed to my leg. I pull it away, and the bleeding has mostly stopped. Already, I can see a faint purplish outline of where I've undoubtedly bruised myself.

Scott is still white. "Want a Band-Aid?" he asks, his voice a little hoarse.

I nod. "Yeah, thanks." He practically leaps up from the tub and opens the vanity, digging around for the box of bandages, probably grateful for an excuse to look away. I'm not mad or offended. I've always known about his squeamishness and don't take it personally.

I put on the Band-Aid he hands me and gather up my supplies. I stand and wince. It feels as though someone's punched me in the thigh. With a grimace, I pull up my yoga pants.

"Can I get you anything?" Scott offers.

I shake my head and give him a hug, soaking up his warmth. "I'll be okay. I'm just going to put some ice on my leg to see if that helps. Lesson learned on that one: go slow."

He kisses my forehead. "Tomorrow will be better."

"I hope so."

"I'll be in the office if you need anything, okay?" I nod and give him a quick kiss on the lips.

I want comfort, so I hobble downstairs, slap an ice pack on my leg, and turn on *Ghost Hunters*. My sense of accomplishment is fading. I have to do this all again tomorrow morning. And again tomorrow after work. And again, and again, for the next ten days or so, before my eggs will be ready to, as Dr. Kane put it, harvest. The idea of harvesting something that's growing inside me makes my skin crawl, and I push the thought away.

Just as I get myself nice and cozy—curled up on the couch under a blanket, ice pack on my leg, people running screaming through an allegedly haunted asylum—my phone buzzes with an incoming text from Mia.

How are you? Have you started with the needles and stuff yet?

I stare at the message, trying to figure out what to say. It's nice of her to ask but I get the sense that she's asking more out of a combination of obligation and guilt than concern. But maybe I'm being overly sensitive and unfair. I mean, she did ask. It's unnerving feeling this uncertain with her. I was already having a hard time talking to her, and now, knowing that she's pregnant, I feel completely at sea.

I answer: I'm good! How are you?

The only answer I can think of that isn't a lie is to dodge the question completely. I don't feel like talking about my "needles and stuff" right now.

Mia: I'm okay. Still super barfy, unfortunately.

Before I can answer, another text comes in.

It sucks. I'm hungry all the time, but also nauseous, and the smell of a lot of food turns me off. And naturally I can't have any of the things I'm craving. No wine, no raw cookie dough, no good cheese, no sushi. It really blows.

I grit my teeth and reply.

That sounds really hard.

Mia: It is! I've tried everything to try to get the nausea to calm down. I have one of those motion sickness bracelets—total waste of money! I've tried aromatherapy, I've tried sucking on hard candies. Nothing works.

My skin prickles, and before I can stop myself, I type out my response.

I can only imagine.

For a couple of minutes, I see the three little dots indicating she's writing a message appear and then disappear, only to reappear several seconds later. Finally, she figures out what to say.

Can I give you some advice?

Again, I don't get the chance to reply before another text comes in.

I know all of the treatments and doctor's visits are stressful for you, and I'm just wondering if you're putting too much pressure on yourself. They say that stress has a detrimental effect on your health, and you've definitely been stressed lately, with your mom and work and everything else. You guys should go on a vacation, or take some kind of break. Then you'll be ready and refreshed for when you do IVF.

I'm not sure how many times I read Mia's message. Anger settles in my chest like hot coals, shimmering, burning, ready to ignite into something that'll consume me in seconds flat. I have no clue how to respond to any of this. She knows everything we've been through, how hard and how long we've tried. Our situation has nothing to do with stress. In a way, I feel like she's blaming me for my own infertility. *Silly Claire, if she'd just relax, all of his would go away!*

I have the strong urge to type two simple words: fuck off. But I don't. I don't type anything at all. I decide to let my lack of reply speak for itself.

After a few minutes, she texts again.

Anyway, I just wanted to give you a heads up that I'm going to take a few days off work. This nausea is killing me. I'm going to sleep, get a massage, and I've got my first OB appointment too. I figure it's better to take the time off than try to discreetly throw up at work, LOL. Oh, and please don't tell anyone at work about my pregnancy. I'm not ready to share publicly yet, and obviously I want to tell people myself.

With a sigh, I text her back.

K, enjoy your time off. Hope you feel better.

That means I'll be working solo on the Mandy Sinclair nursery project for the next few days. We're supposed to get the wallpaper hung and start bringing in some of the furniture by the end of the week—I guess I'll have to handle that all on my own while balancing the monitoring appointments with blood work and ultrasounds, plus the daily injections, plus my other clients, plus planning Mom's party.

I lie back on the couch, my phone on my stomach. My body feels heavy, tired, weary. Worn out and worn down. I feel bombarded by the fertile world—Mia's pregnancy, Mandy Sinclair's nursery. I don't want to think or hear about any of it. I want it to stop. I want it to leave me alone.

12

I stare at the giant bulldog on my mom and Eddie's front lawn. It's seven and a half feet tall, and nearly as wide, with a display sign across its chest, just below its chin. Despite my mom's gallows humor, I hadn't been able to bring myself to put one of her morbid messages on the sign. So instead it just says "We love you Nora!" I hope she likes it.

I'd hoped against hope that we'd be able to have the party outside, but it's too cold. The trees are bare now, dried leaves covering lawns and sidewalks, and the sky is cloudy, threatening rain. For some reason, I'd always envisioned this party outside, in the sunshine. I guess we should've thrown it sooner. For Mom, there are no more warm days.

Symptom-wise, she feels better after stopping chemo, but we can all see how sick she truly is. She's too thin, looking frail and highly breakable, her face gaunt. Her skin is sallow with a yellowish undertone—she's slightly jaundiced because her liver is starting to fail. She's dying in front of us, organ by organ, and there's nothing any of us can do but pretend we're not dying along with her.

I step inside the house and drop my bag by the door. It's got my little med kit inside—I'll have to inject myself with my afternoon shots in a few hours. Thankfully, I haven't had another incident like the one on the first day. I'm getting better at shooting up, apparently.

There are balloons and flowers scattered throughout the house, and the caterers I hired are busy setting up a buffet on the dining room table with all of mom's favorites: chicken wings, guacamole and tortilla chips, deep fried macaroni bites, a cheese platter, and a display of fresh fruit, including a watermelon intricately carved with roses.

Everything looks great, and I hate it. I've been dreading this day, even though I know Mom's been looking forward to it. In fact, I think it's kept her going over the past couple of weeks, even as she's struggled with managing her pain and her waning appetite. So it's worth it just for that. But I still hate it. I hate that we have to do it. I hate what it signifies. I hate that it's here, today.

Eddie's hunched over the stereo in the living room, loading CDs into the five-disc changer from the 90's that they still use. I think most of the CDs are probably from the 90's, too. I peer over his shoulder, watching him load in some of Mom's favorites: Elton John, Queen, The Beatles, Aretha Franklin, and Stevie Wonder all disappear into the rotating mouth of the CD player. I wonder if there'll be certain songs I won't be able to listen to anymore after she's gone.

"Hey, Kiddo," he says when he sees me. He rises and gives me a hug. I want to ask him how he's doing, but I don't because then he'll ask me the same, and I'll probably start crying. For now, I've got my emotions firmly under control, kept in a glass jar. But I know how thin and fragile that glass is. The last thing I need today is to shatter everywhere. Today isn't about me; it's about Mom. "Everything looks great," he continues. "She's going to be so happy when she sees it all."

"She's not here?"

"She wanted to go down to Sawmill Commons. Nancy took her," he says. My "aunt" Nancy, Mom's best friend. My heart hurts as I think of all the people who will miss her. All the people who'll walk around with a hole somewhere inside them where Mom used to be. I swallow against my thickening throat. I think Eddie can sense I need a topic change, because he asks, "Where's Scott?"

"He's on his way. He's picking up our order from the liquor store."

Eddie nods, and we get to work seeing to all the last-minute details—making sure the flowers and balloons are evenly distributed throughout the first floor, hanging glittery gold and silver streamers from the ceiling, arranging framed photos of Mom on every surface.

Eddie has moved Mom's automatic armchair—the one that lifts up and down, making it easier for her to get in and out of—to a place of prominence in the living room, draping it with a couple of her favorite blankets. I dip into the kitchen to check on the food, and see that they've set up the dessert table as well. The small folding table, draped with a bright orange table cloth, is covered with mouth-watering confections. A towering macaron tree sits in the middle, surrounded by cupcakes, cookies, donuts, cake pops, cheesecake squares, and miniature lemon pies. Anything Mom's sweet tooth could ever want.

Scott comes in, a giant cardboard box full of clinking bottles in his arms. Eddie rushes forward to help him with it.

"My hero," I say, clasping my hands together in front of my heart as Eddie takes the box from Scott and hauls it into the kitchen.

"Happy to help, ma'am," says Scott, tipping his imaginary hat at me. I lean forward and kiss him. He slips his arms around my waist and kisses me back. A spark ignites somewhere low in my belly. It's as though my body remembers pleasure and how to feel good, those nerve endings firing automatically, only to be short circuited by my overactive brain.

"Jeez, get a room, why don't you?" says Mom from somewhere behind us. We pull apart, and I can see the amusement twinkling in her eyes. Aunt Nancy is a few steps behind her, and she waves at me. Her shoulder-length brown hair is shot through with white, and her face is warm and kind despite her sharp, angular features. She's taller than my mom with a thin, almost wiry frame. I step forward and give her a hug. Her arms are tight around me, saying everything our mouths won't today. Today isn't a day to dwell on the impending loss, but to celebrate what we've all had with Mom. It's a day to cherish, not mourn, although personally, I'm not sure how to untangle those two ideas.

The doorbell chimes with the arrival of the first guests, and the party starts.

It's dark outside and the house is quiet. Everyone has said their good-byes, maybe for the last time, and I feel deflated. One of the streamers has fallen from the ceiling, hanging down limply, and the helium-filled balloons are starting to sag, just a little. I can relate—it's like pathetic fallacy through party decorations. The tables are no longer laden with food, but picked over platters with scraps remaining. The caterers talk softly amongst themselves as they wash dishes and pack up supplies.

Scott is sitting with Eddie in front of the TV, watching sports high-lights on mute and drinking a beer. After saying goodbye to everyone, Mom went to lie down for a little while. I feel at loose ends, so I decide to go check on her.

The door to her bedroom is ajar, and I knock gently before pushing the door open. Mom's sitting propped up in bed, staring out the dark-ened window, her silhouette outlined in the glow from the streetlamp. She clicks on the bedside lamp, and I can see that her eyes are red and puffy. I walk over and sit down beside her on the bed, not saying anything. She takes my hand in hers and squeezes.

"Today was really good," she eventually says, her voice raspy. "Thank you. I know you didn't want to do it."

"It's not that I didn't want to do it, Mom. I just…I'm sad we needed to do it." My throat tightens and I swallow around the lump lodged there.

"Me too, honey. Me too." She coughs, a deep, racking cough that I've never heard from her before. Still coughing, she reaches over to her nightstand for a tissue, pressing it to her mouth until the coughing subsides. She takes a deep breath, and I can hear a rattling sound when she does.

"Do you want some water?" I ask, my eyes darting back and forth between her pale face and the tissue clutched in her thin, veiny hand. There are little black flecks mixed in with the phlegm she coughed up. Her face has taken on an unnatural waxy sheen.

She shakes her head. "I'm okay."

We both know that's not true, but neither of us says anything. Instead, she sits up a little straighter and points at the closet. "There's a bag in there for you. I had Nancy take me to the Commons earlier to pick it up."

I slip off the bed and open the closet. There's a large white paper shopping bag sitting on the floor, the handles tied together with a bit of red ribbon. I lift it up carefully, and it's surprisingly heavy.

"What is it?" I ask, both wanting to know and fearing what might be inside. Mom smiles.

"Open it. I had it made, just for you."

I feel overwhelmed with an emotion I can't name, and my hands shake a little as I set the bag on the bed and untie the ribbon. Inside is something large and bulky wrapped in white tissue paper. Gingerly, I pull it out and unwrap it.

"A quilt?" I ask. We're not really quilt people. I'm not sure what to say.

Mom leans toward me and helps me spread it out, her thin fingers brushing mine. "These are my memories of you, Claire. Things I've held onto over the years because they meant something to me. This, right here," she says, pointing to a square of worn pink flannel, "is the blanket you were wrapped up in when we brought you home from the hospital. This one," she says, pointing to a white one with yellow and green teddy bears on it, "was part of your crib bedding." She takes me through the squares, one by one, telling me what they are, telling me stories of memories attached to them. They're stories I've heard before, but they take on a new meaning when faced with the physical evidence of how much my mother loved me. Baby blankets and first day of school outfits and Christmas dresses. Touchstones of a childhood. Touchstones of a motherhood, all sewn together into a tangible thing. I run my fingers over the fabric, absorbing the different textures and seeing my young self through my mother's eyes.

"When I think about you," she says, smoothing her hand over the quilt as I've just done, "these are the things I think of. Not just the present, but the memories. Everything you've given me. You made me a mother, and being your mother made me a better person."

Her words crack me open and it's all I can do to keep my messy insides from spilling everywhere. I blink and tears rapidly slip down my cheeks. I swipe at them before they can hit the quilt. Mom rubs her fingers over the scratchy navy blue fabric of my high school graduation gown.

"These are what matter to me, and what nothing can take away from me. These memories of you." She reaches out a hand and cups my cheek. My silent tears leak onto her fingers. "You were the best thing I did, Claire. The absolute best thing." Her voice trembles and her eyes are bright.

I inch forward and wrap my arms around her. "Thank you, Mom. I'll take good care of it." They're the only words I can get out before the pressure in my chest becomes too much; I need to sob just to get some air.

Mom strokes my hair as we cling to each other. "I won't really be gone. I'll be here through you. Remember that you'll always have a part of me with you, okay?" She reaches for another tissue and wipes at her running nose. I notice that it comes away tinged with flecks of blood before she crumples it in her hand. She tucks my hair behind my ear. "I know things are hard right now, and I know I haven't been the most supportive. I'm sorry."

Something tears open inside my chest and I shake my head. "No, Mom, it's fine."

"It's not. You can't change the hand you've been dealt, and no one else can tell you how to play it. But I know you're strong, Claire. You're so strong. Stronger than me. And I know you have it in you to fight for what you want. You don't run from obstacles, and I'm so proud of you for that. No matter what happens, I'm proud of you. No matter what happens, I know you'll be okay."

Her words soothe something deep inside me, as though I've been a boiling kettle for months and months now, and she's suddenly switched me off. I feel still as her words run through me, over and over again. *No matter what happens, I know you'll be okay.* More than anything, I want this to be true.

By the time Scott and I get home, it's late. We scrounge leftovers from the fridge for supper, sitting together and watching the news as we eat reheated pasta and slightly stale garlic bread. I made a salad to go with it, but the lettuce in the fridge was starting to wilt, so even the fresh part of our meal is a bit worse for wear.

Scott sets his plate down beside mine and rubs my shoulder. "Today must've been hard for you."

"It was, but I'm glad we did it. It made Mom so happy."

"She seemed to have a really good time," Scott agrees, rubbing his thumb in little circles.

"She did." My lungs and heart feel a bit crushed as I think about the party, and how for so many, it'll probably be the last time they see her. I don't know how much time she has left, but it can't be much. I think about how badly I want to be able to tell her that I'm pregnant before she dies. To know that she'll live on not just through me, but through my child, even if she's not here to see it happen.

"What was in that bag she gave you?"

My breathing hitches as I think about the quilt. I go and retrieve it from the front hall and spread it out on the dining room table for Scott to see. I'm barely three words into my explanation before the tears are flowing. My skin is hot and itchy, my throat sore. He pulls me into his arms and lets me cry, kissing the top of my head. I stare at the quilt, unable to take my eyes away from it despite the wave of loss it sends cresting over me. I love it, but it's also churning up something inside me, something I'm sure my mom didn't intend.

"Will we ever have this?" I ask Scott, my face half buried in his chest. "These memories of a child, of a life we made and cherished and nourished? All these experiences…we might never get to have them. We might never get to experience this huge part of life."

His arms tighten around me and it takes him a few seconds to speak. He clears his throat softly. "I don't know. I hope we do." I can hear the doubt in his voice. It's subtle, but I know him well enough to find it nonetheless, like a seashell buried underneath layers of fine sand.

"Mom said that a part of her will always live on through me. What does it mean if you and I don't live on through anyone? One day we'll be gone and that'll just be…it." The idea of leaving this planet without a part of me remaining here, alive, is a despairing, depressing one. I want a part of me, a part of Scott to live on. I want a part of Mom to live on, too.

"I don't think it's about what we leave behind, but about what we do with the time we're given," he says.

"You think so?"

"I have to." His voice is rough around the edges, as though he's swallowed sandpaper. I can hear the grit. "I have to." The second time he says it, it's quieter, like he's saying it mostly to himself.

For a few moments we just hold each other, looking at the quilt, the memories, the years of life spread in front of us. "Maybe IVF will work," I say, my voice barely a whisper.

He nods. "Maybe it will." I do have some hope, and I try to cling to that, like a life raft in a storm.

No matter what happens, I know you'll be okay.

Never in my life have I wanted my mom to be right about something so badly.

13

Before

CLAIRE STANDS IN FRONT OF THE SINK IN THE BATHROOM AT work, staring into the mirror, but she's not looking at her reflection. She's not looking at anything. All she can do is replay the conversation from last night. As though her memory has subsumed everything else, dulling all of her other senses.

"Claire?"

She hears Mia's voice from the doorway. She's lost track of time. She has no idea how long she's been standing here, replaying and replaying and replaying her mother's words.

There's no easy way to tell you this, so I'm just going to do it. I have ovarian cancer, and the prognosis isn't good. I'm going to pursue treatment, but the odds aren't in my favor. I'm probably not going to beat this.

She sees Mia in the mirror behind her and turns, avoiding her own reflection, knowing she'll see dark circles and pale skin.

"Are you okay? You don't look well." Mia's smooth brow wrinkles in concern.

"I—" Claire doesn't even know what she's trying to say, but her voice cracks before she can make it any further. Mia pulls her into a hug.

"What's wrong, babe?"

"My mom has cancer." Claire whispers the words into Mia's hair. Mia's arms tighten around her.

"I'm so sorry, Claire. That's awful." She doesn't say anything else, doesn't ask any questions. Just hugs her, holding her tight. Anchoring her. When she pulls away, her own eyes are damp. "Whatever you need, I'm here. Okay? Anything, just name it."

Claire nods, not having the first clue what to ask for. "Just be here with me, okay?"

"Of course. I'm not going anywhere. I'll always be here for you. I love you, C. You'll get through this."

"I love you, too." Claire leans on Mia, grateful to have a friend like her.

Now - November

I'm sitting on the floor of Mandy Sinclair's in-progress nursery, taking my time assembling the white bookshelf with ornate, curving moldings along the top and bottom. It was supposed to come assembled, but instead arrived in an impossibly flat box. I have what feels like a million other things to do, like emails to answer, sketches and concept boards for other clients to work on, meetings—but they'll all have to wait. I stopped by Mandy's to check on progress, intending to simply pop my head in and make sure everything was on track. Then I learned that the wallpaper hadn't been hung yet because the crew hadn't shown up, Mia ordered the wrong wainscoting and it's already been installed, and the rug I desperately wanted is on backorder. So now I'm sitting here, on the floor, putting together a bookshelf just so I have something concrete to focus on. At least I'm doing *something*.

Mentally, I create a to-do list as I insert dowels and twist Allen keys. Call the crew to re-book a time to hang the wallpaper, or find another crew. Have the improper wainscoting removed, re-order the wainscoting agreed on and have it installed ASAP. Source a new rug and get Mandy's approval.

I check the time on my phone. Mia was supposed to be here over half an hour ago, promising she'd stop by on her way back to the office after a client meeting. I mentioned that I'd likely be running behind this morning thanks to my monitoring appointment. I might as well have told her I was getting my nails done for all the reaction it elicited.

I glance over at the crib, sitting in the center of the room. It's empty and bare; it's assembled, but there are no linens, no mobile hanging above. I don't want to look at it, but I can't seem to stop. That empty crib is seared into my brain.

My hand is tired, and I drop the Allen key onto the floor. It makes a soft, metallic *clink* against a bag of screws I haven't opened yet. I lean back on my palms, closing my eyes and taking a deep breath, trying to ignore or dispel or somehow just function alongside the anxiety gripping at me. Everything just feels like too much—work, Mom, fertility treatments, Mia's pregnancy. The pressure of it builds inside me, and I can't seem to untangle one thought from the other. They come and go too quickly, flitting back and forth, knotting together into a snarled mess. If my thoughts were music, they'd be the cacophony of a symphony of musicians tuning their instruments before a performance. My brain is noise.

I sit up and I feel a painful twinge in my abdomen, in what has to be my ovary. It's not a muscular twinge; it's deeper, more tender. The ache peaks and then subsides after a few seconds. I massage my uncomfortably bloated stomach. It's an incredibly strange feeling to suddenly be hyperaware of an organ you never were before. I mean, imagine being able to feel an ache in your liver, to be aware of exactly where your liver is, to move and feel your liver protest. It's weird. It makes my body feel alien. I try to take comfort in the discomfort of it—after all, it's a sign that the drugs are working, that multiple eggs are growing. I try not to think about the upcoming surgery to retrieve them. I try not to dwell on the fact that half my pants don't fit right now thanks to the bloating, which, in all honesty, makes me look like I'm about four months pregnant. I do everything I can to hide my stomach. Today I'm in jeans—what used to be my "eating" jeans because of the extra roominess in them—and a gray V-neck sweater that actually belongs to Scott. I have a flash of guilt as I realize that wearing his sweater is probably the most intimate thing I've done with him in the past couple of weeks. And yet with the injections and the bloating and the blood draws and vaginal ultrasounds, the last thing I feel like doing is getting naked and letting someone, something else inside me.

"Hey, how's it going?" Mandy startles me from my thoughts as she pokes her head into the nursery, a wide smile on her face. As usual, she looks stunningly perfect, her face still made up from her show earlier today. She's wearing a figure-hugging brown and white checked dress with a high neck that looks simple, but with razor-sharp tailoring, giving it an expensive air. The dress seems to cup her growing belly, showcasing it. She is glowing and round and vibrant with new life. She is everything I'm not. I feel a little sick to my stomach. I feel mean and dull and exhausted. I feel empty.

"A bit slower than I'd hoped, I'm afraid. I really am sorry about the wainscoting mix-up. I promise it'll be fixed, and that the wallpaper will be installed within the next day or two. I'm confident we can get back on track by next week and should still be able to finish on time."

Mandy waves a hand. "No worries. I have faith in you." She steps into the room and leans against the doorjamb. "So...have you given any further thought to what we talked about?"

Shit. I'd completely forgotten about it with everything else going on. "The TV segment?"

She nods. "I'm interested, I really am. But life is...honestly, kind of overwhelming right now. I haven't even had time to think it over or talk to my boss." I feel blood rush to my cheeks as my eyes sting just a little.

Mandy comes and sits down on the floor in front of me, graceful despite her large belly. She pokes at a bag of screws. "Are you okay?"

"I…" I try to say *I'm fine*, but I can't. The words won't form. "No. I'm definitely not okay."

"Do you want to talk about it?"

I shake my head slowly. I don't know her. She's practically a stranger. A pregnant stranger. She won't understand. She can't. She'll be another one of those women who looks at me as though I need to get over myself because it can't possibly be as hard as I say it is.

She studies me, assessing me with a journalist's gaze. "You know, I think you and I are a lot alike."

I slide a shelf into the bookcase, hooking it into the protruding dowels, my shields up, my defenses high. "Really? What makes you say that?" I try to keep my tone light. I can't be rude to a client, especially a high profile one like Mandy.

She tilts her head as she continues to study me, one hand resting lightly on her rounded belly. "You work hard, take pride in your job, have the same ambitious spark that I do. I'm guessing that you probably don't want to spend the next thirty years just designing rooms for other people when you're capable of so much more. Not that there's anything wrong with the work you're doing now. I just…I can't see it keeping you fulfilled indefinitely. You'll want more."

I think about how ambitious I used to be and how it's fallen by the wayside in the wake of everything else. It's another little piece of myself that I seem to have lost along the way. I shrug, non-committal, not showing her that she's nailed me. "Sure, maybe eventually. I just have so much on my plate right now that ambition's had to take a back seat." I don't have room for ambition when most days I'm focused on survival. On not letting the weight of everything else pulverize me into dust.

"Or it can see you through, whatever it is you're dealing with. Sometimes it helps to have another focus besides all the obstacles in your life."

I look at gorgeous, smart, successful Mandy Sinclair and wonder what kind of obstacles she's faced. Bitterness rises up like bile in the back of my throat. I know I'm being unfair to her, but then she absently rubs her belly and I withdraw again. So I just nod, taking her unsolicited advice and adding it to the pile.

"You don't watch my show, do you?" she asks. Her tone is casual, neutral. Completely non-confrontational.

"Uh, no, but only because I'm at work when it airs," I say, and it's mainly the truth, although daytime talk has never been something I've gravitated towards.

She lets out a little laugh. "It's okay, Claire. I don't expect everyone in the state to watch my show. Although it'd make my sponsors happy if they did," she adds with a wry twist of her lips. "I only ask because a couple of weeks ago, we did an episode on IVF."

I sit up straighter, my hands stilling, a cold knot forming in the pit of my stomach. I feel naked. "Did Mia say something to you?" I ask.

Mandy shakes her head. "Not at all. We talked about IVF on the show because *I* went through it, and if my infertile chick Spidey senses are right, I think you're going through it too."

My mouth falls open. "How did you know?"

She smiles. "I told you, we're a lot alike. When I came in to the Carlisle and Winter offices, I immediately recognized how uncomfortable you were, how you avoided looking at my stomach. It was clear you didn't want the project, and I had a suspicion as to why. Now that I know you a little better, I see even more subtle signs. The sadness lurking just behind the eyes. The way you get skittish around anything to do with babies or pregnancy. The way you keep other people at a safe distance, not wanting them to see how much you're hurting. I know, and I get it, because that was me too. For years."

I clear my throat and fold my hands in my lap. I not only feel naked, but flayed. Vulnerable and exposed. But also hopeful. Here's an example of what I want, sitting right in front of me. Proof that happy endings are real. "How did you…I mean…what ended up working for you?"

She smiles again, and I can see that she doesn't mind me asking. Granted, she's the proud owner of a baby bump, so maybe it's easy for her to talk about.

"My husband and I tried on our own for almost two years with no success. I think we waited so long to go to the doctor because we were in denial that there might actually be a problem. When we finally did go, they couldn't find anything wrong with either of us and told us we had unexplained infertility, which, I mean, I don't understand how basically saying 'gee, I dunno' is an official medical diagnosis. We tried timed intercourse, and when that didn't work, timed intercourse with Clomid. When that didn't work, we moved onto unmedicated IUIs, then medicated IUIs with Clomid and then injectables. Nothing worked. Meanwhile, it felt as though the entire world around me was getting pregnant, having babies, having second babies, lapping me, and I was just…" She trails off, and her eyes are bright. I can see that even though she's now pregnant, this is all still painful for her. I could be looking into a mirror; I know her emotions. Each and every one, because they're mine, too.

"Alone," I say, finishing her sentence. "You feel as though the world can't see you, can't see this enormous boulder you're dragging around behind you."

She nods. "Exactly. I spent years feeling like a failure as a wife, as a woman. Like my body had betrayed me. I was angry at the world, angry at myself, angry at just about anyone. I wanted someone to blame for this blameless thing that had taken over our lives." She pauses, shaking her head. "I hurt so much, every day, and no one around me seemed to understand why. How could simply not getting pregnant be so freaking awful?"

"But it is," I say quietly. "Because it attacks every aspect of your life. Your marriage, your friendships, your sense of who you are and the idea that you have control over what happens in your life. Seeing babies and pregnant women everywhere is constant salt in a wound that never closes up because to keep trying is to keep re-opening it, month after month."

Mandy wipes at her eye. "It's an unending grief that no one else understands. They don't get how you can grieve something that never was."

I know that these exact words have run through my mind before and goosebumps rise up on my arms. The sensation of looking in a mirror is amplified. I nod, and Mandy continues. "When nothing else worked, we decided to move on to IVF. I didn't respond to the drugs as well as they'd hoped, and they only got a handful of eggs, and we ended up with a single low-quality embryo. We transferred it, even though the odds of success weren't good. Now here we are," she says, gesturing at her belly.

Her story is similar to mine—the years of struggle, the isolation, the grief and sadness, the pain—but I don't know if mine will end the same way. She's on the other side; I'm still in it. I appreciate her sharing her story, but at the same time I can't help but resent her, just a little. As though there's only so much success to go around.

"We've been trying for years too," I say, my words halting and cautious at first. They don't come easily, but I want to unburden myself. I want to share. For the first time in a long time, I feel safe. "The issue is most likely my egg quality, so I spend a lot of time blaming myself. It adds a fun layer to the shit salad we're in," I say, turning to sarcasm to keep my emotions in check. I'm a little shocked at how honest I'm being.

Mandy reaches out and gives my hand a squeeze. I'm caught off guard by the warm gesture, but it relaxes me, and I feel some of the rigidity leave my tired muscles. This is…it's nice, actually. Being able to talk openly and honestly about how much infertility fucking sucks with someone who gets it. With someone who sees me.

"We did several IUIs and are now in the middle of our first round of IVF. I have my egg retrieval in a couple of days," I say. The words are both heavy and hopeful in my mouth.

"The egg retrieval is the hardest part. If they offer you Ativan or Xanax or something, take it."

This makes my stomach tighten with nerves, but I nod, tucking that piece of information away.

"How have you found the hormones?" she asks.

"Not fun, but not unbearable, either. I'm getting used to injecting myself, which I didn't think would happen. It's more…everything else," I say, twirling my hand in a circle, encompassing the room, encompassing us. "My husband is as supportive as he can be, but I don't think he can really understand how all of this makes me feel. It's not his fault. He just can't. It's not his body that's broken and defective. And none of my friends really understand. I'm at the point where I've basically stopped talking about it with them, which only makes me feel alone. On top of that, my mom is really sick. Cancer. She doesn't have much time left." I hadn't planned to bring Mom up, but the words fall out of my mouth before I even know they're there. It makes sense, seeing as she's always there, hovering somewhere in the recesses of my brain.

Mandy lets out a soft little gasp. "Oh, Claire, I'm so sorry. I can't even imagine."

I shake my head, swallowing down the tears clogging my throat. I don't want to talk about Mom right now. I already feel so raw. Sunburned. "How did you get through it? How did you come through on the other side without losing your mind?"

"Ha, well, I think there were days when I did lose my mind. Or at least, it felt like I was losing it. It seemed as though the entire world was fertile; everyone could get pregnant except me."

I nod. Yes. This is my reality, too.

Mandy flashes me a dry smile and continues. "For me, the key was focusing on other things. Things that fulfilled me and made me happy. Things I could control. I dug deep into my ambition, worked harder, drove myself to take the show to the next level. I exercised. I indulged myself with massages and haircuts and expensive makeup." She takes my hand again and meets my gaze. "That's what worked for me. Maybe it'll work for you. I don't know. You need to figure that out. It's an incredibly hard path to walk, especially when you feel like you're walking it alone. What I do know is whether you're successful or not, the only way out is through."

I feel an easing of tension through my whole body at her words. As though she's giving me permission to do whatever I need to do to just make it through. For once, I don't feel guilty for the walls I've built, or that the pain I carry that sometimes leaks out onto those around me. I'm surviving, and that's all I can do.

"Thanks," I say. "It feels nice to talk to someone who gets it."

"Anytime you want to talk, you know where to find me. Even though I'm technically the enemy now," she says, gesturing at her belly.

I laugh, something I almost never do when talking about this stuff. "You're not the enemy, I promise." And it's true. Knowing what she went through, I don't feel the same way about her pregnancy as I do about others. Because she knows; she understands.

Once the bookcase is assembled, I make a few phone calls and finish up for the day. Mia never showed—she ended up going home sick, but then posted a picture of herself getting a pedicure on her Instagram feed. It makes me sad, but honestly, my expectations are pretty low when it comes to Mia these days. I'm hurt by her self-absorption, but more than that, I'm disappointed. I feel let down. I wish I was in a spot where I could be understanding of everything she has on her plate, but I'm not. I'm going through IVF and have a dying mother. She's one of my closest friends—or at least, I thought she was—and she's not able to be here for me right now. I'm not saying she shouldn't be focused on her own pregnancy or excited about it—it just means that life is pulling us in completely different directions right now, and it sucks.

I drive home as the sky darkens, winter beginning to slip its chilly fingers through the air. The leaves are completely gone from the trees now. They lie scattered on the ground in wet, rotting clumps. We're in that transitional phase where even a week can make a big difference. A small zing of panic zips through me as I think about the upcoming holidays. Mom's last Thanksgiving, last Christmas. The possibility of yet another Christmas without a baby. Another set of holidays where my family, my hopes, my dreams, stagnate. It gets harder every year.

I stop and pick up pad Thai for dinner. Scott has a work-related dinner meeting, so I know he won't be home until later. As I wait in the restaurant for my takeout order, I watch the people around me. It's a bit early for dinner, so the restaurant isn't very busy, with only a few tables occupied. A couple in their early twenties, clearly on a date. Two men talking loudly about football as they cram spring rolls into their mouths. A family with two young children, making even more noise than the men. The dad is scrolling through his phone while the mom tries to cajole the toddler into eating something. A baby screams in her arms. It's enough to nearly drown out the new agey, Asian-tinged music playing through the speakers. I can feel the start of a headache—I've been getting a lot, thanks to the hormones—and for once, I'm glad I'm on my own tonight. I take my food and go.

The house is dark and quiet, soothing after the cacophony of the restaurant. I set my food down in the kitchen and then head up to the bathroom so I can go through the routine of my injections. I'm up to six a day now—three in the morning and three in the evening. I'm a bloated human pincushion, my swollen, tender ovaries never letting me forget it.

With quick, efficient movements, I prep my skin and inject myself. Even though I barely feel them anymore, I still wince each time the needle pierces my sensitive, slightly bruised skin. I don't know how to turn that reaction off. Finished, I toss the alcohol wipes into the garbage and put the spent needles into the sharps container, now almost half full.

Sitting on the edge of the tub, I feel strangely Zen. Calm. Like the frenzied storm of emotion always roiling within me has finally quieted.

Everything in my life is still in freefall mode; Mom will die, IVF will either work or it won't, friendships might crumble. But right now, in this moment, I'm okay. I can't do anything about any of that right now. All I can do is be. All I can do is take each minute as it comes and get through it until somehow, someday, I'm on the other side of all of this, whatever that looks like.

I put on sweatpants, fuzzy socks and one of Scott's sweatshirts. It smells like him, his deodorant, his soap, his comforting warmth. I stick my nose into the collar and inhale. It smells like home.

I head back down to the kitchen and take my container of pad Thai to the couch. I wish I could have a glass of wine with it, but with my egg retrieval coming up, I'm no longer allowed to drink. I basically have to follow all the same restrictions as a pregnant woman: no wine, no sushi, limited caffeine, no medications aside from Tylenol. It feels like an extra kick in the teeth, having to basically act as if I'm already pregnant when so much is still up in the air. I start eating and put on an episode of *Ghost Hunters*.

A couple of hours later, when I turn off all the lights and go upstairs, I stop by the office and grab a yellow Post-It note pad and a pen and take them into the bathroom. I scrawl two notes and stick them to the upper corners of the mirror over the sink, where I'll be able to see them every day. My reminders. My mantras. My survival guide.

No matter what happens, I know you'll be okay.

The only way out is through.

14

It's snowing the morning of my egg retrieval. I stand at our bedroom window, my arms wrapped around my middle, my mind still a bit groggy from the sleeping pill I took last night. Frost clings to the roofs of the houses on our street, sparkling and white, and a fine dusting of white powder lays on the ground, coating cars and trees. It's such a small amount that blades of grass poke up through it in defiance, not ready to lie down and let winter take over quite yet. The sky is a pale silvery blue, lightening as the sun rises behind the clouds. Delicate snowflakes fall, swirling gently toward the ground. It's a pretty scene, but one I'm not in the mood to appreciate. I'm too nervous, too caught up in my own thoughts, swirling like the snowflakes outside. The anticipation, the fear, the worry, the hope, all mingling together until I can't tell one from the other.

Scott's taken the day off work to take me to the clinic, and is currently masturbating behind the closed office door. As usual, his contribution to this entire process is sperm in a cup. Today, my contribution is having all the eggs I've grown sucked out of me with a giant needle inserted through my vaginal wall and into my ovaries. Then the embryologists will take my eggs and Scott's sperm and fertilize my hopefully non-shitty eggs one by one, creating life. Doing something we were never able to do on our own. We'll get a report with how many eggs were retrieved and how many were successfully fertilized. We'll get another report on day three with how many are still growing. The goal is to make it to day five, transfer the best one, hope it sticks, and freeze any others for future use. Going into this, I don't know what kind of results to expect. According to my last ultrasound, I have twelve follicles growing, which potentially means twelve eggs. Twelve would be good. A dozen feels like a solid number.

My mind races with what ifs. What if the surgery is painful? What if I have a difficult recovery? What if they're not able to get many eggs? What if the eggs are so shitty they're unusable? What if none of them fertilize? What if they do, but they all die, leaving us with nothing to transfer? What if none of this works? Do we start over again? What if I don't want to start over again? What then?

I step away from the window, shaking my head, trying to push away the what ifs and the anxiety building in my chest, like steam inside a pressure cooker. I dress in yoga pants and an old sweatshirt and brush my hair, pulling it up into a messy bun. I don't bother with any makeup. My empty stomach churns nervously. I'm hungry and wish I could eat breakfast, but I'm not allowed to have anything in my stomach for the procedure, not even water. So instead, I head into the bathroom and rinse my dry mouth out with mouthwash and then take the lone Ativan Dr. Kane prescribed me. As it dissolves under my tongue, my eyes dart back and forth between the two Post-It notes I stuck to the mirror.

I meet Scott downstairs, his cheeks a little flushed and the paper bag in one hand, the top folded neatly over itself.

"What did you watch?" I ask.

"Threesome," he says, grabbing an apple from the bowl on the kitchen island and biting into it. I can smell it, and it makes my mouth water. I feel a bit nauseated with hunger.

"Oh yeah? Two dudes and a girl, right?"

He laughs and shakes his head. "No, Claire." He grins, as though he's remembering something.

A sudden wave of insecurity crests over me. We haven't had sex in weeks, partly by choice (mine) and partly by circumstance. My stomach is bloated, my thighs bruised, and today I look like an absolute princess in my grubby clothes. A sense of failure sticks to me like a film of dried sweat.

Soon—too soon—it's time to go, but thankfully the Ativan is starting to kick in. I don't feel less anxious, necessarily, just more accepting of what's happening. I feel slightly detached as I put my coat on, sit down in the passenger seat of Scott's car, put my seatbelt on. Scott hands me the paper bag and I dutifully tuck it between my thighs.

The drive to the clinic is peaceful. The snow is still falling in tiny white flakes, and I stare at them as they whiz toward the windshield, letting myself become mesmerized by them.

Scott pulls into a spot in the parking lot close to the front doors and helps me out of the car. My fluid filled belly makes getting up diffi-cult sometimes. I'm awkward and clumsy with my non-baby belly.

I sign in at the front desk and Scott hands his sample off to the lab. We're then whisked down a series of hallways I've never noticed before. The receptionist leads us further into the clinic than I've ever been, towards what must be the very back. I follow without question. Hospi-tals—or in this case, fertility clinics—are a little like airports. We're herded in, herded to the appropriate location, herded out by people who've done all of this a thousand times. We're not humans, we're numbers—on tickets, on medical bracelets—and we surrender control, allowing ourselves to be passively led from one location to the next. Blindly trusting that the people whisking us to and fro won't lead us astray.

At the back of the clinic is a room with several plastic-looking recliners, each with a hospital-style curtain dividing them—slightly worn fabric, striped in muted greens and yellows with white mesh along the top. The receptionist hands me off to a nurse, who gestures to one of the chairs and tells me to sit down. Scott takes my coat and hangs it up somewhere. The nurse reviews my chart with me, making sure the information is correct. She takes my blood pressure—unsurprisingly, it's high, despite the Ativan. Then she wraps a paper bracelet with my name and information around my right wrist. I'm given a hospital gown to change into and assigned a locker in which I can store my stuff.

I sit back down in the chair and see that Scott has pulled up a little plastic chair from somewhere. I shiver as the bare skin of my legs makes contact with the cold vinyl of the recliner. Scott takes my hand again and holds it, not saying anything. "Survivor" by Destiny's Child plays through the little speakers nestled into the tiles of the drop ceiling.

"Do you guys do that on purpose?" I ask, and the nurse's head swivels up from the papers she'd been organizing at the little desk several feet away.

"I'm sorry?" She frowns, peering at me.

I point up at the speaker. "The rah rah girl power pop music."

"Oh." She smiles briefly. "We want to make sure our patients are in as positive a mood as possible while here."

I arch an eyebrow and say nothing. I can see Scott biting back a smile out of the corner of my eye. I lean my head back against the headrest and close my eyes. I'm not tired, but my eyelids feel heavy. "Hit Me With Your Best Shot" by Pat Benatar comes on and I start to laugh, a silent quiver making its way through my body, shaking my bones. Scott squeezes my hand tighter, and I open one eye. He's laughing silently too. I squeeze back. There's no one else I'd rather have here with me right now.

Soon, the nurse comes over and inserts an IV in my hand, which hurts more than I'm expecting. After a few minutes, I feel warm and slippery. I'm loose. I'm no longer held together. I close my eyes and doze for a minute, enjoying the sensation. It's nice. Nothing matters. I could bask here for hours.

Scott kisses me on the forehead, and I open my eyes to see another nurse standing in front of me. She says something, and I think the gist of it is that I need to stand up and walk over to the operating room. I guide my IV pole over the floor and shuffle forward, Scott's hand warm on the small of my back. I realize that I forgot to do up the back of my gown, and Scott's holding it closed for me. I suppress a giggle.

The lighting in the operating room is dim. It smells of antiseptic and metal and it's cold. A bed-like table sits near the middle of the room, surrounded by machines and equipment. A chair for Scott is positioned by the head of the table. Monstrously huge stirrups protrude from the end of the table. This is where I'll be splayed, helpless, while I'm probed and poked and drained. A little window is set into the wall nearest the table, closed off with wooden shutters. I know this is where the lab is, where the doctor will pass the liquid filled tubes they've collected to lab techs so they can find the eggs under powerful microscopes. I wonder if everyone in the lab will be able to see my vagina as this is going on. So many people have seen it at this point that I don't really care; I'm just curious.

The nurse helps me climb onto the table and instructs me to lift my legs and lay them in the stirrups. These aren't the typical stirrups, with slots for your heels at the end. They're bigger and higher, and I realize I'm to put my thighs in them so that they cradle the backs of my knees. My socked feet dangle in the air, helpless and adrift. The nurse drapes a sheet over me for modesty and dignity, not that I really have much of either left. I start to shiver and panic begins to claw at me from the inside. I clamp my lips together, my chin shaking. A tear slips free, sliding down over my temple and into my hair. So much is riding on this that I'm pulled into a thousand little pieces by the emotions tugging at me.

"I think she's cold," says Scott, his hand stroking my hair. As Dr. Kane comes in with another man I don't know, a nurse places a warm blanket over me. It helps ease the shivering, but does nothing for the knot of anxiety right in the center of my chest. In this moment, I'm scared of everything the future holds. Future pain, future failure. I'm standing on a precipice, staring into the dark below.

Dr. Kane pats my leg as she passes and opens the window into the lab, chatting with one of the technicians. The nurse speaks with the man. I want to scream at them all to get on with it. I feel like I've been lying here for hours.

The man's face comes into my field of vision. Between the dim lighting and his seafoam green cap and face mask, I can't really tell what he looks like, which unnerves me.

"Hello, Claire. I'm Dr. Evans. I'll be looking after your medications today. I'm going to inject a pain reliever as well as a strong sedative into your IV now. You might feel a slight burning sensation as the drugs first enter your blood stream. Don't be alarmed; that's normal. We'll do our best to keep you as comfortable as possible. Okay?"

I manage to nod, agreeing, giving permission. As if I have some kind of say in all of this. As if I have any permission left to give. Scott strokes my hair again from his spot behind me. A rush of buzzing warmth spreads from my hand, up my arm, and into my body. I close my eyes, breathing

"...doing really well, Claire, I know it hurts." Dr. Kane's voice. Something is stabbing me in my abdomen, the pain cold and sharp. Relentless. It's not a throbbing pain, but a constant drag of agony through my insides. I hear a low, guttural moaning sound and realize it's coming from me. "Push more Fentanyl," she says. The pain starts to glow and

Beeping and low murmurs of voices surround me. Scott is there, his hand on my head. I know his hands; I can feel him behind me. I try to move, relieved it's over, and hands made of steel hold me in place. "Hold still, Claire, we're almost done the first ovary." Dr. Kane's firm voice. I make a horrible strangled sound as the needle moves inside me, scraping me raw from the inside out. I feel movement behind me

I'm both sinking and floating at the same time, struggling against some invisible force to see, to speak, to be. I can't tell if I'm free or trapped in this silent, black space. I don't like this place. I don't want to be here anymore. I can't

"Seven eggs from the right ovary," says a watery voice from somewhere far away. I feel a hand squeezing my shoulder. My eyes flutter open. Dr. Kane is hunched between my legs. She moves the ultrasound probe, the one with the long, long, long needle on the end inside me and I almost scream. I can feel it, puncturing me, invading me, violating me.

"Push another round of Fentanyl," she says, sounding annoyed. I'm

Scott's hand brushes something away from my temple. "Shh, it's okay, sweetheart. Don't cry. I think they're almost finished." Air moves through the room and I can tell my cheeks are wet. I'm shaking again and can't seem to get a good breath. I'm spending all my effort on not letting out the sob building inside me. A sob of pain and grief, of helplessness and fear. More bees buzz into my blood and Scott says

I slowly open my eyes and then immediately close them again. I'm back in the recliner room with its fluorescent lights. I ache. My hand. My abdomen. My vagina. I have blankets wrapped around me, and it's hard to keep my eyes open, but I do. I manage to lift my head, even though it weighs about a thousand pounds, and look around the room.

Scott stands about ten feet away, his arms crossed as he listens to Dr. Kane. I can't hear what he's saying. After another moment, Scott turns away from her and heads back toward me. He smiles he sees that I'm awake.

"How are you feeling?" he asks, rubbing my arm through the mound of blankets.

"Sore. I didn't think I would feel as much as I did." I start to shiver despite all the blankets as flashes of pain-laden memory come back to me. I force myself to swallow, not wanting to think about it.

Scott rubs a reassuring circle on my arm. "You did great, sweetheart."

"How many eggs?" I ask, my throat froggy and dry.

Scott smiles. "Ten."

I relax back into the chair. Ten is good. In five days, we might actually end up with something to transfer. For the first time, there might actually be life on this planet that is half me and half Scott.

I let my eyes fall closed again.

15

Two.

Two low-quality embryos. After five days, that's all we're left with. We'd started with ten eggs, eight fertilized, and then received inappropriately cheerful updates as one by one, almost all of them arrested. Died. Stopped growing.

"Why did so many of them…arrest?" I ask the nurse over the phone, using the term she'd used instead of saying died, which is more truthful, less sterile, but more painful. I'm sitting at my desk, sketching out a room for a new potential client. I let the canary yellow Prismacolor marker drop to the paper, where it leaves a small blot of more intense color on the curtains I'd been shading. Shit. I hastily put the cap back on the marker.

"According to the embryologist's report, your eggs were very…" There's a pause and I hear the sound of rustling paper from her end. "Fragile."

"Fragile? What does that mean, exactly?"

Another pause. "I think it means that they were of generally poor quality. They didn't withstand the retrieval and fertilization process very well."

"Oh." We knew, or least suspected this already. I shouldn't be so disappointed, so…surprised isn't the right word. Dismayed, maybe. "But we can still move forward with the transfer this afternoon?" *Please don't tell me I've been shoving estrogen up my vagina for nothing.*

"Yes, there's no reason not to. We'll freeze the other for future use."

I thank her for calling and set my phone down on my desk. As I stare at the snowflakes falling outside, I think about the two embryos sitting in the lab at the clinic. Two embryos that could become our children. If they work. If everything goes right. I have a hard time believing in everything going right. I force myself to return to my sketch, trying to keep my mind busy and distracted.

I hear a commotion from the back of the room and see a group of women surrounding Mia, hugging her and jumping up and down as Mia pats her stomach. She's through the first trimester now and telling people. I stay at my desk and don't join the fray. Mia's getting enough attention; she doesn't need my insincere enthusiasm. She knows I had my egg retrieval five days ago. She hasn't said a word about it. Now that she's pregnant, I feel farther apart from her than ever before.

Instead, I pick up my phone and text Becca, who's been my go-to person over the past five days. She checked in with me every day to see how my recovery was going and let me vent about my frustrations without judgment or unsolicited advice. She understands how I feel about Mia's surprise pregnancy and doesn't make me feel bad for my sometimes ugly and uncharitable thoughts.

Mia's announced at work. Cat's out of the bag now.

Becca: Did she tell you she was doing that today?

Of course not.

Becca: Listen, do you want me to talk to her? I don't want this hanging over our Friendsgiving dinner.

There's another eruption of squeals and laughter from the back of the room. I glance over at Mia's desk and notice a new picture beside her monitor: a framed ultrasound pic. I immediately look away. Those shadowy white and gray images haunt me, mock me, with their promise, their confidence, their ability to remind me in a microsecond of what I'm struggling for.

I text Becca back.

If you can think of a tactful way of asking her to tone it down a little while not making her feel bad, go for it.

Becca: She's making this harder for you than it has to be. I'm happy for her, and she has every right to be excited, but you're her friend, and I don't appreciate the way she's completely neglecting you during a difficult time.

Claire: To be fair, I'm neglecting her just as much.

I set my phone down just as another text comes in. This one's from Mandy.

My producer wants to book you on the show for late January. Does that work? I really want to fit the segment in before I go on mat leave in early Feb.

My stomach does a little lurch. Mandy actually wants to have me on her show, to profile me and my work, and showcase the now finished nursery we've designed for her. I glance over at Mia, a twinge of guilt pulling at me that I'm doing this without her. I text Mandy back.

That sounds great. Thanks so much for the opportunity. I really appreciate it!

Mandy: Anytime! You're a talented designer and I think you'll be great on the show. BTW, how are you doing? How did everything with the retrieval go?

Claire: We've got two embryos, and we're doing a fresh transfer this afternoon.

Mandy: Good luck! I'll be thinking of you.

I glance down at my phone and then over at Mia again. I can almost feel, can almost see the divide widening between the two of us, our friendship being pulled at the seams from opposing directions. Maybe I need to stop dwelling on how I feel Mia's let me down and spend more energy appreciating the people in my corner, people like

Becca and Mandy. Maybe I need to own the fact that I'm probably letting her down too.

I pick up the marker and finish my sketch, and then call Scott.

I'm going to pee my pants.

Honestly, that's how I feel, sitting in the clinic's waiting room with Scott, my leg bouncing up and down, sweat prickling along my hairline as I concentrate on holding my bladder. It's uncomfortably full—a necessity of the embryo transfer procedure.

As usual, the clinic's waiting room contains a handful of people, everyone surreptitiously avoiding eye contact with anyone else. The news plays in a constant loop on the flat screen TV, the fireplace is off. The two receptionists answer the phone when it rings, typing and chatting between calls. A delivery man comes in with a stack of boxes on a dolly, all marked with Bowerman Medical Supply.

I stand, unable to sit still any longer, and rove across the room. A large purple book—it looks like a guest book of some kind—sits on a coffee table at the far end of the waiting room. I don't remember ever seeing it before, so I pick it up, looking for a distraction from my aching bladder.

The book is large and filled with thick, creamy paper, divided into sections. At the beginning of each section, a question is printed in brown scrolling font, and it looks like patients are anonymously filling in their answers. I flip through the sections, skimming through handwritten stories about why people chose this particular clinic, individual diagnoses, even success stories. Most of the entries are signed with a first name only, sometimes with a single letter. I keep flipping, mesmerized by the collage of handwriting, differing ink colors dancing before me. There are so many of us. My breath catches a little when I reach a section near the back of the book. The question is simple, eternal.

Why do you want to be a mother?

The answers are varied in length, in content. I scan down the page and then turn it, taking them all in.

To continue my family line. – Jess

Because I want to nurture and love a child. – Ashanti

I long physically for a baby. It's only natural. – Nicole

To give my son a sibling. – Silvia

Because I love my husband and want to have a baby with him. – Bipasha

I want to fill my heart with love. – E.

My childless life feels empty and meaningless. – Luisa

Because I adore children. – Megan

Each one of these sentences resonates, vibrating through me until I've absorbed them. Until they reverberate so strongly that they meld together, coalescing into an indescribable feeling of yearning. I close the book and set it down, glancing around the room again at the people waiting. They suddenly seem so much more real, so much more tangible than extras in the background of a movie.

"Claire Stanhope?" A nurse with a clipboard beckons me and Scott down one of the clinic's familiar hallways and into one of the regular exam rooms. She gestures at the table. "Go ahead and undress from the waist down. There's a sheet to cover yourself with. Dr. Kane will be in shortly to perform your transfer." She smiles perfunctorily. "Good luck."

Scott sits down in the little plastic chair pushed against the wall, and I hand him my coat and tote. He doesn't say anything as I shimmy out of my skinny black pants and underwear, balling them up and shoving them into my bag. Being naked from the waist down always makes me feel undignified, like Porky Pig or something, and I scurry over to the table and peel the paper thin sheet open, wrapping it around my waist.

"I still can't believe we only got two," says Scott, staring at an invisible spot on the wall. "With ten eggs, I thought we'd have more. I thought the big hurdle would be how many eggs we got."

"I know. I guess it doesn't matter how many eggs you get when they're all rotten."

He doesn't seem to hear my self-pitying comment. "I know it only takes one to work, but I was hoping we'd get more chances out of this, you know?" He pushes a hand through his hair. I can feel the sadness and frustration coming off of him in ripples.

"If these two don't work, then what?" I ask. I shift on the table, the paper crinkling under my ass, as I try to find a position that will alleviate some of the pressure on my screaming bladder. "Superwoman" by Alicia Keys plays softly on the clinic's speakers.

Scott picks at a piece of invisible lint on his suit jacket. "I don't know. We don't need to figure that out today, though."

"I know we don't, but I want to know what the plan is going forward." Plans, even hypothetical ones, calm me, prevent my mind from spiraling out of control and into dark, remote places.

"I don't think there is a plan right now, Claire. Let's just take it one thing at a time and cross that bridge if and when we come to it. I don't know what more I can say." There's a slight sharpness to his voice, and I bite my lip, sitting on my hands. He's just as tense and nervous about all this as I am. It's getting harder and harder to comfort each other when we're both hurting, both trying to cope with the same wound.

There's a sharp knock on the door and then Dr. Kane enters, clipboard in hand.

"Hello, Claire. Okay?"

I shrug and nod. "I'm all right," I say. It's a half-truth and the best I can do right now.

She studies the papers attached to her clipboard, flipping through them with her perfectly manicured nails. "So I see we've got two embryos, a 3BB and a 2BC. Today we'll transfer the higher quality one of the two—the 3BB—and freeze the other."

I don't know a lot about how the embryos are graded. It was explained at the information night, but it was near the end of the presentation and I'd started to tune out, already overwhelmed with it all. What I remember is that a higher number is better, with five being the best, and matching letters are better than non-matching letters. I think A is better than B or C? I couldn't tell you what the letters indicate, though. But even with my limited knowledge, hearing that we have a 3BB and a 2BC makes my heart sink. Those ratings don't sound very promising, and I feel a little of the hope I had left start to slowly drain out of me, like a tire with a small hole.

A nurse comes in and helps me lie back on the table while Dr. Kane opens the wooden shutters to the lab, just like during my egg retrieval. The nurse dims the harsh light in the room to a soft glow and then brings over another clipboard with a consent form for both me and Scott to sign. I don't even read it, I just sign it. What it says doesn't matter—it's not as if I'm going to see something in there I disagree with, pull my feet out of the stirrups and march out.

The embryologist reads off our information and we confirm that it's all accurate, and once the embryo is loaded in the catheter, we double check all of the information again to make sure this is in fact *our* embryo. I think about the couple of books and movies I've read or watched that made light of having the wrong embryo transferred. I can't even imagine the trauma of that. The violation, the way lives would suddenly be twisted inside out. Fuck those stories.

I try to relax, focusing on the ceiling tiles as Dr. Kane slips the speculum in. To my right is a large ultrasound monitor, and the nurse squirts goop low on my abdomen, pressing firmly down with the ultrasound wand.

Once I'm sufficiently splayed, Dr. Kane takes the catheter, and with the guidance of the ultrasound, threads it through my cervix and into my uterus. The pressure on my bladder from the ultrasound wand is excruciating. I'm tense with the effort of holding it. I wonder how many women have peed on this table, unable to stop themselves. I hope I'm not one of them.

I feel a slight scratching inside me, similar to an IUI, but it quickly fades. Other than the unshakable, relentless need to pee, the procedure feels like nothing. Scott glances up from his phone occasionally. He looks bored.

But then something happens. The nurse turns the ultrasound screen towards me, so that if I crane my neck at an awkward angle, I can see it. There, in those shivery black and white and gray tones, is our little embryo. A round collection of living cells made up of me and Scott, now inside me. It seems to glow, white and pure and full of promise. There's a flash of white as the catheter releases the embryo.

I stare at it, unable to tear my eyes away from the screen. This is by far the closest I've ever come to being pregnant. As far as I know, I've never had a living embryo in my uterus before. I feel a rush of something—hope, maybe even love, paired with a fierce protectiveness—for this tiny little thing inside me. For the first time in a long time—possibly even ever—my hope is stronger than my doubt. It's alive, and it's inside me, exactly where it needs to be. How can this not work? Of course it's going to work. We've struggled long enough. It's our turn.

I'm finally, actually, going to get pregnant. I'll know what it's like to complain about sore boobs and morning sickness, to watch my little bump get bigger and bigger, to feel the baby move inside me. I'll know what it's like to hold our baby in my arms as we playfully argue over whose features are more prominent. I'll finally emerge from this shadowy land of infertility and into the sunshine with everyone else. I'll be able to tell my mom. This path, every element of it, is so clear to me now, because this is going to work.

I look up and see that Scott's fixated on the screen too. He's rapt, staring at the little white dot that could become our child. *That will become our child.*

"Would you like a picture?" the nurse asks, gesturing at the screen.

I nod, clearing my throat before I speak. "Yes, please."

She presses a button and prints one off, handing it to Scott. He takes it carefully, gently, worried about disturbing it. As though it, too, is alive and just as fragile.

Dr. Kane withdraws her instruments and stands, pulling off her gloves. "All done. You can get dressed and then go empty your bladder. We'll see you in two weeks for your blood test. Good luck."

The nurse wipes the goop off of my stomach with scratchy paper towels, and when she's finished, I pull my shirt down and rest a hand on my abdomen.

"Welcome aboard," I whisper.

16

Two weeks of waiting. That's fourteen days. 336 hours. 20,160 minutes. Over a million seconds, each one ticking by slower than the one before. It sounds like a song from *Rent*.

I've decided I'm going to wait the full two weeks this time and not test at home. Home pregnancy tests are bad luck for me, and this time, everything's different. This time, hope buoys me, carrying me through each agonizing minute, each never ending day. Bad luck and home pregnancy tests with their blue lines that never give me the answer I want are a thing of the past. I touch my abdomen almost constantly, imagining the life growing there. Letting myself believe. Actually believing. I feel renewed. I feel certain. I might even feel smug, which could very well be one of my first pregnancy symptoms.

I say the words to myself in the mirror every morning, savoring them and the rush of adrenaline they bring while I fantasize about how I'm going to tell Scott. While I fantasize about everything that lies ahead.

I think I might be pregnant.

The remnants of our Thanksgiving dinner sit on my mom's dining room table, picked over plates with bits of food in front of empty chairs. The scents of turkey and pumpkin pie still hang in the air, mingling with the tinge of woodsmoke coming from the fireplace in the living room.

"Do you remember where the tree is?" Mom asks as I help her into her recliner in the living room. Her voice has lost its power, and I have to bend close to hear her. Her breathing is shallow and rapid as she settles into her chair. The trek from the dining room to her spot in front of the fire is too far for her to walk on her own now. I wrap her favorite blue shawl around her painfully thin shoulders, letting my hands linger for a moment as I try to rub some warmth, some comfort into her bones.

Eddie emerges from the kitchen, a dish towel thrown over one shoulder. "I'll get it in a second, honey."

Scott rises from where he was crouched in front of the fire, prodding at it with the metal poker. "I'll get it," he says, setting the poker back into its stand. "I think I remember where it is."

This is our tradition—every year after Thanksgiving dinner, we get the Christmas tree out and put it up in the same corner of the living room, by the fireplace. Mom's always been a Christmas fanatic, and for her, the season starts the second we've all finished our last bites of pumpkin pie. Despite the cheery atmosphere—the fire, the food, Frank Sinatra crooning away in the background—an air of melancholy has settled over everything, like a fine layer of dust that I can't brush away. This will be Mom's last Christmas. We're all thinking it, but no one's saying it because it doesn't need to be said. We all know.

I want to tell her that I think I might be pregnant. I want to give her that. But I hold back because of the chance that I'm not. It feels like a small chance, but it's one I'm not willing to take. I can't give her false hope. I can't give her the gift of a future grandchild and then take it away. I touch my stomach, my palm splayed over it, warm, almost feverish with hope. I have to wait until I know for sure. Until what I think I know is confirmed.

With Mom settled, I duck into the kitchen to help Eddie with the dishes. The counter is strewn with plates and serving platters, half-full serving dishes, and what remains of our turkey. Normally, turkey dinner is Mom's thing, but Eddie and I put together this year's dinner. Eddie was in charge of the turkey, the stuffing and the mashed potatoes. I made green bean casserole, sweet potatoes, and a pumpkin pie—well, as much as putting store bought pumpkin pie filling into a store bought pie shell counts as "making" it.

Eddie turns, holding out the turkey's wishbone to me. "Feeling lucky?" he asks. From the living room, Mom coughs, a deep, bone rattling cough that shudders through the whole house. I feel it in my own chest, a sickly constriction that makes it hard to breathe properly. I nod. We pull and I come away with the winning half.

"It doesn't matter," I say, meeting his eyes. "We both want the same thing." The same impossible thing.

His eyes soften with sadness and then he nods, setting the wishbone back down on the counter and then returning to the dishes. I work on clearing the table, and then pick up a clean dish towel and set about drying the mounting pile in the dishrack.

We work in silence for several minutes, listening to Mom direct Scott as to the exact placement of the tree, telling him to move it to the right, to fan the branches out more. Our holly jolly dictator, as usual.

"I don't think she has much time now," Eddie says, his eyes focused on the darkened, blank window in front of him.

I take my time drying off a ceramic serving platter, chasing down each last drop of water, studying the delicate pattern of leaves and berries decorating the rim. "No, I don't think so," I agree. "That cough sounds awful."

He nods. "I think it's in her lungs now. Sometimes she wakes up at night because she can't breathe." He takes a deep breath, as though reminding himself that he can breathe, even if she can't. "Like she's drowning."

Her body is a cage now, with no escape except the final, ultimate one. Death is the only mercy left to her. I lean into this idea in a way I haven't allowed myself to before. I have to, because it's coming.

Eddie pulls his hands out of the soapy water and rests them on the counter, splayed out on either side of him as though he can't hold himself up anymore. I set the platter down and touch his arm. He turns his face away from me. The slight juddering movement of his shoulders gives him away though, and when he speaks, I can hear the tears in his voice.

"I don't know how much longer I can do this, Claire. I…" He trails off, shaking his head. "It's so hard to watch her, to look after her, to worry constantly, to put on this brave face for her."

I throw my dish towel over my shoulder and wrap my arms around him. I feel awful that I haven't really thought about the toll being her full-time caretaker has taken on him. He's always been so steady, so dependable, that his struggles usually go unnoticed. But he doesn't deserve to feel this way, to feel overwhelmed and exhausted and helpless.

"Let me make some phone calls, okay? There are people who can help. Personal support workers, and nurses, and housekeepers…you shouldn't have to deal with this all on your own. It's okay to need help, Ed."

"I didn't want you to think that I didn't want to do it anymore," he says, his voice thin and raspy like tissue paper.

I rub his arm. "No one thinks that. We all know how much you've done for her, but it's reaching a point where you can't do it alone, and that's okay."

He nods, and I can feel the relief trickle through him as his muscles relax.

We finish the dishes and then head into the living room to let Mom bossily tell us where each ornament goes, one last time.

December - Now

Things I have Googled over the past ten days, in no particular order:

- Early pregnancy symptoms
- Early pregnancy cramps
- Early signs of pregnancy
- Implantation bleeding
- Diarrhea early pregnancy sign
- Headache early pregnancy sign
- Bad breath early pregnancy sign
- Change in cervical mucus pregnant
- Fatigue early pregnancy
- How many weeks pregnant does morning sickness start
- IVF success rates first transfer

I'll probably think of more before it's time for my blood test next week, although I should probably put down my phone and step away from the Google. I think I'm driving myself nuts, imagining all these symptoms when I don't know anything for sure. Maybe I just want it so badly that my hope, my need for this to work, is manifesting itself physically. Like a psychosomatic pregnancy, built on nothing but desperation and search algorithms.

I feel as though I'm held together by razor thin threads made of insubstantial stuff. I'm held together by wishes, shimmering and intangible. A puff of air could undo me, so precarious is my hold on…well, on everything.

I am a mess.

Allison's gorgeously minimalist penthouse smells like pine and vanilla, with the scent of ham underneath. We don't do turkey for our annual Friendsgiving dinner—Allison hates it and won't be convinced it isn't disgusting. I kick my shoes off by the front door and hang my coat on the stainless-steel geometric coat tree positioned between two framed abstract art prints.

"Hey!" I call as I make my way deeper inside, my cheesy potatoes in their Pyrex dish clutched in my hands, a big Ziploc of gingerbread cookies perched on top of the tinfoil. Music and voices pull me into the kitchen, where the other three are gathered around the marble-topped island, drinking wine.

Mia smiles at me and gestures at her glass. "This is cranberry juice," she says, as if I'd asked for an explanation. I hoist a smile onto my face and set my things down on the counter, by the rest of the food.

Over the past couple of weeks, I've taken some space from Mia, unsure how to handle our strained friendship, her pregnancy, and my IVF attempt all at once. Trying to keep up a normal level of communication with her would've felt like trying to untangle a knot by pulling tighter on the opposing ends—all action and effort only to make things worse. Sadly, I'm not even sure she's noticed that I've pulled away. Sometimes I wonder if I'm the only one who misses us and what we used to have. But I don't fight against it anymore. It's just the way things are between us right now, the way things have to be.

I grab an empty glass and help myself to some of Mia's cranberry juice. Allison arches an eyebrow at me.

"Not drinking?" she asks.

I shake my head. "Nope. Can't because of the hormone medication."

This seems to satisfy everyone and we all head into the living room, where Allison has a shrimp ring and a cheeseball set up on her glass coffee table. Everything in her penthouse is shades of white and gray, with steel, glass, and bamboo elements.

"So, Mia, how's everything going?" asks Allison, sipping her wine.

Mia beams and pats her now visible little baby bump. My stomach churns and I look away. Becca catches my gaze with hers and shoots me a sympathetic smile. I smile back, grateful for the small gesture of kindness.

Mia launches into a detailed description of everything that's happened—her last ultrasound, how excited Tom and the kids are, how she still can't quite believe she's pregnant, followed by a detailed recounting of all of her symptoms. I don't know how to respond. I can't be the happy, excited friend she needs right now. That she deserves. Just like she can't be what I need. We're both too wrapped up in our own lives.

I pick at the food on the table and sip my juice as Mia goes on about gender predictions and names and comparisons between her other two pregnancies and this one. She then moves on to nursery planning, and I can't listen to any more. Pressure builds inside me, like a dropped soda can, and needing relief, I pop the top.

"Speaking of nurseries," I say, knowing I shouldn't say any of this, but wanting to say it all the same, "Mandy Sinclair was so happy with how hers turned out that she invited me to come on her show."

Mia's face falls, and I feel both satisfied and horrible. "Just you?" she asks, nibbling at a cracker, her eyes wide and uncertain.

"She and I kind of bonded," I say with a shrug. "You missed a lot of the project because you weren't feeling well. I'm sure if she'd gotten to know you more, she'd have included you too." I'm not really sure how much of this is true, but I say it anyway.

"Oh," says Mia, nodding a little too quickly. "I see." She takes a breath and smiles, but I can tell it's forced. "Well, good for you. That's really exciting. When?"

"In January."

"Very cool," she says in a way that tells me she doesn't think it's cool at all. I feel bad that my news hurt her, but a part of me—the bitchy, insensitive, childish part, mostly—is satisfied that I've given her a little taste of how she makes me feel. I eat a shrimp and then pick at a cuticle as the satisfaction quickly fades and I'm left feeling like a jerk. Me sticking my foot in my mouth doesn't magically erase all the times Mia's done it.

Becca rescues the conversation, steering us back into the safer waters of celebrity gossip. Mia excuses herself and heads for the bathroom. Allison pokes my arm as soon as Mia's out of earshot.

"Really, Claire? You didn't need to tell her like that." Her voice is a low hiss.

I nod. "I know. It just kind of slipped out."

"I think you really made her feel bad."

Something in me snaps. My face is suddenly hot, my pulse thrumming through my temples. "Do you give her a hard time for how much she talks about her accidental pregnancy in front of her infertile friend?"

Allison opens and closes her mouth, her face blank.

Becca holds up her hands. "I think we could all stand to be a little bit more sensitive to what everyone's dealing with." She clears her throat softly. "But Claire's right. Yes, what she said probably hurt Mia's feelings, but it's not fair to only stand up for Mia when Claire's hurting too, and frankly on a much deeper level."

Allison sniffs. "I didn't realize it was a competition."

Becca smiles and gentles her voice even further. "No one said that. I just think that Mia isn't the only one due sensitivity and consideration here."

Allison shakes her head. "I mean, you're doing IVF. You'll be fine. I don't think it gives you the right to rain all over Mia's parade, just because you have to try harder."

I take a deep breath, wanting to steady my voice before I speak. "It's not about trying harder. This isn't one of those things where if I just work hard enough, it'll happen. It's not a meritocracy."

Becca squeezes my arm in solidarity. Allison shrugs. "I don't know. I don't want kids, so I guess I just don't get it."

"If you don't get it, then maybe don't judge," says Becca softly. Mia returns and Allison heads into the kitchen to refill her wine. Great. Another friendship I've managed to damage.

"So, I have some news," says Becca once Allison returns. The vibe in the room is decidedly less festive now. "I'm moving to Italy."

"What?" I gasp out. I set down the shrimp I'd been about to bite into. Everyone is staring at her.

"I need to give this thing with Giancarlo a chance. I'm going to go in January, and I'm planning to stay for at least six months. I'm not selling the store, but I've hired someone to take over while I'm gone."

Selfishly, my first thought is that my one ally is leaving. I want to beg her not to go, but I can't. She deserves to be happy.

"What will you do while you're there?" asks Mia, her body angled away from me.

Becca shrugs. "Whatever I feel like, I guess. Giancarlo will be working, so I'm sure I'll have lots of time to explore on my own."

"Does he live in Rome?" asks Allison in a detached tone.

Becca shakes her head. "No, Venice."

Mia clutches a hand to her chest. "Oh, that's even more romantic!"

I lean over and pull Becca into a hug. "I'm happy for you, even if I'm sad to see you go."

The conversation continues to swirl around me, and all I can think about is how piece by piece, my world is disassembling itself, and I don't know how to put it back together into something new.

17

I PULL INTO A SPACE IN THE TARGET PARKING LOT, TIRED AFTER another week of work. Tired after spending the week making polite but strained conversation with both Mia and Allison while trying to focus on my current clients. Tired after obsessing day in and day out about if there's life inside of me. Tired after spending hours on the phone arranging for help for Mom and Eddie—a housekeeper to come every other week, a nurse to come once a week to check on her and adjust her pain medications as necessary, and a personal support worker to come every other day to help her bathe and look after herself. Tired, tired, tired.

The afternoon sky is gray and quickly darkening, threatening more snow, the temperature just below freezing and dropping. I'm listening to Mariah Carey's Christmas album, normally my favorite, trying to pull myself into the Christmas spirit, but I'm just not feeling it this year. My mom is dying, I'm in the trenches of infertility, and I'm losing friends to both geography and circumstance. Not exactly a recipe for a merry mood.

But I'm trying, dammit, so here I am, at Target on a Friday after leaving work early, to buy wrapping paper, ribbon, and probably about a dozen things I don't actually need because that always seems to happen whenever I shop here. Maybe they've got some nice picture frames. I haven't added to my collection in a little while.

For a minute, I let myself fantasize about using one for my own ultrasound picture, the way Mia's done. I don't think I'd actually do this —no one needs to see the inside of my uterus, especially my co-workers —but I let my imagination linger there all the same. I absently trace my fingers over the inside of my left elbow, feeling for the little lump of cotton held there with medical tape. My two weeks are finally up, and this is the real reason I left work early and why I'm at Target. I couldn't focus, and knew I needed a distraction as I wait for the phone call that might—that *will*—change everything.

I shut the car off and just as I'm undoing my seatbelt, I hear my phone beep from inside my purse. I pull it out and see that I have a missed call and a voicemail from the clinic. *From two freaking hours ago.* My stomach flips over on itself and my heart starts to pound erratically in my chest as I dial in to my voicemail. I have to turn the volume on my phone up because of the blood surging through my ears. With a shaking hand, I enter my pin and then rest my hand on my stomach. My palm is damp, clammy.

"Hi Claire, this is nurse Stephanie calling from the clinic." Her voice is bright and my hopes soar. My entire body buzzes. "I have your test results here, and I'm sorry to tell you that the result was negative. You can discontinue your progesterone, and your period should start within the next few days. Have a nice weekend!"

Have a nice weekend! The chipper words echo through my ears as my head seems to float away from my body, which has gone completely numb. I look down to where my hand is still splayed on my stomach and drop it down to my side. I stare out my windshield at the nearby row of red shopping carts until my vision starts to blur, my mind blank.

I'm not pregnant. I'm still empty. Always was. My imaginary symptoms were all in my head. I'd wished so hard that I'd convinced myself, maybe even convinced my body that things were different this time. But they're not. Once again, I'm not pregnant. As usual. As always.

Well.

On autopilot, I slide my phone back into my purse, and then step out of my car, shutting the door behind me. I inhale a deep breath of frosty air, but it does nothing to shake me out of my haze. Shouldn't I be crying? I blink a few times, waiting, but there are no tears. There's only this vast, yawning nothingness. I stand beside my car, watching as a woman settles her toddler into the backseat of her SUV. It's suddenly harder to breathe. I hate her. I hate myself. I hate my empty uterus.

I force my feet to move, walking slowly through the parking lot. The car parked beside me has one of those obnoxious "baby on board" magnetic bumper stickers. Something bubbles up inside me, an uncontrollable bitterness, frothing and spilling over like potion in a cauldron. Before I can stop myself, I reach out and peel it off.

Oh, that feels good. Cathartic. Soothing. Like I'm somehow leveling the playing field. I stuff it in my coat pocket and look for more. I want more of this catharsis. More of this childish revenge.

I walk through the parking lot, row by row, taking each colorful proclamation of procreation and motherhood I can find. There are so many, more than I'd have expected. But I shouldn't be surprised. After all, nearly everyone but me can have a child.

My coat pockets start to bulge with pink and blue bottles, yellow diamonds, pink and blue crowns, so I start shoving them in my purse. Each one I peel off is pure satisfaction. I'm erasing these outward signs of fertility, these tiny little reminders that slice me open like paper cuts every time I see them.

The wind picks up and my face stings. I realize that tears are now rolling down my cheeks, but I don't wipe them away. I snatch a "precious cargo on board" magnet with little baby feet on it, wanting to rip it in two. It feels so good. Petty revenge from the lowest road.

I've gone through nearly the entire parking lot, and I march up to the entrance of the store, dumping everything in my pockets into the garbage can there. I'm sobbing now, almost uncontrollably. My body aches. I can't catch my breath. I wish I were still numb, because then I wouldn't have to find a way to breathe through this crushing disappointment, to survive yet another heartbreak. Two women heading into the store stare at me. I must look like a lunatic. I don't care. Right now, I need to be a lunatic. My survival depends on it.

With my pockets now empty, I walk back to my car, gulping air and trying to rein in my hiccupping sobs. I lay my forehead on the steering wheel and let everything out, an anguished moan that turns into a scream, echoing in the close confines of the car.

I don't know how long I sit there, pushing all of the pain out of my body until a somewhat pleasant numbness returns. I think about telling Scott that it didn't work, of having to break his heart and dash his hopes yet again. I think about trying again with our one remaining embryo and where it'll leave us if it doesn't work. I think about how Mandy got pregnant on her first transfer, jealousy coating the back of my throat like bile. I think about Mia and feel lonely. I think about Mom and feel lost. I think about the path I'm on and how it's eating me alive from the inside out, like a flesh-eating disease.

I start the car and drive home. Fuck wrapping paper.

My face is still raw, my throat still swollen when I step inside. I'm back on autopilot, treating each small action as a task completed and a small amount of distance put between me and the initial pain. I set my keys on the table by the door. I kick off my boots. I undo my coat and hang it in the closet. I pull my phone out of my purse and slip it into my pocket. There, that's at least forty-five seconds gone.

"Claire?" Scott calls from upstairs. "Did you get wrapping paper?"

"No, sorry, I forgot." The lie comes easily.

Scott comes down the stairs, stopping halfway when he sees me. One look at me, and I know he knows. His eyes meet mine, and I shake my head, confirming what's already creeping through him.

I try to smile, my lips quavering unsteadily. "We can try again with the other one." I'm trying to be brave. To not need the comfort. To provide some, for once in my life.

He nods and pulls me against him, kissing the top of my head. "I'm so sorry, sweetheart. Fuck." He breathes out the last word on a sigh, its weariness and exhaustion and heartache almost palpable. Like something I can reach out and touch, taste. Bristly and sweetly sour.

We stand the entryway like that, neither of us speaking. All I can think about is what happened in the Target parking lot, and before I can hold it back, I start to laugh. Scott pulls back, one eyebrow raised.

"Would you care to share with the class?" he asks.

"I—I stopped at Target and that's when I heard the message and I just...I stole a bunch of those obnoxious baby on board bumper stickers from people's cars." I'm laughing so hard I can't quite catch my breath. What I've done is now insanely, deliriously funny to me.

Scott stares at me. "Oh-*kay*," he says, the word long and drawn out and full of judgment. I stop laughing. He opens and closes his mouth and then turns and goes back upstairs. I hear the door to the office slam.

I can feel Mia behind me before I see her. I've worked with her and been friends with her for long enough that I'm attuned to the sound of her footsteps, the way she carries herself. I'm used to an underlying, unconscious awareness of her presence. It's sad how a presence that used to light me up now makes me tense and anxious.

"Hey," she says, stepping into my field of vision. My cheeks go hot.

We haven't spoken since Friendsgiving, over a week ago now. She seems to have swapped me out for Allison, the two of them often heading out for coffee or lunch, leaving me behind.

"Hey," I answer, looking up from my laptop where I'm trying to source furniture for the Aurora Construction project we won.

"Can we go somewhere to talk? One of the meeting rooms, maybe?" she asks, her arms crossed in front of her.

I close my laptop. "Sure." We do need to clear the air. I know I shouldn't have blurted out my news about the TV show the way I did. I owe her an apology. I also owe her the truth about how hard it is for me to handle her pregnancy and how much she shares. I want to salvage this, salvage us, and so I need to be honest.

She turns and I follow her to the smallest meeting room. It's in the far back corner, and even though the walls are clear glass, it's the most private of the meeting spaces because it's tucked away out of view.

Mia sits down in one of the chairs and I study her, a flood of warmth engulfing my chest. It's a yearning, almost, for the way things used to be before everything changed. Before I couldn't get pregnant and she did completely by accident. Her shiny blond hair is straight today, falling over her shoulders in a golden sheet. She's wearing less makeup than usual, but her skin is still glowing. Her face is a little fuller, gently rounding out some of the pointier edges of her chin and jaw. She's wearing a black sweater dress, her little bump barely visible. Memories, one after the other, flit by as I look at her. Getting drunk together in a hotel room at a design conference and staying up all night talking about anything and everything. Taking her to a sex shop and helping her pick out a vibrator when she admitted that she'd never actually owned one. Celebrating career successes with champagne and cupcakes. Brainstorming design solutions together and cheering each other on through difficult projects. Texting nearly every day, no secrets, no boundaries, between us. My infertility has been the first and only thing I've struggled to talk about with her because she's struggled to understand. For the first time, Mia hasn't been able to give me what I need. For the first time, I haven't been able to do that for her, either, and I'm not sure where that leaves us.

But the truth is, I love her. I love us, our friendship and what we have—or, at least, what we had. As hard as this all is, as shitty as things have been, I don't want it to be over. I don't want to lose her. I've taken our friendship, our closeness for granted. I see that now, in a way I didn't before. I suddenly feel very, very lonely.

"I'm sorry for taking the TV gig without including you in it," I say, sinking down into the chair across from her. She tucks a strand of hair behind her ear and looks up at a spot on the wall somewhere above my head. After a second, she nods.

"I mean, I worked on that nursery project too. It felt like you were deliberately pushing me out," she says, not meeting my eyes. "Which… I was really hurt by that."

I lean forward a little, wishing she'd look at me. "For what it's worth, that's not at all the way it went down. While I was working with Mandy, I found out that she got pregnant through IVF and—" Mia rolls her eyes. I pause, my stomach knotting, but I choose to ignore it. "Anyway, we bonded over that and she invited me on her show."

Mia frowns. "I don't really see how her going through IVF is relevant to you pretending you designed that nursery all by yourself, when you didn't."

"I never pretended that. The invitation came from Mandy, and it's her show. You were sick and not around much, so she didn't have the chance to get to know you. It wasn't personal, or intended as a slight of any kind."

Mia examines a fingernail and doesn't say anything for what feels like a long time. Finally, she looks up, and her gaze is raw, open. "You've been a shitty friend ever since I got pregnant, Claire. Yeah, it sucks that you can't get pregnant, but can't you just be happy for me?"

And there it is, in two sentences. Our friendship, hanging in the balance. I pick my next words carefully, my heart throbbing in my chest. I can feel every beat under my skin.

"You haven't exactly been there for me, either, Mia. It's been hard, not being able to talk to you about this huge thing in my life. And then to have you upset with me because I'm struggling with hearing all about your pregnancy, which is really difficult for me...that's shitty, too."

"What are you talking about? You talk about your infertility *all the time*." And there it is again, the undercurrent of irritation, of annoyance.

"Because it's a massive part of what's going on in my life right now." I take a breath, my cheeks warm, my chest tight, my stomach full of cement. "And I think I kept bringing it up with you because I wanted you to understand. For whatever reason, the less you understood, the harder I tried make you get it. It just...it mattered to me that you get it."

Mia scoffs. "I *do* understand. How can I not when it's practically all you talk about?"

"But that's just it, Mia. You don't. And maybe it's not fair of me to expect you to because you've never been in my shoes. I don't know." I let out a long, slow breath, shaking my head. "It's not that I'm not happy for you. I am, somewhere deep inside me. Of course I am. But this is so fucking hard for me, Mia. You already have two kids. You weren't even trying. You get annoyed when I talk about how hard all of this is for me. And it hurts, because out of everyone on the planet, I thought you'd be there for me. I thought you'd get it. All I wanted was to lean on you."

She stares at me, an unreadable expression on her face. "Well, I'm sorry I didn't live up to your expectations, but you let me down, too. It hurts when your best friend pulls away just because she's so caught up in what she doesn't have that she can't be happy for you. I was so excited to share this with you, and you're basically telling me I'm a bitch for thinking that I could."

"Please don't put words in my mouth. No one is a bitch." My jaw tightens and I feel the hint of a tension headache pulling at my temples.

She sighs and crosses her arms in front of her chest. "I just don't think it's fair that you're upset with me when you've essentially done exactly the same thing to me."

With a sudden flash of clarity, I know. She will never understand. She will never see that my situation and hers aren't the same. I might as well have been tilting at windmills all this time.

"You don't get it, Mia. I'm sorry that I haven't been there for you the way you would've liked but...but you get to move. And I'm just stuck."

"What does that mean?"

"You get to have everything I've ever wanted without even trying. You get to move forward in life, almost effortlessly, while I spin my wheels. Stuck. Do you have any idea how hard that is to watch? When I'm going through month after month of failure, failed treatment after failed treatment? I want to be happy for you, and somewhere deep down I am, but I'm too fucking sad for me to get there."

"So is that why you took the TV show appearance? So you'd have something I didn't have? To even the score?" Her voice is getting louder. I press a hand to my forehead. Everything I just said, that was my truth, the core of everything I've struggled with. And she still can't see where I'm coming from. She never will. I need to accept that.

"I don't know! Maybe. I don't know. But one TV appearance isn't the same thing. I'm sorry I didn't include you, but it's just not the same thing."

A silence falls over the room. I sit back in my chair. My head isn't spinning; my thoughts are choppy, single words. Mia. Infertility. Pregnancy. Selfish. Invisible. Hopeless. Unfair. Loss.

"If you can't be happy for me, you're not the friend I thought you were, Claire."

"If you can't understand why what you're asking is unfair, you're not the friend I thought you were." My throat burns as I speak, as though the words, even though they're true, are scraping me raw from the inside.

Mia stands. "I guess not." She turns and leaves the room. I sit back in my chair and stare at the ceiling.

"Fuck." I say the word quietly, letting it carry the weight of everything crashing down on me.

18

I feel like I'm going to throw up as I walk through the hospital's sliding glass doors. Heat blasts me in the face as I set foot onto the soggy mat just inside the entrance, and I stamp my feet, adding the slush from my own boots to the soupy mess. I unzip my coat, too warm, and head to the elevators around the corner. A sparkly gold and silver garland hangs over each elevator, and a brightly lit Christmas tree stands in the corner, looking out of place against the pale yellow cinder block walls. The festive glitter among the drab hospital décor somehow makes it even more depressing. A reminder of the time of year and everything it encompasses, juxtaposed against unending reminders of where you are, and what that means.

I step onto the elevator with several other people: hospital staff, chatting amongst themselves, eager visitors clutching flowers and balloons, a pale-faced man in a wheelchair being pushed by his tired looking wife. It hits me that there's a stark division; the happy hospital people, and the downtrodden. There is no in between. Visits are either cheery or bleak. I envy the cheery people, with their flowers and smiles and air of excitement or relief. I understand the bleak ones, because I am one.

I emerge onto the third floor and double check my phone, re-reading the text message from Eddie. Room 3C. The wide wooden door is shut and I stand in front of it, breathing in the scents of rubbing alcohol and lemon floor cleaner. I tilt my head back and shake out my hands, warming up, preparing myself for however bad it is on the other side. I carefully school my face into a neutral expression because I don't want her to worry about me. Worrying is my job now, not hers. Her parental burden has shifted to me; our roles are no longer the same and never will be. If I'm honest, they haven't been for a long time now. I knock once before pushing open the door.

I'm struck by how small Mom looks in her hospital bed, surrounded by machines and tubes. Her light blue hospital gown has slipped down her shoulder, revealing her frail collarbone. Her eyes are closed, her breathing shallow. Her mouth is open, her lips cracked and dry. She's not wearing one of her scarves, and her scalp is shiny and smooth against the pillow.

"What happened?" I whisper as Eddie wraps me in a hug. He tips his chin toward the door and we step out into the hallway. He rubs a hand over his hair, and as he moves, I notice how big his sweater is on him.

"She wasn't feeling well yesterday, and she spiked a fever overnight. She was slipping in and out of consciousness when I called the ambulance. Her white blood cell count is low. She has an infection, and her body's struggling to fight it off." He glances at the door and sighs. "Her immune system's depleted after all of the chemo she went through. She's getting weaker and sicker." He meets my eyes; his are watery and bloodshot. "Her body's shutting down, Claire."

I stand very still as I let this sink in. I knew this was coming. I could've scripted it. This is not a shock, or a surprise. This is what was always going to happen. And yet I can't stop myself from panicking, from wanting to find a scenario where this doesn't end the way we all know it will.

"So what now?" I ask, swallowing around the golf ball-sized lump in my throat.

"They did blood tests and swabs to figure out exactly what kind of infection she has. They've got her on IV antibiotics and fluids, and depending on the test results, they may change her antibiotic to something else, or just add it to what they're already giving her."

"And then what?"

Eddie shakes his head slowly. "We wait. It could take a week or more for her body to begin to fight off the infection, if she's even able. We just have to wait and see."

I nod and we go back into the room, not saying anything, not disrupting the quiet, letting her rest. Eddie sits back down in the armchair in the corner, sinking into it with a tired sigh, and I perch on the windowsill. I look out at the street below, at the slow-moving traffic, the plaza across the street with the coffee shop and the Chinese food restaurant and the convenience store. Holiday lights flash in the windows, and garlands hang from the traffic lights at the nearby intersection. I try to count the cars as they go by, but there are too many. Life moving around me, just beyond this still hospital room, where the only sounds are the soft beeps and whirrs from the machines monitoring Mom. The light filtering in through the window is pale and gray. Sickly. Cold and barren. This is how it starts, the beginning of the end. I know I've said that before, but this time it's really for real. Any denial I've been clinging to is gone.

I fish my phone out of my purse and text Scott an update, and then automatically begin to text Mia. I stop myself after the first few words. We haven't spoken since our fight several days ago. I don't know when we'll speak again with how we left things. I delete the few words I've written and put my phone away.

I feel overwhelmingly, unbearably lost. None of this is how I thought anything would go. Even when Mom was diagnosed, I didn't think she'd die. I didn't think the cancer would win. Losing her felt remote, impossible. I didn't think I'd have trouble getting pregnant, and even then, I was so sure IVF would work for us. I never thought Mia and I would have such a massive falling out that there'd be a chasm between us, neither of us able to cross to the other side because of the hands we'd been dealt.

I always assumed everything would be fine; that things would work out exactly the way I wanted them to. Now, I feel foolish for believing that. For assuming that bad things only happen to other people. The truth is, they happen to everyone, all the time.

Mom stirs in her bed, letting out a small, raspy moan. Eddie and I both leap up from our seats, each taking a spot on either side of her bed. She opens her eyes and blinks slowly. Then she reaches out a thin, veiny hand to each of us, grasping our hands with her bony fingers.

"Well, doesn't this suck?" she says, somehow managing a wry grin. My heart crumbles like old stone, little tiny pieces falling away, bit by bit. I give her fingers a gentle squeeze, avoiding the IV protruding from the back of her hand.

"It's just an infection," I say, keeping my tone light. "With some antibiotics, they'll get you sorted out."

Eddie runs a hand over her bare scalp and she closes her eyes again, leaning into his touch. She doesn't say anything, and neither does Eddie. We all know what I've said is half-true, at best. She'll never be sorted out. Not in any way that means she gets to stay.

"You know," she says, her eyes still closed, "having cancer wasn't so bad. It was the trying to get rid of it that's killed me."

I press my lips together, searching for something to say. For the right words, even though I'm pretty sure there are no right words right now. Eddie sniffs and wipes at his eyes, glancing up at the ceiling as though he's stored some secret reserve of strength there. The sadness in the room starts to solidify, becoming a presence, like a fourth person.

Mom gently clears her throat and turns her face up to me. "Tell me something good," she says. Still fighting. Not letting the pain and inevitability grip her so tightly that it extinguishes her light.

"Scott and I are doing another embryo transfer soon," I say. The words are out of my mouth before I can stop them, before I can even fully process them. Scott and I haven't talked about when we'll try again with our remaining frozen embryo. I'd thought maybe we'd wait until the spring. But now I know I want to move forward with it as soon as possible. I want to give her something, even if it's a tiny something, to hope for. Or maybe I'm the one who needs something to hope for.

Mom looks up at me, and her eyes are bright. "Well, you'll have to keep me posted," she says, almost sounding like herself, breezy and carefree.

"I will," I promise, just wishing I could keep her, period.

It's midnight, and I can't sleep, probably because I can't figure out how to stop dragging my brain through the quicksand of my thoughts, all of them pulling at me, sucking and cloying until I'm surrounded by them. Until I can't move, can't do anything because of them. Stuck. Always stuck.

I stayed at the hospital until Mom shooed both Eddie and I away. Eddie hadn't wanted to go home, so I sat with him in one of the hospital's little cafés and watched as he picked at a turkey sandwich he clearly didn't have the stomach for. We sat in silence, nothing left to say. As the sky had faded from a soft gray to a woolen black, I headed home, remembering too late that Scott was at a work dinner and wouldn't be home until later, dreading the oppressive quiet of our empty house. So I'd ordered a pizza, opened a bottle of red wine, and tried to fall asleep on the couch waiting up for him, old episodes of *Ghost Hunters* on TV. I don't know if it's a sign of resilience, or the adaptability of humans, or what, but it strikes me as both odd and somehow reassuring that I can still do these normal things despite the fact that my world is falling down around me. The world as I know it is about to be swept away, and I'm eating pizza and drinking wine. My adult life might turn out very differently than I'd imagined, and I'm half-watching trashy TV while scrolling through Instagram on my phone.

Shortly after I'd crawled into bed, the bedroom door opens and I see Scott's silhouette against the dim light of the hallway. He closes the door softly behind him and he heads for the bathroom. The door snicks shut behind him and I hear the sounds of running water and his electric toothbrush. A few minutes later, I see him fumble towards his side of the bed.

"It's okay, I'm awake," I whisper. The lamp on his side of the bed flares to life, bathing the bedroom in soft, yellow light. His tie is loose around his neck, his shirt untucked and his pants undone. I stare at him, taking in everything about him, as though I haven't looked at him thousands of times. As though I don't have him memorized. The dark gleam of his hair, the kindness in his deep brown eyes, the sturdiness of his shoulders, the strength of his hands, the masculine grace of his movements. The little scar on his chin. His nails, chewed down as always. I stare, and I know that what I feel is love, but on an even deeper level, it's gratitude. He's here. My anchor. My safe, soft place. In this moment, the gratitude that I have him, that at least this part of my life isn't being ripped away from me, is almost overwhelming.

"What?" he asks with a tired grin, unbuttoning his shirt and tossing it carelessly onto a chair in the corner.

I shake my head, my tangled hair tickling my cheek. "Nothing. How was your meeting?"

"Fine. Long. A good reminder of why I hate clubs. Too loud, too crowded."

"You sound old," I tease, and he smiles.

"That's because I *am* old," he says, pulling off his undershirt.

"Positively ancient," I agree and he makes a face at me. Despite the weariness clinging to me, I smile. The tension between us seems to have faded, and I'm grateful.

"How's your mom?" He steps out of his pants and tosses them onto the chair, the belt buckle clanking. Stripped down to his boxers, he turns the light off and slips into bed. I reach for him and without having to ask, without having to want, even for a second, his arms are around me. Lying in the dark, surrounded by blankets and pillows and Scott's strong arms, I feel settled. As though my entire being had been one giant itch and I've finally been scratched.

"Not good. The infection's serious, and she might not have the strength to fight it off."

He exhales and kisses the top of my head, holding me tighter. "I'm sorry, Claire. Just tell me what you need, okay? I'm here."

"Right now, that's all I need. Only you, here, now."

He doesn't say anything, just runs a hand up and down my back. We're belly to belly, and as I shift against him, I feel him stir in his boxers. A tingling heat works its way over my skin, warming me from the inside out. It's a feeling I've missed; a feeling I thought maybe I'd lost.

"I don't want to wait until spring to transfer our other embryo," I say, blurting it out into the darkness. "I don't want to wait."

"Okay," he says, almost immediately. "We don't need to wait." He says it in a way that tells me he knows what I'm not saying. That Mom will be gone by spring, and I don't want to wait until after she dies.

I tilt my face up to his and kiss him. "I love you," I say, breathing him in.

His palm rests against my cheek, and he kisses me again. "I love you, too. No matter what. You know that, right? Baby or no baby. I love you."

Something softens inside me, a warm melting I haven't felt in I don't even know how long. For the first time in a long time, Scott and I make love without any pressure, or insecurities, or the pain of loss and wanting clinging to us.

It's just us. Only us. And it's good.

Christmas morning dawns with a smear of pastels across the sky. Blush pink, soft lavender, and hints of dove gray mingle together in the stretched out streaks of clouds clinging to the horizon. A couple inches of fresh snow coat the ground, glistening and pristine, as yet undisturbed. The bare branches of the trees lining our street are still, dusted with white. The street is quiet, empty of traffic. It's a beautiful morning, and yet for me, this year, it holds none of the hope, none of the promise, none of the joy of years past.

Scott kisses the nape of my neck and a mug of coffee appears in front of me. I manage a small smile and gratefully wrap my chilled fingers around its warmth.

"I keep thinking that by next Christmas, we'll have a baby," I say, staring down at my coffee, watching it blur as my eyes sting.

"Me too," he says. He wraps his arms around me from behind, and I lean into the sturdiness of him.

"This is the first Christmas that I'm…I'm not thinking that anymore."

"We're still trying," he says, his voice a little tight. I just nod. He's thinking it too, but his unrelenting optimism won't let him say it out loud. And that's okay. I can say it.

"I don't know if I can face today." My voice breaks a little on the last word. We're going to stop by the hospital to spend some time with Mom, and then we're driving two hours to Scott's sister's house. It'll be a big gathering, with lots of kids running around and well-meaning but nosy relatives asking us about the state of my uterus. I dread it more and more every year, not because I don't like Scott's family, but because I never feel more alone than when I'm the only childless woman in a room full of happy people.

"You can," he says, tightening his arms around me. "I'll be beside you the whole time. And you're stronger than you think."

I tilt my head back and look up at him. "Maybe I'm just good at faking it."

He shakes his head. "No. You've had more shit thrown at you over the past couple of years than most people have to deal with, and you're still standing. Still fighting, still trying."

"If I'm so strong, why does it all hurt so much?"

He sighs, taking a moment to weigh my question. "Because strength doesn't protect you from getting hurt. It gives you the ability to keep going despite the pain. And you're still going." He lowers his voice, almost a whisper. "We're not out yet."

I take a sip of my coffee and mull over whether or not I think what he's said is true. A few little flakes fall from the sky, dancing in front of the living room window, swirling down until they disappear against the sheet of white on the ground. For a long time, we stand in front of the window, not saying anything. The house is quiet, and I wonder if it'll be this quiet forever. The silence hangs in the air, like a tomb, holding the ghost of a family that hasn't come to be.

After another few minutes, he kisses me on the head once more. "I'm going to jump in the shower."

"Okay," I say. Still staring out the window, I listen to his footsteps as he heads upstairs, the creak of the floorboards, the shuddering of the pipes as he turns the shower on. I pull my phone out of the pocket of my robe and text Mia. We didn't exchange gifts this year, for the first time since I've known her.

Merry Christmas, Mia. I hope you have a wonderful day with your family.

I hit send, and then add, I miss you. I stare at the three words and then slowly reverse the cursor, deleting them one letter at a time. I slip my phone back into my pocket and head upstairs to dress and face the day ahead. As I do, I send up a silent prayer that Scott's sister has enough wine to get me through.

19

January - Now

CHRISTMAS CRAWLED BY, AND SO DID NEW YEAR'S, WITHOUT THE usual festive cheer. Early January brought more snow, and the sluggish progression of days so typical of mid-winter. Cold air, sludge covered roads, dark evenings, and darker nights. A sort of wakeful hibernation, everyone bundled against the harsh season, surviving. Persevering until spring, one day, one week at a time.

Over the past few weeks, Mom got better, and then worse, and then a little better, never leaving the hospital, the infection setting up camp in her body. I don't know if she'll ever go home again. For now, that's the goal, but she insisted on adding her name to the waiting list for a bed in a nearby hospice.

Hospice. The word, despite its smooth sibilance, feels gritty in my mouth anytime I'm forced to say it. And yet I know it's all we have left to hope for—a comfortable, dignified end.

Mia never returned my Christmas morning text. Not that I'd expected her to. But still. Now we avoid each other at work, each giving the other a wide berth. I miss her. I miss Becca. I'm lonely.

It's only been a couple of weeks since Scott and I decided to move forward with our frozen embryo transfer, but it's felt like months. But finally, after the slow stretch of time we've endured, Scott and I are sitting in the clinic's waiting room. My bladder is full, and idiot that I am, I'm starting to let myself hope again. Getting back on the roller-coaster of my own free will even though it made me hurl last time. A glutton for punishment because of the allure of the potential reward.

"Claire Stanhope?" A nurse with a clipboard calls me, and Scott and I stand. My stomach clenches, nerves flaring through me. Not about the procedure, but about the potential outcome, and what it'll mean for us. Scott gives my sweaty hand a gentle squeeze before falling into step behind me. I follow the nurse down the hallway, nearly tripping over my own feet when she veers suddenly left instead of heading right toward one of the procedure rooms as I'd been expecting. Hearing my faltering steps, she glances over her shoulder. "Dr. Kane needs to speak with you in her office." She doesn't offer more than that, and I don't ask. Instead, I turn to look at Scott, who shrugs affably. I don't feel affable. No, I feel like I've eaten about ten pounds of rock shards, and they're all tumbling around inside me. This deviation from the norm can't be good.

The nurse ushers us into Dr. Kane's office, and Scott and I sink silently into the two chairs facing her vacant desk. My bladder is so full that I cross my legs and try to focus on my breathing. I reach out and thread my fingers through Scott's.

"Jeez, did we not pay the bill they sent us or something?" I say, trying for levity and failing miserably. Scott seems to have picked up on the fact that something is up, because he just shakes his head.

"No, I paid it. You saw me write the check."

The office door swings open and Dr. Kane enters, looking polished and pristine as always. She gives us a perfunctory smile as she slides behind her ornate mahogany desk. Pictures of her kids line a shelf behind her. She opens the file folder in her hand, glances down at the lone sheet inside and closes it again, her slender fingers tenting over it.

"I'm very sorry, but your embryo didn't survive the thawing process. We won't be able to move forward with the transfer today."

I feel like someone's dumped a bucket of ice water over my head. I'm numb. My chest hurts. I can't think or speak, only sputter. In the space of a handful of seconds, I can feel everything I'd hoped for slipping away, pulling out of my tenuous grasp until my hands are empty. I look at Scott, and he's completely crestfallen. I can see the hurt, the disappointment, etched onto his face. As for me, my heart doesn't break. It doesn't shatter. It implodes, caving in on itself until there's nothing left but dust and rubble. The debris of my heart. The debris of my hopes, my future family. A dusty ruin of something that never was.

"Oh," I finally manage to say. "Oh."

"Is that normal, for that to happen?" Scott asks, leaning forward in his seat, chasing answers. I wonder if the answers even matter.

Dr. Kane tilts her head. "I wouldn't say it's normal, no, but it does happen, especially with low quality embryos."

"So what do we do now?" he asks. He looks at me again, and all I can do is blink. I feel like an astronaut, floating in space. Untethered.

Dr. Kane folds her hands and rests her elbows on her desk. "With the concern over your egg quality," she says, nodding meaningfully at me, "as well as the lack of success with this retrieval and transfer cycle, I'd strongly suggest considering donor eggs."

"Donor eggs." I repeat the two words tonelessly. "So, not mine."

"That's right," she says, and retrieves a pamphlet from a drawer in her desk. She holds it out to me, but I don't take it. After several seconds, Scott does.

I stand. "Excuse me, I need to use the rest room." I bolt out of the room on unsteady legs, weaving my way back to the front of the clinic and slamming the bathroom door behind me. I tug my pants down violently, the undone zipper scraping the skin on my legs, and sit down on the toilet, emptying my bladder, because there's no point.

No point. Nothing. I will never have a child that's mine. That has my eyes, or my hair, or my pointy chin. I can be a host for Scott's child with a stranger. I can contribute. But not participate in the conception. Because I'm defective. Broken, and empty, and the proof is that my genetic material can't be passed on to some poor, undeserving kid.

Loss swallows me up, encasing me and coating me. Never will there be a child on this planet who's a part of me. Never will there be a child who's part me, part Scott. That child will never, ever exist. It feels like a death.

I flush, wash my hands, and rearrange my clothes. I avoid my own face in the mirror, scared of what I'll see there. I step out into the hall, but I don't walk back to Dr. Kane's office, where I assume Scott is still peppering her with questions. Instead, I head back to the waiting room, making a beeline for the purple book. I flip quickly to the page I can't stop thinking about: why do you want to be a mother? I pick up the pen and write my answer.

I'm not sure I do anymore. – Claire

I twirl the stem of the wineglass between my fingers, the base of the glass scraping unevenly against the dining room table. David Bowie's playing on the Bluetooth speaker, and I'm staring out the window. The sky is gray, almost white, bare tree branches swaying gently in the cold wind. Everything looks blank and barren. A sympathetic landscape if there ever was one.

Scott pulls out the chair nearest me and sits down, gently laying out the pamphlet from the clinic on the table between us.

"We should talk about this," he says, tapping his finger against the pamphlet. "This might be a good option."

"A good option?" I stare at him. He might as well have just suggested we move to Mars. "That's easy for you to say. You're not the one who's being erased from the genetic equation."

Scott's eyebrows knit together and he opens his mouth a little. I can tell he doesn't know what to say to that, and I feel smugly satisfied.

Probably not the healthiest response, but I'm too raw to be delicate right now.

"So...you don't want to talk about it," he ventures, sliding the pamphlet away from me and folding it up.

"I don't know, Scott. I don't know what to think or how to feel about any of this. I need time. I need..." My voice cracks and I take a generous sip of my wine. "I need to grieve," I say, and as I say the words out loud, I know it's true. "I..." I shake my head, sighing. "I'm not saying we can't talk about this ever, but right now, I just need to be sad. I don't have room for anything else."

He nods. "I'm sorry. I don't mean to push you."

I glance at him and feel like a jerk at how discouraged he looks. For once, my glass half empty realism has successfully beaten down his inexorable optimism. For as long as Scott's been the buoyant one, I might have just sunk us. It makes the finish line, the one where we call it and abandon our flat-lining hopes of having our own biological child, feel that much closer.

I take another sip of wine, regrouping. He's right, we do need to talk. As much as I want to retreat to lick my wounds, that's not fair to him.

"I'm sorry. I don't mean to be a bitch."

"You're not." But his voice is flat, unconvincing.

"How would you feel?" I ask, not wanting to dig into how he feels about me right now. Instead, I just want him to understand because I'm not sure that he does. "If it were the other way around, and we were talking about donor sperm instead of donor eggs? If our only hope of getting pregnant would be for me to get pregnant with another man's baby?"

He purses his lips together and stares at his hands. "I don't know," he says after several seconds.

I angle my body toward him and lace my fingers with his. "I don't just want any baby. I want *our* baby." Tears prick at my eyes and I clear my throat, but it's no use. My nose is already running. I try to sniffle delicately, but it comes out as a loud snuffling snort. "We could potentially still have a baby, but knowing I'd be cut out, genetically speaking…it really hurts, Scott, in a way I'm struggling to explain. I want something, someone, that will never exist." He squeezes my hand, not saying anything. "There are other options, but I…I need time to…" I can't finish my sentence because I'm crying. My chest is tight, my eyes are burning, my throat is closing up. "Everything is just…it's just *gone*."

Scott pulls me into his lap and wraps his arms around me. "I'm sorry, Claire. I'm so fucking sorry."

He holds me tight and I sob against him, trying to figure out how to live with this yearning inside me for something that will never come to be. It doesn't feel real.

"What if this is the end of the road for us?" I ask.

"What if it is?"

"I don't know if I'm okay with that. I don't know if I'm ready. But…" I pull back and wipe at my eyes. The back of my hand comes away with a black smear. "But I don't know if I can keep going. If I want to keep going. I don't know what I want anymore. Maybe all of this is a sign. I don't think it's supposed to be this fucking hard." He doesn't say anything, and I force myself to ask the question that's been eating at me for a while now. "Do you regret marrying me?" God, I feel so pathetic, so desperate for reassurance, so awful for fearing Scott's answer.

Scott slips a hand under my chin and forces me to meet his eyes. "No. Never. I want us, and that hasn't changed."

"Even if I want to give up?"

Scott takes a second before he answers, and then he shakes his head, as though he's made up his mind about something. "Saying that you've had enough after everything you've been through to try to get pregnant is hardly giving up, Claire."

I feel the tiniest flicker of relief at the idea of saying no more, but also a tremendous sense of guilt and loss. I rest my head against Scott's shoulder, letting the internal tug of war play out. Not knowing what side will win.

"I don't know anymore," I say, my voice hoarse. I feel like all I say is *I don't know.*

"That's okay," he says, stroking my back. "I don't know either. But we'll figure it out. Eventually."

20

February - Now

MOM'S ALMOST UNRECOGNIZABLE IN HER HOSPITAL BED, surrounded by whirring, beeping machines. There's a fine coating of fuzzy gray hair on her head, and she's lost so much weight that the skin on her face is sagging, melting away as though it has nothing left to hang on to. She looks deflated. Emptied out and sucked dry. Her lips are cracked; little flakes of the black bile she's been coughing up cling to them. Her breaths are shallow and wet sounding, with more and more space between them. The nurses have been keeping her sedated because of how much she struggles to breathe while awake. I want to talk to her, but I can't watch her struggle.

This person in the bed, it's hard to see her as my mother. It's not how I picture her when I think of her, and I already know it's not how I'll choose to remember her. I'll remember her curls, her kind face full of warmth, her laugh, the smell of her perfume, her sometimes twisted sense of humor. Most of all, I'll remember the way she loved me, and the way I loved her, and try to take some small measure in comfort in knowing that that love isn't gone, and never will be. I refuse to remember her as this cancer-riddled shell of a person. This isn't who she was, even if it's who she is now, in the end.

The flat screen TV mounted to the wall is on, HGTV playing on mute. The room felt too somber with it shut off, but the chatter was annoying, too. Eddie's sitting in the other chair on the opposite side of the room, his face drawn with exhaustion and heartache, staring blankly at the TV as a house is transformed from ramshackle to sparkling and chic. The door opens and Scott steps in, a tray of coffees and a paper bag in his hands. He hands me my cup and a muffin from the bag before passing the tray and bag to Eddie. He takes it and stares at it, as though he's not quite sure what he's just been given.

"Breakfast," says Scott, leaning against the heating unit attached to the wall by the door. Eddie nods and mechanically takes a bite of his muffin. Mine tastes like sawdust.

We sit together in silence, a kind of hollow purgatory, for a while. An hour? Longer? I don't know. I have no sense of time right now, only of being suspended. Waiting. I'm good at waiting now, at giving myself over to the stillness of it. Embracing its impermanence.

A nurse raps gently on the door and then enters. She checks the machines around Mom's bed, making a few adjustments, and placing a fresh Fentanyl patch on her shoulder. Mom takes a loud, shuddering, gasping breath, her body almost convulsing as it struggles for air, and then she sinks back down into sleep, her chest rising with each shallow breath.

"I don't think it will be long now," says the nurse quietly. "Many patients have one last bit of strength before they die, and are able to pull themselves out of sedation, even if it's just for a minute or two. Be ready for that so you can say goodbye." She squeezes my shoulder as she leaves.

More time passes. I know this because the shows on the TV begin and end, begin and end. The quality of the light outside changes as the hours tick by. We wait, together in the room, alone with our unspoken thoughts.

I'm not sure what time it is when Mom takes a rasping breath and her eyes flutter open. Immediately, Eddie and I are on either side of her, both of us grasping one of her thin, brittle hands. I feel Scott behind me, his hand warm and reassuring on the small of my back. For several seconds, she simply blinks and struggles to breathe. She moans and clears her throat, over and over again. She sounds like she's drowning in her own body.

Eddie uses the remote to tilt the bed up, helping her into a sitting position. She groans and coughs, gurgling and struggling. Eddie grabs a handful of tissue and holds it in front of her mouth. She coughs and manages to spit, coating the white with the black inside her. He tenderly wipes her mouth clean.

She turns her head toward Eddie. "Love you," she says, her voice froggy, inhuman. Unrecognizable as my mother's. "Always." Eddie doesn't try to disguise the tears slipping down his unshaven cheeks. He raises her hand to his mouth and kisses it.

"Love you, too. Always," he says. The room blurs in front of me and I blink furiously. My nose drips and I wipe it on the back of my sleeve. Mom's head swivels weakly toward me. Her grip on my hand tightens.

"Love you."

"I love you too, Mom." I'm crying now. I can't hold it back. She struggles to say something else, but her voice is lost in the gurgling sounds coming from her throat, her chest. I lean closer.

"Not the end of the world," she rasps. "Not the end of the world." I nod, even though I'm not sure if she's talking about me or her or something else altogether. I nod, even though I don't agree with her. It *is* the end of the world. Hers, and mine, and Eddie's.

After another moment, she sinks back into unconsciousness and her breathing becomes shallower, each breath costing her energy she no longer has. They come slower, farther and farther apart. We don't let go of her hands, staying with her until the end, not letting her move into the unknown alone. Eddie leans down and kisses her forehead.

"It's okay, sweetheart. You can go. It's okay. You don't have to fight anymore. We love you, and it's okay for you to go."

She takes a breath, but this time there's no exhale. Just stillness.

A few hours after Mom's funeral, I'm standing alone in the back room of her favorite restaurant, surrounded by the noise of voices and dishes and music, holding a cup of coffee. I'm tired; more than tired. I feel drunk with fatigue, completely wrung out after the past couple of days. I just want to go home and crawl into bed for a week or two. I want to lie on the couch and watch *Ghost Hunters* and eat a sheet cake by myself. I want to cuddle up with Scott and fall into a sleep so deep I don't dream. But I can't. I have to stay here and socialize. Then I have to go back to the funeral home with Eddie and collect all of the pictures we had on display for the visitation. I promised Eddie I'd come over in a day or two to help him start organizing all of Mom's stuff—what to keep, what to donate, what I'd like to have.

Death is exhausting.

"Claire?" I turn and see Mia standing a few feet away. Her blond hair is up in a bun, and she's wearing a simple black dress with a gray cardigan over top. Her belly is bigger than the last time I saw her, a perfect little bump. She looks unsure of herself, her fingers twisted together in front of her, her lower lip caught between her teeth. She meets my eyes, licks her lips. "I'm so sorry about your mom."

I nod. "Thanks. Me too." I set my coffee down on a nearby table, warmth tugging at me at the sight of her. I pull a well-used tissue out of my sleeve and wipe at my nose. I'm surprised she's here, but also touched. "It was really nice of you to come."

She nods back. "I've—I've been thinking about you a lot. How are you?" She's so hesitant, so careful. Despite everything between us, I'm glad to see her.

"I'm okay. Hanging in there." I offer her a small smile. She smiles back. "How are you?"

"I'm good. I'm…" She glances off to the side. "I'm sorry I haven't really been around."

"I haven't exactly been around, either."

"No, but you've got a much better excuse than I do. I mean, if you needed some space from me and…" She trails off and clears her throat. The air between us is thick, stifling and stuffy with awkwardness. "Listen, I've had some time to think and I just…I should've respected that more. I didn't understand. I was so caught up in myself that I just kind of…I could've been a better friend to you, and I'm sorry that I wasn't."

I study her for a minute. Maybe I haven't lost Mia. "I'm sorry I couldn't be there for you the way you deserved." I meet her olive branch with one of my own, hoping maybe we can build a bridge out of them.

She reaches out a hand and squeezes my arm. "Shit, no, please don't feel bad. I can't even imagine having to deal with everything you've had thrown at you. I'm so sorry that you've had such a tough go. It's so unfair."

"How…what made you…" I shrug, hoping I don't need to finish my question.

"When you pulled away, it made me think about what it must be like for you. I think maybe I took you, took our friendship for granted. I don't want to lose you, to lose us. Claire, you mean so much to me, and I don't want this to come between us. We can fix this. I can do better." She steps forward and pulls me into a hug. "I fucked up. I'm sorry." Something inside me dissolves, melting the frost around the edges of my heart. My arms go around her and for a moment, we simply hold each other.

"I think I took our friendship for granted, too," I say. "I'm sorry that I hurt you. I'm really sorry, Mia. I could've been a better friend, and I regret letting all of my own shit get in the way of that." I feel her nod against me.

After a moment, she steps back. "How did the TV show thing go?"

"I didn't do it. It was complicated, with Mom and everything and I just didn't feel right about it. Because you were right—it was *our* project, and I should've advocated for that."

She shrugs. "I get why you didn't. But thank you. For sticking up for me in the end. I appreciate that."

I nod again, shifting my weight. A draft blows down on me from the vent on the ceiling and I rub my hands over my arms.

"Anyway," she continues, "I wanted you to know that I'm sorry, and that I miss you. I'm sorry about your mom, and if there's anything I can do, please let me know. Seriously, anything you need." She moves forward and gives me another brief hug. "Love you, C. Give me a call if and when you feel like it, okay?" She pulls away and gives me another soft smile before turning to go. Our once unshakable bond is damaged, but for the first time in months, it doesn't feel as if it's beyond repair.

I walk to the table at the back of the room and pour myself another cup of coffee. A chair scrapes loudly against the floor. Laughter erupts from a small group on the other side of the room; I see Nancy at the center of the group, probably telling one of her many Nora stories. I think about walking across the room to join them, but I'm too tired.

I sit and sip my coffee, Mom's words echoing through my head. *Not the end of the world.*

21

March - Now

For the past two weeks, my life has been about death. Losing Mom, which I knew was inevitable, but that doesn't make the pain any less sharp. Losing our only remaining embryo, our expensive IVF attempt ending in utter failure. A part of me also saw that as inevitable.

And as if those two deaths aren't enough, I'm mourning myself. Who I thought I would be, and the life that Scott and I would have. That future, so golden and alluring in its promise of happiness and fulfillment, is also dead. Dead like Mom. Dead like my fertility.

I wake up every morning and I feel like I'm dying, too. I shuffle through each day, a mindless grief zombie, and I feel like I'm dying.

I've been spending a lot of time people watching. Sitting inside Grinders Café, a latte and a cookie I don't really want on the table in front of me, I squint out the window. It's cold, but sunny, the snow melting and sending rivulets of water cascading over the cobblestone courtyard. Two women sit at the table next to me, a mother and daughter, if I had to guess. They're a generation apart, and they seem close. Affectionate. The mother is telling an animated story, the daughter listening, leaning forward, head tilted. An ache flares up in my chest.

Two men walk by outside, holding hands. They pause in front of the window display in Becca's store, leaning back as they study it. After a moment, they go inside, chatting happily.

A young girl walks quickly across my field of vision, a laptop bag slung over her slender, hunched shoulder, earbuds stuffed into her ears, drowning out the world around her. She disappears inside the bookstore, her long, dark brown hair swooshing along behind her.

An elderly woman shuffles slowly by, leaning on her cane for support. She stops for a second and looks up, at what, I'm not sure. She's still, and then she smiles. With a little nod, she continues on.

I want to reach out and touch each of these people. I want to know what kind of pain they've endured. What kind of losses they've suffered. I want to know, because I want to know how to be okay.

Each day bleeds into the next, and I try to shoehorn myself into a routine designed to keep me from thinking or feeling too much. Getting up at the crack of dawn and hitting the gym. Working all day, taking on project after project, saying yes to everything. Cleaning the house and cooking dinner after work. Watching a movie with Scott. Reading. Going to bed. All in the hopes that my grief is like a fire, and if I just keep moving, I'll eventually smother it out. I'll starve it of oxygen by refusing to feed it. Refusing to acknowledge it. Filling my time with anything and everything to avoid the nothingness buried beneath the surface.

"Claire? Hey, you have a sec?" Scott asks me as I bustle in through the front door, my arms full of groceries. I stopped by the market on the way home so I can spend the next two hours cooking an elaborate dinner I probably won't eat.

"Uh, sure," I say, toeing off my black ankle boots and juggling my grocery bags, purse, and laptop bag. He steps forward and takes the groceries from me, disappearing into the kitchen with them. I'm just hanging up my coat in our newly organized closet—I'd spent a few hours purging, installing a new organizer, and then arranging every-thing by season and then by color within each season—when Scott takes it from me, tosses it on the bench and takes my hand. Without a word he leads me into the living room and guides me onto the couch. He sits down beside me.

"You need to stop," he says simply, his hands dangling between his legs. His face is serious, his gaze unflinching as he watches me for a reaction.

"Stop?" I ask, being deliberately obtuse. I know what he's talking about, but I don't want to acknowledge that I'm doing this all on purpose. I'm not covering up my grief with action, I'm just an efficient whirlwind of productivity. Nothing wrong with that, right? That's what I want him to think, what I want him to see. But it's useless. I know that he sees the truth. He knows me too well.

"Yeah. Stop. You're on the go from the second you get up, and I know exactly what you're doing, Claire. You think that if you stay busy, you won't have to deal with anything you're feeling."

I let out a little breath. "Well, it's working. I'm doing fine. I'm fine." Despite my best efforts, my voice is brittle, chipped.

"No, you're not. And you wouldn't know if you *are* fine because you haven't stopped moving for five seconds. As much as you might want to, you can't outrun this."

"I'm not outrunning it. I'm surviving."

He shakes his head, his lips pressed into a thin, determined line. "No, you're avoiding."

"Maybe avoiding *is* surviving." I arch an eyebrow and force myself to meet his gaze. His warm brown eyes and the sympathy shining in them kills me, just a little. I don't want to be pitied.

"No, Claire. Not the same thing. It's not healthy."

I lean back into the couch cushions and cross my arms over my chest. "So, what? You want me to sit around feeling sorry for myself instead? Because that's not healthy either."

"That's not what I said. But you have to admit that what you're doing now…" His hands grasp at the air between his legs, as though he's searching for something. "I'm worried about you. You need some time, some space, to breathe. To process. To actually work through something."

"Maybe I don't want to work through it."

"What are you scared of?" He rubs a hand across my back, and I feel all the fight go out of me. All of my stubbornness melts, like snow in spring, trickling away.

"That once I lift the lid off the box, I won't be able to put it back on," I say, my voice sounding small. "I don't want to get sucked under missing Mom, grieving for our family. I don't want to lose myself to that." My throat tightens, my eyes burn sharply. I meet his gaze. As always, his brown eyes are steady. Full of love. Holding me together. Holding us together.

"You won't. But you can't just leave the box closed forever, either, as tempting as that might be. You can't let things eat at you and fester. It'll be that much harder when the lid eventually comes off because every-thing's boiling over."

I tip my head back and stare at the ceiling. Blood pounds at my temples, and my chest aches. I feel tired, hollow. More than hollow. A deep, yawning emptiness that I don't know how to fill up again. "I don't know what I'm supposed to do."

Scott pulls me into his arms and settles my head on his chest. "I don't know either. I think you just have to live through it, without running yourself into the ground."

"How are you coping?" I ask. I'm not the only one who's lost something here. I have such a hard time remembering that. Because I really am the worst sometimes. Once a taker, always a taker.

He shrugs. "Day by day, I guess. I mean, we haven't decided anything for sure."

"Maybe we both need some time to really process. Time away from everything. If I'm away, I'll have no choice but to stop." An idea takes root and I bite my lip. She did say to ask for anything I need. Anything that might help.

"Maybe, yeah," he agrees.

We sit together in silence for a while before finally getting up off the couch to make dinner. I pull my phone out of my purse and text Mia.

I have a favor to ask you.

———

Mia and Tom's beach house is just as beautiful as I remember. I'd always thought they were crazy for buying it—it's a three hour flight away, and they barely have time to use it. I know they rent it out most of the year, but still. It seemed like an extravagant purchase, but it's one I'm grateful for now. And thanks to Mia's generosity, it's ours for the next week.

As we pull up in our rental car, I take in the cozy house on flood stilts standing only a few hundred feet back from the ocean. Cheery blue siding and white trim give it a fresh, contemporary look. Palm trees line the yard on either side. Scott parks the car under one of the raised sections of the house and we start unpacking everything, bringing suitcases and groceries into the house.

We take our time settling in, putting away groceries, setting out toiletries, refolding clothes and tucking them into dresser drawers. The house is quiet, save for the rhythmic shush of the waves. I slide open the door to the balcony off of the master bedroom and step outside. The house isn't far enough south that it's hot out, but it's a balmy sixty degrees—much warmer than the twenty-five we'd left behind at home. It's cloudy, with a gentle breeze ruffling the palm fronds. I wrap my arms around myself and take a deep breath, inhaling the damp, salty air. I'm glad it's cloudy. It feels cozier this way, somehow. More secluded.

Scott steps onto the balcony and wraps his arms around me, kissing the back of my head. I lean into him. I'm always leaning into him. Leaning on him. I turn my head slightly so he can hear me over the waves.

"I don't know what I'd do without you," I say.

"Good thing you'll never need to find out."

I turn in his arms and lean against the railing. "I'm serious. You're always so…so steady. You keep it together. You keep me together. It feels unfair, how much you've had to do that over the past few months."

He shrugs and smiles. "Things have been hard. It's my turn to carry the weight for both of us."

"But I feel like I've been selfish."

He cups my face in his hands and kisses me. His touch is strong, warm. It's home. "Don't worry, you'll get the chance to be the strong one when I have a mid-life crisis in ten years and buy a motorcycle. I'll go bald, get a pot belly. Maybe I'll blow all our money on some crazy pyramid scheme."

I twist my lips into a smile. None of this will happen, or at least, none of it's very likely. He's trying to make me feel better for being the taker in the relationship. Even now, he's giving me this. "Deal."

We don't shake on it because we don't need to.

Scott sings as he cooks dinner, and I wander through the house with a glass of wine. It's tastefully decorated in shades of blues and greens with white accents. There are no personal touches—no family photos or anything like that because of how often they rent it out. I wonder if they'll sell it with the new baby coming.

My stomach gives a sick little turn as I remember Mia's pregnancy. Somehow, I'd managed to put it out of my mind, and remembering almost feels like finding out about it all over again. The same thing happens with Mom. Sometimes I wake up, and I forget, and then I remember and it's like I've lost her all over again.

I don't know how any of this is supposed to get better, how it's supposed to heal when the wound just keeps opening itself up over and over again.

I step into our bedroom and rifle through my bag for the phone charger, but can't find it, so I check Scott's bag. I pull it out, but it's tangled with something, and as I free it from the bag, the brochure Dr. Kane gave us—the one about donor eggs—pops free. I go still when I see it. He obviously brought it with the intention of bringing it up again. Seeing the brochure, with its picture of a woman's hands cupping a pair of tiny baby feet, I know immediately what my answer is. I pick it up and head downstairs. It crinkles slightly in my hand as I walk, the glossy paper sticking to my palm.

The kitchen smells like garlic and tomatoes, the kind of comforting smells that cling to your bones. I set the brochure down gently on the counter.

"I found this in your bag."

He stops stirring for a second and then nods. "Yeah. I thought maybe we could talk about it."

"I can't, Scott."

"You can't talk about it?"

"No, listen." I turn the burner on the stove down and take his hands, leading him to the table. We sit down and I take a sip of my wine. "Right now, for now, I need to stop." I feel ten pounds lighter as soon as the words are out of my mouth. Scott doesn't say anything, his expression unreadable. Blank, almost.

"So that's it, we're done, it's over?" I can hear the dejection in his voice, can see how much pain and longing he's been holding back for my sake. To not make this harder on me.

"I'm not saying never, ever. I'm not saying we can't ever talk about starting treatments again. But for now, for the foreseeable future, I need to stop. I can't do this anymore. I just need...I need to heal. And I can't do that if we're still putting ourselves through this."

"Okay," he says slowly, glancing down. "If that's what you want."

"It's what I need." If I'm going to figure out how to be okay, I have to get off this roller coaster. I have to stop tormenting myself with what I can't have.

"Is this because of the whole donor egg thing?"

I shrug. "Partly, yeah. It's a big deal, and I'm not really in a position to even figure out how I feel about that right now. Like I said, I'm not saying we can't ever talk about this again, but right now, I need to stop."

"For how long?"

"I don't know. Maybe forever. I don't know. But for now, I'm done." As relieved as I feel, a tightness pulls at my chest and I have to blink back tears. They fall anyway. I don't know why I'm always so hellbent on fighting them.

Scott reaches up and wipes one away with his thumb. His eyes are wet, too.

"I'm so sorry," I say, laying my hand over his.

"Don't be." He shakes his head, a sad smile tugging at his lips. "It's not like we didn't try."

"This might not be the end. It might just be a pause." I'm not ready to shut the door completely. For now, I'm okay with leaving it just the slightest bit ajar.

He nods. "I can't ask you do to more than you've already done, Claire. If you've had enough, I..." He pulls away and wipes at his eyes.

"I'm so sorry," I say again, wrapping my arms around him. "I wanted to give you this."

His shoulders shake. "I know. I know you did."

"But for now, I think we need to try to accept that it just might not be in the cards for us. Right now, I'm not ready to think about donor eggs or adoption or anything like that. Maybe I'll feel differently in the future, when I've had the chance to heal, to process everything. I don't know. I can't predict that. So I need to know that you're okay if it's only ever just us."

He pulls me against him and I bury my head in his neck, breathing in his scent. "I choose you, Claire. Always. Baby or no baby. We'll be okay."

22

Scott and I spend our days quietly. Tiptoeing around our grief. Whispering so as not to disturb what lies sleeping. We immerse ourselves in the mundane. Drinking coffee in the mornings. Walking on the beach. We head into town and walk some more, eating on restaurant patios and browsing in kitschy stores. We spend one rainy afternoon at the aquarium. We go to the movies. We peruse the stalls at a little farmer's market, picking out fruit and vegetables and meat and eggs and then cooking together.

We string these activities together into a day. Into a few days. Breath by breath, minute by minute, marching resolutely forward. Infertility has taught us how to wait, and minute by minute, we're learning to survive.

I rinse the final wine glass from tonight's dinner under the tap, set it gently in the drying rack, and then rinse the soapy water off my hands. I'm full of steak and baked potato and grilled veggies, and I feel content. Not happy, or satisfied, or okay in any real way, but content in this moment. I am fed. I am warm. I am safe. I am loved. Right now, that's enough.

I dry my hands on the towel looped over the oven door and then listen for Scott. I can't hear any sounds from the TV in the living room, so I head upstairs, looking for him. I find him in our bedroom. The lights are off, the balcony doors open, the curtains fluttering in the evening breeze. Scott sits on the bed, staring out the open doors. He turns slightly as he hears me in the doorway, and in the changing light, I can see that his face is wet.

"Scott?" My voice is tiny in the semidarkness.

He hastily wipes at his eyes and then rubs his hands on his thighs. "Hey." He swipes at his nose and looks out the doors again.

I am made of grief, but also of guilt. I've done this to him. I've taken away something he always wanted. I don't know what to say.

I cross the room and lay my hand on his shoulder. His muscles are tense beneath my fingers, bunched with everything he hasn't been telling me.

"Talk to me," I say. I want to fix it. Fix him. Fix us.

He shakes his head. "I'm okay."

"No, you're not. You're sitting in the dark with tears running down your face. Definitely not okay."

"It's fine. I don't…"

"You don't what?"

He sighs deeply, and his shoulders sag, as though they're carrying a heavy weight. They have been, I see. My weight.

"I'm so sorry, Scott."

He raises a hand and then gently sets it on my knee. I lay mine over top of his. "Don't be. I'm sorry. I didn't want you to see me like this."

"What? Upset?"

"I need to be strong for you. We can't both fall apart. You lost your mom. You've been through so much. It's my job to be your glue, and—"

I cut him off with a soft touch on his cheek. "You're allowed to fall apart. It's okay to let me be the strong one sometimes. You've lost something, too. I'm not so fragile that you can't lean on me."

He leans his head on my shoulder and clings to me, letting it all out. I hold him, glad that I'm able to give him this after everything he's given me. We're in this together, just like we promised years ago. For better or worse, through thick and thin, good times and bad. I'm relieved that that promise hasn't changed despite what we've lost.

Scott is jogging. This is new, but maybe it's what he needs. To blow off steam, to keep his mind busy. In any case, he's out and the house is empty.

The sun is setting, and I walk out through the back doors, not bothering to put shoes on. The sand is cool between my toes, squelching and molding around my feet as I walk. I inhale a deep breath, the salty air sticking to my skin.

I stop about ten feet back from the water and plunk myself down on the sand. Wetness seeps through my yoga pants, but I don't care. I pull my knees up to my chest and rest my hands on them, staring out at the vast expanse before me. The sun is disappearing behind the house, casting the beach with golden strips of light, and painting the underbellies of the clouds a cotton candy pink.

I rest my chin on my knees and think about Mom. I think about the baby we'll probably never have. It strikes me that there's gratitude in loss; you just have to know where to look for it. It's there, in my memories of Mom, in who I am because of her. It's there, in my marriage. It's there, in me. Without all of this, maybe I would never know how strong I am. I wouldn't know just how much I can survive. I wouldn't have nearly unending faith in my marriage.

My heart can handle a lot of disappointment, I've learned. It's actually scary and miraculous just how much. Our hearts are resilient.

Expansive and irrepressible. Mom taught me that. Infertility taught me that.

Memories of Mom flit through my mind, like a movie montage. Playing in the snow with her as a little girl. Swimming at the lake in the summer. Spending a rainy day playing board games and making cookies. Pushing her away as a teenager, wondering why she was out to ruin my life. Longing for her as an adult. Laughing together. Singing in the car. Arguing about curfews and parties and boys.

She was my guiding light, and she's gone. I can't fix that, or change it. All I can do is live. One breath, one minute, one day at a time.

Not the end of the world.

Tears roll down my face and I feel restless. I push myself up and start walking down the beach, faster and faster until I'm full out running, my legs and arms pumping, sand spraying up behind me. My heart pounds in my chest, my throat burns with lactic acid.

I'm running, but I'm not running away. Not anymore. I'm running toward something. Something unknown. Something I'd never thought I could have.

EPILOGUE

May – Now

I, Claire Stanhope, am about to go to a baby shower completely of my own free will. Not because I have to, but because I want to. Gold star for Claire.

I pull my sunglasses off of my face and slip them into my purse as I step inside the little bistro. Pale yellow and mint green balloons float on either side of the doorway, swaying merrily in the warm, late spring breeze. Voices and music greet me as I step inside. I gently set my gift bag—containing a muslin blanket, pacifiers, and a couple of cute, gender neutral outfits—down on the table with the other gifts. I figure I don't get full points for this. I mean, yes, I bought baby stuff, but I ordered it online instead of going to an actual baby store. But still. I'm trying. Trying to move forward. Trying to be okay. Just trying in general.

"Claire!" I spin at the sound of a familiar voice.

"Oh my God, Becca! I thought you were still in Italy!" I pull her in for a hug and then step back, appraising her. "You look amazing." And it's true, she does. Her hair is a bit longer, her skin has a sun-kissed glow, and she's put on about ten pounds in all the right places. "Venice obviously agrees with you."

She smiles. "It does. I love it there. But I miss my life here, too. And I wanted to be here for Mia."

I take her hand and give it a squeeze. "Me too." She squeezes back.

"I'm glad you guys are okay."

"We're working on it." And it's true, we are. Mia's trying to be more understanding, more sensitive. And I'm trying to be more supportive. It's not always easy. And we're not perfect. But we're trying, and that's what counts.

Before I can respond, Mia rushes over. She looks absolutely beautiful, practically luminescent in her floral print dress. Her belly is smooth and round, like half a basketball. I force myself to look at it and brace myself for the usual onslaught of ugliness. Jealousy and bitterness and resentment. I hold my breath, waiting for it. And it's there. I can feel it, deep below the surface. But it feels so much smaller than before. Maybe because I'm not holding a magnifying glass up to it anymore.

Mia and Becca squeal over each other, jumping and hugging before Becca turns to help herself to the food laid out on a table on the other side of the room.

"I'm glad you came," Mia says, her hand on my shoulder. "I would've understood if you didn't want or weren't able to, or, you know…" Her voice trails off and she gestures awkwardly.

"I'm glad I came, too," I say. And I mean it.

When I step inside the front door a few hours later, Scott takes my bag from me and gives me a kiss. "I'm proud of you. That couldn't have been easy."

I pause, considering. "It wasn't, but it also wasn't as hard as I thought it might be." I shrug. "Maybe there's a certain power in letting go."

He smiles. "Maybe there is." He kisses me again, with more heat this time, but we're interrupted by a small bark and the feeling of sharp claws on my leg.

"Hello, Monty," I say in my most disgusting, syrupy sweet voice. I bend down to scratch his soft little head, burying my fingers in his fur. He paws at me with his enormous feet. He's small now, but he'll be a full-sized golden retriever by the end of the year.

"Hey, did you pick up our pictures?" I ask. Monty flops over, belly up, and I scratch up and down his stomach. One happy leg kicks rhythmically in the air.

"I did. They're on the dining room table."

"Thanks." I give Monty one last scratch and then head into the dining room, where a stack of carefully selected photographs sits on the table, along with my collection of empty picture frames. I pull out the chair and sit down, spreading the pictures in front of me. Me and Mom at my college graduation. Me and Scott on our wedding day, on our honeymoon. Me and Eddie. More recent ones, like our trip to London. Mia and I with Mandy Sinclair after we appeared on her show— together—last month. Scott with Monty the day we brought him home.

One by one, I slip the pictures in the frames, filling them with memories. Filling them with the proof that Scott and I can build a life we love, with or without kids. That we can still find meaning and happiness in our everyday lives. I feel renewed, not pinned down by grief, but fueled by the need to prove that our inevitable extinction doesn't mean that our lives don't matter while we're here.

I likely won't be a mom. I'm going to miss out on one of life's most significant experiences, but that means I have more room for other dreams. For career, travel, whatever I want.

Despite this, the grief and the loss are still there, and I know that to some degree, they probably always will be. Looking at all of these pictures, I can clearly see what's missing. But I'm getting better at living alongside it. At not letting it define me. At building my life around it.

Despite it. Maybe even because of it. Grief isn't something you get over, but something you integrate into your life. The life after. The life going forward. It becomes a part of you.

When I was a kid, I thought that the good guys always won. That the desired outcome was the inevitable one, despite the obstacles faced along the way. I took comfort knowing that Darth Vader would never actually defeat Luke Skywalker; of course Dorothy would be reunited with her family. I miss the days when my worldview was sunnily positive. But the truth is, life doesn't work like that. Sometimes the worst possible outcome comes to pass; sometimes we fail. We lose. We're defeated and will never achieve whatever heroic goal we were pursuing. Our instinct is to rail against the injustice of this, to cling to the Hollywood version of our lives we'd always assumed was ours for the taking. Letting go and finding a new way forward is hard. But in the choosing of that path, maybe all isn't lost after all.

Maybe that's how you find something new.

AFTERWORD

If you or someone you care about is struggling with infertility, please visit www.resolve.org to learn more about infertility and the treatments available, as well as find out where to get help and support.

Did you enjoy
this book?

*Please leave
a review!*

Reviews help
authors more
than you know!

FREE DOWNLOAD

Download Tara's story Reload for free!

Get started here: https://www.tara-wyatt.com/newsletter

OTHER BOOKS BY TARA WYATT

Stealing Home

Wild Card

Royal Treatment

Nailed

When Snowflakes Fall

Like Fresh Fallen Snow

Until the Sun Sets

Can't Help Falling in Love:

The Complete Graysons Trilogy

Necessary Risk

Primal Instinct

Chain Reaction

Stripped

* * *

Co-written with Harper St. George:

Dirty Boxing

Take Down

No Contest

For complete information on all of Tara's books,
visit www.tara-wyatt.com/books.

ABOUT THE AUTHOR

Tara Wyatt is the award-winning author of over a dozen romance novels. *Little Blue Lines* is her first foray into women's fiction. An infertility survivor, Tara lives in Hamilton, Ontario, Canada with her family.

Don't miss out on a sale or new release!
Join Tara's newsletter: www.tara-wyatt.com/newsletter

For regular updates and to stay in the loop, follow Tara on Facebook:
www.faceboook.com/tarawyattauthor

You can also connect with Tara on Instagram:
www.instagram.com/taradwyatt

Follow Tara on BookBub:
www.bookbub.com/authors/tara-wyatt